# SUSAN SCARLETT
## UNDER THE RAINBOW

SUSAN Scarlett is a pseudonym of the author Noel Streatfeild (1895-1986). She was born in Sussex, England, the second of five surviving children of William Champion Streatfeild, later the Bishop of Lewes, and Janet Venn. As a child she showed an interest in acting, and upon reaching adulthood sought a career in theatre, which she pursued for ten years, in addition to modelling. Her familiarity with the stage was the basis for many of her popular books.

Her first children's book was *Ballet Shoes* (1936), which launched a successful career writing for children. In addition to children's books and memoirs, she also wrote fiction for adults, including romantic novels under the name 'Susan Scarlett'. The twelve Susan Scarlett novels are now republished by Dean Street Press.

Noel Streatfeild was appointed an Officer of the Order of the British Empire (OBE) in 1983.

# ADULT FICTION BY NOEL STREATFEILD

As Noel Streatfeild

*The Whicharts* (1931)

*Parson's Nine* (1932)

*Tops and Bottoms* (1933)

*A Shepherdess of Sheep* (1934)

*It Pays to be Good* (1936)

*Caroline England* (1937)

*Luke* (1939)

*The Winter is Past* (1940)

*I Ordered a Table for Six* (1942)

*Myra Carroll* (1944)

*Saplings* (1945)

*Grass in Piccadilly* (1947)

*Mothering Sunday* (1950)

*Aunt Clara* (1952)

*Judith* (1956)

*The Silent Speaker* (1961)

As Susan Scarlett
(All available from Dean Street Press)

*Clothes-Pegs* (1939)

*Sally-Ann* (1939)

*Peter and Paul* (1940)

*Ten Way Street* (1940)

*The Man in the Dark* (1940)

*Babbacombe's* (1941)

*Under the Rainbow* (1942)

*Summer Pudding* (1943)

*Murder While You Work* (1944)

*Poppies for England* (1948)

*Pirouette* (1948)

*Love in a Mist* (1951)

# SUSAN SCARLETT

# UNDER THE RAINBOW

With an introduction
by Elizabeth Crawford

DEAN STREET PRESS

*A Furrowed Middlebrow Book*
FM91

Published by Dean Street Press 2022

Copyright © 1942 The Estate of Noel Streatfeild

Introduction copyright © 2022 Elizabeth Crawford

All Rights Reserved

The right of Noel Streatfeild to be identified as the Author of the Work
has been asserted by her estate in accordance with the Copyright,
Designs and Patents Act 1988.

First published in 1942 by Hodder & Stoughton

Cover by DSP

ISBN 978 1 915393 20 3

www.deanstreetpress.co.uk

# Introduction

WHEN reviewing *Clothes-Pegs*, Susan Scarlett's first novel, the *Nottingham Journal* (4 April 1939) praised the 'clean, clear atmosphere carefully produced by a writer who shows a rich experience in her writing and a charm which should make this first effort in the realm of the novel the forerunner of other attractive works'. Other reviewers, however, appeared alert to the fact that *Clothes-Pegs* was not the work of a tyro novelist but one whom *The Hastings & St Leonards Observer* (4 February 1939) described as 'already well-known', while explaining that this 'bright, clear, generous work', was 'her first novel of this type'. It is possible that the reviewer for this paper had some knowledge of the true identity of the author for, under her real name, Noel Streatfeild had, as the daughter of the one-time vicar of St Peter's Church in St Leonards, featured in its pages on a number of occasions.

By the time she was reincarnated as 'Susan Scarlett', Noel Streatfeild (1897-1986) had published six novels for adults and three for children, one of which had recently won the prestigious Carnegie Medal. Under her own name she continued publishing for another 40 years, while Susan Scarlett had a briefer existence, never acknowledged by her only begetter. Having found the story easy to write, Noel Streatfeild had thought little of *Ballet Shoes*, her acclaimed first novel for children, and, similarly, may have felt Susan Scarlett too facile a writer with whom to be identified. For Susan Scarlett's stories were, as the *Daily Telegraph* (24 February 1939) wrote of *Clothes-Pegs*, 'definitely unreal, delightfully impossible'. They were fairy tales, with realistic backgrounds, categorised as perfect 'reading for Black-out nights' for the 'lady of the house' (*Aberdeen Press and Journal*, 16 October 1939). As Susan Scarlett, Noel Streatfeild was able to offer daydreams to her readers, exploiting her varied experiences and interests to create, as her publisher advertised, 'light, bright, brilliant present-day romances'.

*

Noel Streatfeild was the second of the four surviving children of parents who had inherited upper-middle class values and expectations without, on a clergy salary, the financial means of realising them. Rebellious and extrovert, in her childhood and youth she had found many aspects of vicarage life unappealing, resenting both the restrictions thought necessary to ensure that a vicar's daughter behaved in a manner appropriate to the family's status, and the genteel impecuniousness and unworldliness that deprived her of, in particular, the finer clothes she craved. Her lack of scholarly application had unfitted her for any suitable occupation, but, after the end of the First World War, during which she spent time as a volunteer nurse and as a munition worker, she did persuade her parents to let her realise her dream of becoming an actress. Her stage career, which lasted ten years, was not totally unsuccessful but, as she was to describe on *Desert Island Discs*, it was while passing the Great Barrier Reef on her return from an Australian theatrical tour that she decided she had little future as an actress and would, instead, become a writer. A necessary sense of discipline having been instilled in her by life both in the vicarage and on the stage, she set to work and in 1931 produced *The Whicharts*, a creditable first novel.

By 1937 Noel was turning her thoughts towards Hollywood, with the hope of gaining work as a scriptwriter, and sometime that year, before setting sail for what proved to be a short, unfruitful trip, she entered, as 'Susan Scarlett', into a contract with the publishing firm of Hodder and Stoughton. The advance of £50 she received, against a novel entitled *Peter and Paul*, may even have helped finance her visit. However, the Hodder costing ledger makes clear that this novel was not delivered when expected, so that in January 1939 it was with *Clothes-Pegs* that Susan Scarlett made her debut. For both this and *Peter and Paul* (January 1940) Noel drew on her experience of occasional employment as a model in a fashion house, work for which, as she later explained, tall, thin actresses were much in demand in the 1920s.

Both *Clothes-Pegs* and *Peter and Paul* have as their settings Mayfair modiste establishments (Hanover Square and Bruton Street respectively), while the second Susan Scarlett novel, *Sally-Ann* (October 1939) is set in a beauty salon in nearby Dover Street. Noel was clearly familiar with establishments such as this, having, under her stage name 'Noelle Sonning', been photographed to advertise in *The Sphere* (22 November 1924) the skills of M. Emile of Conduit Street who had 'strongly waved and fluffed her hair to give a "bobbed" effect'. *Sally-Ann* and *Clothes-Pegs* both feature a lovely, young, lower-class 'Cinderella', who, despite living with her family in, respectively, Chelsea (the rougher part) and suburban 'Coulsden' (by which may, or may not, be meant Coulsdon in the Croydon area, south of London), meets, through her Mayfair employment, an upper-class 'Prince Charming'. The theme is varied in *Peter and Paul* for, in this case, twins Pauline and Petronella are, in the words of the reviewer in the *Birmingham Gazette* (5 February 1940), 'launched into the world with jobs in a London fashion shop after a childhood hedged, as it were, by the vicarage privet'. As we have seen, the trajectory from staid vicarage to glamorous Mayfair, with, for one twin, a further move onwards to Hollywood, was to have been the subject of Susan Scarlett's debut, but perhaps it was felt that her initial readership might more readily identify with a heroine who began the journey to a fairy-tale destiny from an address such as '110 Mercia Lane, Coulsden'.

As the privations of war began to take effect, Susan Scarlett ensured that her readers were supplied with ample and loving descriptions of the worldly goods that were becoming all but unobtainable. The novels revel in all forms of dress, from under-wear, 'sheer triple ninon step-ins, cut on the cross, so that they fitted like a glove' (*Clothes-Pegs*), through daywear, 'The frock was blue. The colour of harebells. Made of some silk and wool material. It had perfect cut.' (*Peter and Paul*), to costumes, such as 'a brocaded evening coat; it was almost military in cut, with squared shoulders and a little tailored collar, very tailored at the waist, where it went in to flare out to the floor' (*Sally-Ann*), suitable to wear while dining at the Berkeley or the Ivy, establishments to which her heroines – and her readers – were introduced. Such details and the satisfying plots, in which innocent loveliness triumphs against the machinations of Society beauties, did indeed prove popular. Initial print runs of 2000 or 2500 soon sold out and reprints and cheaper editions were ordered. For instance, by the time it went out of print at the end of 1943, *Clothes-Pegs* had sold a total of 13,500 copies, providing welcome royalties for Noel and a definite profit for Hodder.

Susan Scarlett novels appeared in quick succession, particularly in the early years of the war, promoted to readers as a brand; 'You enjoyed *Clothes-Pegs*. You will love Susan Scarlett's *Sally-Ann*', ran an advertisement in the *Observer* (5 November 1939). Both *Sally-Ann* and a fourth novel, *Ten Way Street* (1940), published barely five months after *Peter and Paul*, reached a hitherto untapped audience, each being serialised daily in the *Dundee Courier*. It is thought that others of the twelve Susan Scarlett novels appeared as serials in women's magazines, but it has proved possible to identify only one, her eleventh, *Pirouette*, which appeared, lusciously illustrated, in *Woman* in January and February 1948, some months before its book publication. In this novel, trailed as 'An enthralling story – set against the glittering fairyland background of the ballet', Susan Scarlett benefited from Noel Streatfeild's knowledge of the world of dance, while giving her post-war readers a young heroine who chose a husband over a promising career. For, common to most of the Susan Scarlett novels is the fact that the central figure is, before falling into the arms of her 'Prince Charming', a worker, whether, as we have seen, a Mayfair mannequin or beauty specialist, or a children's nanny, 'trained' in *Ten Way Street*, or, as in *Under the Rainbow* (1942), the untrained minder of vicarage orphans; in *The Man in the Dark* (1941) a paid companion to a blinded motor car racer; in *Babbacombe's* (1941) a department store assistant; in *Murder While You Work* (1944) a munition worker; in *Poppies for England* (1948) a member of a concert party; or, in *Pirouette*, a ballet dancer. There are only two exceptions, the first being the heroine of *Summer Pudding* (1943) who, bombed out of the London office in which she worked, has been forced to retreat to an archetypal southern English village. The other is *Love in a Mist* (1951), the final Susan Scarlett novel, in which, with the zeitgeist returning women to hearth and home, the central character is a housewife and mother, albeit one, an American, who, prompted by a too-earnest interest in child psychology, popular in the post-war years, attempts to cure what she perceives as her four-year-old son's neuroses with the rather radical treatment of film stardom.

Between 1938 and 1951, while writing as Susan Scarlett, Noel Streatfeild also published a dozen or so novels under her own name, some for children, some for adults. This was despite having no permanent home after 1941 when her flat was bombed, and while undertaking arduous volunteer work, both as an air raid warden close to home in Mayfair, and as a provider of tea and sympathy in an impoverished area of south-east London. Susan Scarlett certainly helped with Noel's expenses over this period, garnering, for instance, an advance of £300 for *Love in a Mist*. Although there were to be no new Susan Scarlett novels, in the 1950s Hodder reissued cheap editions of *Babbacombe's*, *Pirouette*, and *Under the Rainbow*, the 60,000 copies of the latter only finally exhausted in 1959.

During the 'Susan Scarlett' years, some of the darkest of the 20th century, the adjectives applied most commonly to her novels were 'light' and 'bright'. While immersed in a Susan Scarlett novel her readers, whether book buyers or library borrowers, were able momentarily to forget their everyday cares and suspend disbelief, for as the reviewer in the *Daily Telegraph* (8 February 1941) declared, 'Miss Scarlett has a way with her; she makes us accept the most unlikely things'.

Elizabeth Crawford

# Chapter One

The Saltings was a village in three parts. Lying snug in a warm curve of the Sussex Downs was Saltings proper. Across the downland and stretching along a valley on the far side was Lower Saltings. Over yet another curve, where fields and woodlands met at the down edge, was Upper Saltings.

Saltings was enchanting. If it had not been so ungetatable it would have been crammed with tourists all the summer through. A Norman church, grey and weathered, sat in a churchyard so green by comparison with the surrounding yellow-grey of the downs that, from the crest of the hills, it looked like an emerald. Because the grass grew so lush and old Ben, who was sexton, was also a milker and often giving a hand to the farmers, sheep grazed in the churchyard. To those who saw Saltings first on a hot day in summer—when heat shimmered in the hollows—that churchyard, and those sheep, and the surrounding cottages with their flaming gardens, stood for ever as a picture of peaceful England.

Lower Saltings was, as it were, a poor relation of Saltings. The Saltings' villagers spoke of any person who lived there as "They from Lower down." The farmers whose farms lay everywhere between the three Saltings gave their address as "of Saltings," or "of Upper Saltings." It would have been considered locally to reduce the value of a farm to have it known as attached to Lower Saltings. Lower Saltings was an excrescence caused by the ambition of some landowner to make bricks from the local clay. It was an industry started during the Great War and had prospered then, was carried on in a half-hearted way for a few years, and had died completely in 1930. To make the bricks, workmen were imported and housed in jerry-built rows of cottages, each attached to its neighbour as if it would fall down if left to itself. The imported workmen had been townsmen and had always taken hardly to country ways, and now, reduced to a sad level of poverty, being on the dole and with no future, they sank and were in many cases what the Saltings people thought them—a dirty, thriftless lot, who could not be bothered to cook good food, but ate wastefully out of tins, and spent what little money they possessed riding by bus into the nearest town, which was Lewes, in order to go to the pictures.

Upper Saltings was the smart relation of Saltings, but a smart relation who had come down in the world, and had little left to show of the great days she had seen. In Upper Saltings lay the large estates and those smaller houses, but still large to Saltings, built on those pieces of land the estates were forced to sell. Now all the estates but one were empty or at best half-closed. There were people in the new houses which had been built, but they were only folk of moderate means. The old days when the vicar of Saltings had merely to ride down to Upper Saltings for any help he needed had gone forever.

When Martin Richards came as vicar to the three Saltings, he was thirty-five. Since his school-days he had known his vocation. He would be a priest, and he would work in a really poor district. He would live as simply as his neighbours and, as one of themselves, find the way to their souls. He had his way. His first curacy had been in South London, and when he had been ordained priest, he had been given a parish lying along the Thames, where his people were dockside labourers and factory hands, living on the meanest incomes and frequently unemployed. There he had carried out his promise to himself. In that parish there was no real vicarage, and he took two little rooms in a tenement. But ideals are one thing, and strength quite another. At first Martin refused to notice that he was breaking down. One winter it was pleurisy, and another pneumonia, and by degrees he found himself reduced to half his work. Desperate, he went to his doctor and implored him to plug something into him that would give him back his strength, but his doctor had spoken his mind.

"I can't do it. You may as well face the truth. Stop on here, in this low-lying district, over-working yourself, and letting yourself in for one illness after another, and you'll find yourself an invalid."

"But I must work here," Martin protested. "This is my world, and these are my people."

The doctor shrugged his shoulders.

"It's for you to decide. I am telling you the truth; I should have thought that God would prefer a healthy man to serve him in air in which he could live, and give of his best, but if you don't think so, I can't over-ride your conscience, you must stop on; but you will see my words come true."

Before the next winter, and before Martin had had time to decide what was right, he broke down again. This time it was influenza; there were endless complications, and he was two months in bed. Before he was out again his Bishop came to see him.

"You'll have to give it up, Martin. I'm fond of you, and we need men like you in the diocese. Some day it may be you'll have the strength to come back to us. In the meantime, I would suggest you take on a small village, and get back your health."

Martin had accepted the three Saltings because of the sea air, because his Bishop had taken the trouble to arrange he should be offered them, but most of all because of Lower Saltings. There, he saw, with a glad quickening of heart, were just the people he was dedicated to serve. He nearly had a fit when he first saw the vicarage. It was one of those enormous vicarages built in the early days of the last century, when the vicar always had a large family, when the cost of living was far lower, and when the vicar was usually a younger son with just sufficient allowed him by his father to enable him to keep a horse, officially for riding round his parish, but actually for hunting two days a week. It was built on three floors, with kitchens suitable for preparing meals for banquets, with gigantic living-rooms, and with a lovely, straggling garden.

The Rural Dean had motored Martin over to see the parish and, at first sight of the vicarage, Martin had turned to him quite pale with horror.

"I can't live here. I'll find a couple of rooms in a cottage."

The Rural Dean shook his head.

"They won't like it if you do. Old Dickson lived here for fifty years you must remember, and they're used to somebody in the vicarage."

"But he's dead."

"Only a month ago; he's very much a green memory."

"But I don't think a priest should live in a place this size; it puts him out of touch with his people."

The Rural Dean laughed.

"Don't you believe it! Go and live in a cottage and they'll think you're peculiar, and sooner or later there'll be letters to the Bishop."

Martin knew that he knew nothing of Sussex villages, and the Rural Dean everything, and he gave in. He was also almost pushed into the vicarage by his predecessor's housekeeper—a widow called Mrs. Ramage, known to everybody in the Saltings as Vicarage Bertha.

Bertha was fat and unendingly cheerful. She had black hair which, in spite of the fact that she was nearing sixty, showed very little grey. She had gay black eyes which had caused a lot of trouble when she had been a girl, and cheeks shining like a highly coloured apple. She had borne ten children, all of whom had grown up and married, and most of whom had gone overseas. She had not noticed that she was alone in the world until the old vicar had died, and the six weeks that followed his death and Martin's arrival were the most unpleasant she had ever known. There had been a moment, more serious than she had grasped, when Martin had wondered if he ought to engage her, whether it was suitable for him to be alone with her in the vicarage, but it had ended by Bertha engaging him.

"It's where I've mostly lived, and I know how to run it. Besides, sir, I shouldn't consider anything else, for you're one as wants a lot of mothering if I may say so."

"But . . ." Martin tried to explain, turning pink. "Well, you see there'll be only myself here."

Bertha suddenly got on to what he meant, and roared out her hearty laugh.

"Lor' bless you, sir, there's nobody to think ill of that. Why, they call me Vicarage Bertha here about. Besides, sir, I'm nearly sixty and long past the gentlemen."

Bertha, once she got Martin safely into the vicarage, took possession of him. On a wet day she would see him coming up the drive and wait for him in the hall, and as he came in, push him unceremoniously into a chair and drag off his shoes to feel his socks, and if they were wet she stood for no nonsense.

"Up to your room and change them. Top left-hand drawer. It's not so long since we buried Reverend Dickson, and we don't want to be starting on you."

It was the same with his meals. When he was tired or absent-minded, she stood over him watching every mouthful.

"Down it goes, even if you want to leave it on your plate; I don't want to hang over a hot stove cooking for one as lets my work go to waste."

Bertha was not the only one to fuss over Martin. The villagers, in the usual way of villagers, received their new vicar with great caution, but almost at once the women began to have a soft corner for him. He looked so fragile, and though he had no idea of it, and would have been disgusted if he had known it, he was exceedingly good looking.

"He do look delicate surely, poor gentleman," they said to each other at the Women's Institute.

"And Vicarage Bertha says he doan't eat more than would keep a fly."

It was not, however, delicacy or good looks which won Martin his place in the hearts of the three Saltings. The old vicar was not long dead, and though he, as a keen apiarist, had cared more for his bees than his people's souls, he had been set in his ways, and it needed great delicacy to introduce changes. But Martin, though he did not know Sussex, had so strong a vein of tolerance and humanity, that no people, were strange to him, and he quickly grasped the slow, solid thinking of his parish. Besides, some sendees he knew needed to be rendered to everybody, whether they lived in a downland village or in a tenement by the Thames. He knew what it meant to have company to sit up with you when there was bad sickness in a house. He knew what words could comfort when there was death. He understood how a man or woman might come to talk a trouble out, and then sit tongue-tied, and that patience would be rewarded, and the words be found in the end, if you sat easily, just waiting.

When he had his people's love and not before, he introduced his changes. He worked all three villages, even Lower Saltings, up to quite a different standard of church going. He started clubs for the boys and girls, particularly of Lower Saltings, and persuaded the people of Saltings, and Upper Saltings, to help him with them. And, a matter which had scarcely been mentioned by the old vicar, he took it for granted that all his boys and girls would be confirmed when they reached a suitable age. He was given in to, and, with humour, he accepted the fact, because he was liked and respected.

"Well, I never reckoned to have my Mary done; my Rose weren't never confirmed, but Vicar he fancies it, and he be a good man surely. My Dan says ''Tis better to give in, and no harm done anyways'."

It was after Martin had been at Saltings a year that his old aunt, Miss Connie Matthews—a spinster living on a tiny income— lost everything in a bank smash. Martin was not one to query whether he liked or disliked people. Miss Connie Matthews was his mother's sister; she was a funny old lady who needed humouring. He had gone to see her when he could, and if he had registered a sigh of thankfulness each time he left her little house and her grumbles behind him, he had not realised why he sighed. It was, therefore, natural to him, when she was left penniless, to invite the old lady to the vicarage. He had to go about it tactfully, for though she might be poor, she was certainly not going to admit that her coming to the vicarage was anything but a favour. She was a thin woman, with wrinkles all over her face like the marks of birds' feet in the snow; she had grey hair, drawn angrily back into a little hard bun, and she always wore black: a black coat and skirt with, in winter, a black felt hat, and in summer, a black straw one. There was also a brooch somewhere about her made of jet.

Martin had gone to see her to make his proposal. Aunt Connie sat very upright on a high-backed chair, her large, flat black shoes placed squarely on the carpet, and listened to him with her eyebrows slightly raised. There was nothing in her demeanour to show that she knew that she could not pay another quarter's rent, that there was barely enough food to eat in the house, and that her furniture was to be sold. When she had heard his invitation, she nodded to him kindly:

"Very well, my dear boy. I am your poor mother's sister, and one of your few relatives. I have long thought that you needed a woman to run your vicarage."

Martin thought of Bertha, and spoke hurriedly:

"Oh, there's no thought of that. I've a housekeeper; she's called Bertha." He saw his aunt's stern eyes on him, so he added, hastily: "She was the last vicar's housekeeper, and she's sixty, and I've told her about you, and she's quite prepared to look after us both."

Aunt Connie had a habit of snapping out "What-what!" when she was displeased. She snapped it out now.

"What-what! If I am in your house, I shall do the looking after. I never have left anything to servants, and shall not start now."

The first meeting between Aunt Connie and Bertha was typical of all their meetings. Bertha had gone up to her room to tidy herself. She never failed to get pleasure from that attic. She could still feel cold when she remembered the day of "Reverend Dickson's" funeral, when she had packed and left it; and still recall the glow of her homecoming on the day of Martin's arrival, when she saw her battered tin trunk back in its place and she went round the walls, finding the old nails, hanging up the enlarged portrait of her husband and, under it, the smaller one of his grave, and the wedding groups of her various children, and stood on the dressing-table the framed snapshots of the grandchildren. As she heard Martin's car outside she ran a comb through her hair and came bustling importantly down the stairs, humming "Rock of ages cleft for me." Bertha always hummed hymns, and no one could stop her. "It comes natural," she would say, cheerfully, "and no wonder, seeing where my kitchen is, for there's never a service I can't hear, let alone the choir practices."

Martin had bought a little old Morris car, for his parish was too scattered for him to visit on foot. It was a windy, creaking, rickety car, which had had hard use before ever it came into Martin's hands. In the three villages it was known as "Jimson." Jimson had been a carrier who had shouted before he had neared the Saltings to let the villagers know that he was coming. Jimson had now retired from the carrying business, so to the villagers the car took on his work. It did a lot of fetching for all of them, and it certainly always let them know it was coming. Martin helped Aunt Connie out of it and threw open the vicarage door, and Bertha, smiling radiantly, came forward to meet her.

"Good afternoon, 'm. I hope you had a pleasant journey. I'll just put on the kettle; you'll be wanting a cup of tea."

Aunt Connie withdrew herself further inside her black coat and skirt, and gave Bertha a look which she hoped put her in her place once for all.

"When I'm ready for tea, I will ring. And it's China. I felt sure there would be none in the house, so in my bag here I have the remains of a small packet. Two teaspoonfuls only. Never one for the pot."

Bertha could not believe that Aunt Connie meant to be as cold as she sounded. She gave a jolly laugh.

"Bless you, 'm, you can't ring! Why there's never been a bell in the house that has rung."

"That," said Aunt Connie, in an acid voice, "must be attended to."

In the months that followed, Aunt Connie tried to attend to a hundred things in the house and parish, but she was not an attractive woman, and she had an unfortunate manner, and she was impeded at every turn. For one thing, Bertha was very well loved locally, and her stories of the vicarage fights were retailed with gusto in every kitchen in the village.

"Came stalking in, if you please, and took the pepper-pot out of Vicarage Bertha's hands, just as she was flavouring the soup, and said that she did not want any pepper used, and that Bertha was too fond of the pepper pot. And not a better soup-maker in the village."

"Came to Vicarage Bertha and said she was to get a man in right away to see to the bells, and wouldn't believe it when Bertha said it would cost a lot of poor vicar's money, and all the bell-wires hanging down like so much twine."

"Up and said why wasn't her bedroom done, and when Vicarage Bertha said Monday was her day for turning out vicar's study, and always had been, she said it was for her to make the decisions in that house, and Bertha would do as she was told."

Martin, egged on by his aunt, sent for Bertha, and had a solemn talk with her in his study.

"My aunt is an old lady, Bertha, and has been used to her own house. I want her to be happy, so I think we must do things her way."

Bertha stood beside his desk, her eyes twinkling.

"Seventy next birthday, that's ten years older than me, and though I grant you she looks nearer twenty-five years older, she don't need all that humouring for a ten years' difference."

"She has always had her own home," Martin repeated, firmly, "and it's very hard for her to take to new ways."

"That comes of being a spinster, sir," said Bertha. "I never knew one yet that didn't get crochety. It seems as if it tried them more with age."

Martin had noticed from the moment of Aunt Connie's arrival that Bertha suffered from an unshakable belief that he and she were allies, fighting an enemy.

"But, Bertha," he said, severely, "that's not the way to speak of Miss Matthews."

Bertha made clicking sounds with her tongue.

"There I go, running on as usual. Reverend Dickson, he never minded, but I forget you are different." She paused for a moment, and then added: "But that's what it is, sir, being a spinster as done it."

Martin never could find himself really cross with Bertha. But for all his affection for her, he had to take Aunt Connie's side; he used his sternest voice: "Now look, Bertha, I quite realise you have run this vicarage for years; but for all that, you've got to give way now. It's hard for you, but that kind of discipline is good for us all. Miss Matthews' orders must be obeyed."

Bertha looked mutinous:

"What's sauce for the goose is sauce for the gander; there's others I could mention that could do with a bit of discipline." Then she smiled: "Never mind, don't you worry, sir; when I was a child my mother used to see to the old bodies down at the almshouses, and I got so used to their funny, crusty ways, that it's stayed with me all my life. I reckon there isn't an old woman born that I couldn't handle."

One of Bertha's biggest assets in life was that she always knew the right moment to make an exit. She made one now, with the self-satisfied smile of a maid who knows that she has done the right thing and given in.

Bertha and Aunt Connie were not the only women to try and rule Martin's life. In Upper Saltings, on the one estate that was properly kept up, lived Veronica Lady Blacke. Veronica's husband had been not only a big landowner, a fine breeder of cattle, but he had, as well, made money in the City. His credit was good and the baronetcy an old one, and his name looked well as chairman of companies. Outside these interests, he had also made considerable money in the jute business. When he died, Veronica was only twenty-eight, very attractive to look at, and exceedingly rich. Veronica's beauty was of the really English type, fair hair, blue eyes, with a pink and white complexion, but it was essentially the kind of beauty that belongs to a young girl. By the time she was thirty, it had begun to fade, and was helped out most successfully by her hairdressers and her beauty specialist. At first sight, the effect of her was lovely; she was slim, she dressed exquisitely, and her colouring was perfect. It was only when you got a little closer, that you noticed the hard gleam of the gold in her touched-up hair, and the rather deliberate make-up. Behind her limpid blue eyes, there was strain as if she were determined to get the best out of the world and, although she could buy it, uncertain as to where the best lay.

Veronica was a puzzle, even to herself. She had not loved Charles, her husband, but he had been a baronet, and he had been rich, and from the angle of the small, one-maided flat in Kensington in which she had been brought up, he was a catch. She had, however, a strong sense of duty, and having married Charles, she made him very happy. It was only when Charles was killed hunting, and she found herself a widow, that Veronica realised how much she had disliked her married life. After the funeral, she felt like a person who had been shut up in a stuffy room, and come out to take a breath of fresh air. She said to herself, stretching, as it were, metaphorical arms to the sky: "Now I can live."

Unfortunately for Veronica, the fact that she was free to do what she liked, and had the money to go where she would, did not mean that she had the faintest idea at first what she really wanted. She enjoyed being a Lady Bountiful, she loved showering kindnesses on people, and she enjoyed the eternal gratitude which she was sure they felt. She liked going to a committee and hearing the local people discuss a small fête to raise money for a fund and then, suddenly, sweeping it all aside, exclaiming: "Don't bother to get it up; I'll give you the money and then you can be all spared the bother." She supposed that she was loved for this kind of thing, and, indeed, nobody in the three Saltings denied that she was generous, but, she never got affection. Upper Saltings said:

"I wish Lady Blacke didn't think she could buy everybody.".

Saltings said:

"She'm mean well, but she do be one to throw her money about."

Lower Saltings said:

"Go and pitch the tale to Lady Blacke; if you thank 'er often enough you can get anything out of 'er."

When Martin came to Saltings, life for Veronica changed; she saw suddenly what she had meant to herself when she had said: "Now I can live." Not in her wildest dreams had she supposed that she would want to marry a poor clergyman, but almost from her first glimpse of Martin, she knew that she did not care whether he was the butcher, the baker or the candlestick-maker, for he was the man for her. Even while she admitted in her heart that she wanted him, her brain acknowledged how appallingly difficult it was going to be to get Martin's thoughts turned to marriage. Unbelievable though it seemed to her, in spite of his good looks and his charm, he never regarded women from a marrying point of view. Veronica could not kid herself that she was anything to Martin but Lady Blacke, to whom he could turn at any moment of want or need in his parish. He liked her; he enjoyed talking to her; he sometimes stayed to lunch with her, but, no matter how often she saw him, Veronica could never get him to consider her just simply as a woman.

The coming of Aunt Connie was good news to Veronica. It had been difficult for her to go much to the vicarage. Martin never entertained, and she had small excuse for running in and out and, moreover, Bertha regarded her visits in an obstructionist spirit.

"Yes, m'lady," she would say, doubtfully, "he is in, but he's tired and working on his sermon."

Veronica had tried every method with Bertha; little presents for her to send to her grandchildren; offers of the car to take her into Lewes shopping; invitations to come and get fruit and vegetables from the Manor House garden. Though Bertha accepted a few of these offerings, she remained sternly independent of them.

"Smarmy," she would say, "That's what she seems to me, smarmy. Too smarmy by half, and I don't hold with it."

But Aunt Connie was of a different metal, and Veronica saw at once what card to play there. To Aunt Connie, she talked about the wonderful difference it had made to Martin since she had come to live in the house; of how much better it was in a vicarage to have a woman to run things; of how easily servants got above themselves if given their head; and when these valuable talks had borne fruit, she did little services which were skilfully disguised not to look like services at all.

"It will be such a bore for me driving all that way alone, and I do hate shopping by myself, I suppose you are too busy to take pity, on me and come with me?"

"I suppose you couldn't find a use for all this black material? I had it when I was first a widow and it really seems a shame to waste it."

Having made her effort with Aunt Connie, Veronica got her reward. She felt she deserved it, for Aunt Connie had been very trying, but she had put her exactly where she wanted her to be. In and out of the vicarage all day long, so used to the house that in no time she had discarded the only bell which rang, which was the front door, and walked in, unannounced, treating the place like a second home.

Though, officially, her visits were to Aunt Connie, she very seldom came away without seeing Martin, and, as she told herself, becoming so much a figure in his life that, surely, soon, he would begin to look for her, and wonder how he had lived his life when she was not about.

In Saltings, tucked away behind the post office, was a gem of an Elizabethan cottage. In it lived Sterndale Adam. Sterndale was a schoolmaster in Lewes, but he and Martin had been at Cambridge together, and had remained friends ever since. When Martin came to the Saltings, Sterndale had leased the Elizabethan cottage. The extra trip to and fro, every day to Lewes was more than compensated for by the charm of his little house and the real pleasure he and Martin got from picking up their old friendship. Most nights Sterndale would walk to the vicarage, or Martin would walk to Sterndale's cottage, and they would sit together for an hour, smoking their pipes, sometimes whetting their brains on each other, but more often resting in a cosy, comfortable silence.

Martin had been at the Saltings nearly two years, when tragedy came to him.

Living at the other end of Sussex, he had a sister, Sylvia, who was married to an artist. Sylvia had had a hard struggle, the artist did not do well; there were two children; a delicate, small girl, called Polly, aged nine, and a boy, Andrew, who was eleven and away at school. Sylvia and her children had always been an anxiety to Martin, and he had spared her a small allowance to help her to keep things going.

It was on a summer morning in June, that Fred Peters, the local policeman, got off his bicycle at the vicarage and propped it against the wall. Fred was policeman to more than the Saltings; he was, in fact, policeman for six villages, but the Saltings looked upon him as their own, for he lived in Saltings village. Fred was sad at heart about his visit. He liked Martin. There had been a bad time in his house seven months back when their baby had died, and his wife, Rosie, distraught, had turned against him. Fred could well remember Martin's visits and what he had said, and how, in the end, Rosie had come to see sense. Unwillingly, he rang the vicarage bell and asked for Martin. Bertha was always slightly obstructive with the police.

"Now, what's the trouble, Fred? I know the back light went out on Jimson last night, but it's being seen to."

Fred shook his head.

"It isn't that, 'tis bad news. They rang me from Rye and asked me to see him."

Martin was in his study, Fred stood just inside the door, twisting his helmet awkwardly between his lingers.

"It's bad news, sir. You have a sister, a Mrs. Ronald." Martin nodded. "She and her husband was out motoring this morning, sir, and on a cross road a lorry hit them. They were both killed."

Martin said nothing for a moment; his face had gone greenish-white, he put a hand on the mantelpiece. Poor, silly little Sylvia, torn out of life so suddenly.

"What about the child, Polly?" he asked. "Was she with them?"

"No, sir. That's what the constable rang up about special, sir. Apart from me telling you what had happened, he said, it was the little girl. She hadn't been told and there was the boy at school, somebody did ought to tell him."

Martin never forgot that hurried trip across Sussex in Jimson; the country was looking so lovely it seemed that tragedy was out of keeping with such a world, and he never forgot the journey back with little Polly by his side. Polly had been sent to stay with friends until after the funeral, and Martin had left breaking the news to her until this homeward drive. He stopped the car beside a field which was golden with buttercups. He looked down at the child's rusty brown curls and thin, intelligent face.

"Have you wondered, Polly, why you are coming to stay with me?"

Polly drew her eyes unwillingly from the glow of the buttercups.

"No, Uncle Martin. Mummie said I'd go and stay with you one day."

"Didn't you wonder why you were sent away for two or three days?"

She turned her enquiring eyes to his:

"No, Mummie and Daddy often go away; they have to when he's going to paint something."

Martin felt for words.

"But this time, Polly, they are not coming back." Polly looked puzzled.

"Not never?"

He felt his way slowly.

"No. You know your father was a man who found himself with a bigger idea of the things he wanted to paint than God had given him the power to carry out."

Polly nodded.

"I know. Mummie was always stopping him tearing his pictures up."

Martin went slowly on.

"And it was difficult for your mother, too; she didn't like to see your father always disappointed in himself, and he was, you know, Polly. But God understood and he didn't want him to go on being disappointed, or your mother to be worried, so he has taken them away to heaven where every artist's dreams come true. There will be no picture now that your father wants to paint, but is better, much better, than anything he ever hoped."

Polly pondered a moment, then she asked in a little voice:

"You mean Mummie and Daddy are dead, Uncle Martin?"

Martin put his arm round her.

"Yes, Polly, and you are coming to live with me, and though it's going to be difficult for you because one can't help missing people very much, you are going to be brave and try not to mind, because they are much happier where they are."

Polly's face was red and he could see she was going to cry. He took her on his knee. After a time, she choked:

"Minding too much would be like me minding Andrew being asked to a party instead of me."

Martin kissed her:

"Yes, that's right."

Polly cried again, and then sniffed.

"Who's going to look after me?"

Martin, in taking Polly to the vicarage, had not very carefully considered that point.

"I have your great-aunt there, my Cousin Connie." Polly rubbed her eyes.

"But if she's your aunt, isn't she very, very old?"

Martin, considering Aunt Connie, could not deny it.

"Well, she is rather, but as well there's Bertha; she's my housekeeper. You'll like her."

"How old is Bertha?"

"Sixty," said Martin, unwillingly.

"Sixty!"

The age seemed to finish Polly's self-control. She laid her head against Martin's sleeve and sobbed as if her heart would break. Between her sobs she moaned:

"I don't want to be mean. I do want Mummie and Daddy to be happy, but I do want them to come back and look after me."

That conversation with Polly made Martin even more observant of her welfare than he would normally have been. He saw, with satisfaction, Bertha take the child to her motherly heart, and knew that, as far as she was concerned, Polly was content, for after a day or two, he often heard scraps of gay conversation, and sometimes hymn singing, coming from the kitchen. He would not in the ordinary way have supposed that hymn-singing showed any sign of cheering up on the part of Polly, but he knew it meant gaiety on the part of Bertha and so was glad to hear Polly's childish pipe joining in.

Things were, though, very much less successful where Aunt Connie was concerned. Aunt Connie belonged to the old school; she believed children should be seen and not heard; she believed in their never speaking unless spoken to, when grown-ups were in the room; she believed in nothing being left on the plate; and she believed, sub-consciously, that a child who is at that moment contented with something must be a child who is doing the wrong thing, and must, therefore, be promptly set to do something else.

Because their two systems were diametrically opposed and a war was anyway always being waged between Aunt Connie and Bertha, it rose to the fury of a prairie fire over Polly.

Bertha knew that a well-fed child, whose inside was properly cared for, and who got enough sleep, would automatically be a happy child, "and what," she asked Aunt Connie, and when Aunt Connie failed to answer, practically every inhabitant of Saltings, "could anyone want more for an orphan child, than that it should be happy?" "Happiness," Aunt Connie would say grimly to Martin, "takes too big a place in Bertha's mind. What a child needs is discipline; this child is too inclined to run wild and scarcely knows the meaning of obedience."

The result was that all day long poor little Polly trotted to and fro in answer to first one command, and then another. "Come in, my precious," Bertha would call, "and have a nice piece of this cake." "Put that cake down at once," Aunt Connie would scream, "you are a very disobedient child. How often have I to tell you not to eat between meals?" "You don't want any socks on a morning like this," Bertha would say. "Just put on your sand-shoes and run out and play." "Polly, come here," Aunt Connie would call. "Where are your socks?" "Bertha said . . ." Polly would begin to falter, but Aunt Connie would never allow her to finish. "Orders are taken from me in this house. Don't let me find you disobedient again or I shall be forced to punish you severely."

Veronica too, had to have a finger in Polly's pie.

Her attentions took the form of endless kindnesses. She was really sorry for the child and liked to give her little treats and presents, and though, of course, the knowledge that her goodness to his niece must please Martin, she was, nevertheless, quite sincere in her sympathy for the child. But Polly, as is the way of small children, could not be bought by treats and presents. With Veronica she was always on the defensive and remained shy and unresponsive.

When Polly had been living in the vicarage for three weeks, Martin came upon her, lying face down under an apple tree, at the far end of the garden, crying in a hopeless, unchildlike way. Full of pity, he pulled her up and put his arms round her.

"What is it?"

It was a long time before Polly could get sufficient control of her voice to speak, and then mostly it was a reiterated "I want Mummie and Daddy." But between these statements little facts were sobbed out.

"I don't belong to nobody here; before, just Mummie told me what to do, and now it's everybody. I don't mean to be bad; I never was bad at Rye, but here nobody couldn't be good. Bertha says something, then Aunt Connie says I shouldn't, and nothing nice ever happens."

Martin held her closer.

"But you've enjoyed going into Lewes and Eastbourne shopping and doing things with Lady Blacke, haven't you?"

There was a louder wail than ever from Polly.

"No. I don't like her not at all, I don't." She turned passionately to Martin. "She says things nice and does things nice, but her eyes are nasty all the time."

That night Martin was down at Sterndale's cottage, and told him exactly what Polly had said.

"There is no question," he finished up, "but I will have to get somebody to look after her. What sort of person do you suppose I ought to get?"

Sterndale scratched his head.

"That sort of thing a woman would know. I could ask my headmaster's wife, but she's an awful old stick. Don't you know any woman who's clever at that sort of thing?"

Martin's face suddenly lit up.

"Mrs. Bramble!"

"Who is she?"

Martin smiled affectionately at a memory.

"One of the best women God ever made. She used to come down to my slum parish three days a week to run things for my mothers. She had her hand in a hundred pies. She's a grand beggar; I never asked her for a penny piece, but she got it out of somebody. She moved in every conceivable circle, and knew everybody. I'm sure she could find the right person for Polly." Sterndale got up and Martin looked after him. "Where are you going?"

"To get the London telephone directory. I suppose your Mrs. Bramble lives in London, doesn't she?"

Martin looked flustered.

"I thought of writing."

"I shouldn't," said Sterndale. "The kid's unhappy, so you can't get on to it too quickly. B-R-A—Bramble, here you are I Does your Mrs. Bramble live in Eaton Place?" Martin nodded, and Sterndale picked up the receiver. He looked at Martin with a grin. "It's after seven o'clock, so it only costs a bob, and it's well worth it. You might be able to fix up something right away."

Mrs. Bramble was in, and delighted to hear Martin's voice. She could not at first be got off inquiring after his health and his welfare, but at last Martin got in what he had to say, and she listened in silence, At the end there was a pause, and he asked if she was still on the line.

"Yes, but I'm thinking. I suppose you want a lot of references for someone like that? I mean, for such a position of responsibility?"

Martin laughed.

"I only want one reference, and that will be from you."

"Do you promise that? I tell you why I ask: I have a girl in mind who should be perfect for you, but she's got no particular training. This would be her first job of the kind, and you would have to accept the fact that she's suitable from me." Martin laughed again.

"When I think of all the workers you found for me and how good they were, I'm not likely to quibble at that."

"All the same, you'll have to meet her." Mrs. Bramble's voice was decided. "Can you run up to London to-morrow to lunch, and I'll get her to see you at my club? The same old Otis where you've lunched before."

"I could," Martin agreed. "What time?"

"One o'clock. Oh, and by the way, the girl's name is Judith Griffiths."

The Otis Club had a special little room which was reserved by members for private interviews, and it was there that Martin first saw Judy. Mrs. Bramble led him into the room, laughing, and pushed him into an arm-chair.

"You look for all the world as if you were going to see the dentist, but Judy isn't a bit frightening, and in any ease, it's you that are interviewing her, and not she you."

Martin nodded.

"I'm an idiot, but I always feel at my worst with women."

Mrs. Bramble gave him a shrewd look.

"I dare say it's as well. Nature's protective colouring, perhaps. Now I'll fetch Judy."

"But you'll stay, won't you?" Martin pleaded.

Mrs. Bramble shook her head.

"Certainly not. You are engaging her, not I; and mind now that you ask her sensible questions."

When the door opened again, Martin got up. In the opening stood a girl of twenty-five. She was not exactly pretty, but her mid-brown hair had charming lights in it, and curled naturally, and there was a generous width between her grey-green eyes, and generosity in the curve of her mouth. She was a little thing, and yet the word which flew to Martin's mind about her was "valiant." There was also something else about her face which drew her to him. It was not the blank face of a woman who lacked experience; at some time there had been suffering. There were as yet no lines, but Martin's discerning priest's eye could see where the muscles had tightened to force a smile which had not come from the heart. There was something, too, in the eyes which, although they were now clear and shining, seemed as if they might have cried a good deal in their time.

He said gently:

"Miss Judith Griffiths?"

She nodded, and smiled. It was a lovely smile, the sort that lights up the whole face and makes you feel that you have found a friend whom you can trust.

"That's right. I'm Judy Griffiths."

Martin pulled forward a chair for her.

"Mrs. Bramble has told you what I want?" Judy sat down.

"Yes. And has she told you that I have no qualifications of any kind, and that she is my only reference?"

"Yes—" he hesitated. "Polly is a nice child. I'm sure you'll like her, but you will have to be a little tactful at first. I've an old aunt who needs humouring—she likes to feel that she is running the house—and there's a housekeeper called Bertha, and she likes to feel she's running it, too. I didn't mind who ran it until Polly came to me, but now, of course, it matters very much. You see, there is not only her, but there is her brother, Andrew—he'll be with me in the holidays. Polly said a very dreadful thing, Miss Griffiths; she said, and she was crying at the time: 'I don't belong to nobody here; before, just Mummie told me what to do, and now it's everybody'."

Judy's eyes clouded with sympathy.

"Poor little thing, I know just what she meant." Martin looked at her thankfully.

"I feel sure you do. I don't think it's going to be very easy for you; I don't want to upset my aunt, but the children must come first, and what you think necessary for their happiness, that you'll have to carry out."

He was surprised at the light in her face.

"I'd love to come to-morrow. I'll go straight home now and pack."

He looked at her doubtfully.

"It's perhaps a little lonely. There is nothing much that goes on in the three Saltings, except simple country things. Saltings is a beautiful village, but I'm afraid that's all we can offer you."

Judy took a deep breath, and her eyes seemed to be looking through the walls, out of London, and over the hills and far away.

She turned to him impulsively:

"You can't think how badly I want this job, and how certain it is that I shall give all that I have in me to Polly and her brother. I so badly need people to care for."

Before she left the club, Judy went to Mrs. Bramble and flung her arms round her.

"Darling, I can't thank you enough. It sounds exactly what I need. He says it's lonely—funny he should have chosen that word; if he only knew that loneliness to me meant peace."

Mrs. Bramble kissed her.

"Don't forget, Judy, that mere peace of surroundings does not make for peace of heart." She took her hand. "As Martin tells me you are going down to-morrow, and as I am going abroad, it will be some time before I see you again. So I am going to say something that I want you to remember. You have your own part to play in your own healing; make your heart receptive, don't feel it's wrong to be comforted, deliberately try to put the past behind you. Will you promise?"

Judy spoke in a strangled voice; her eyes were full of tears.

"I can't promise, but I will try."

## CHAPTER TWO

THE railway station of the three Saltings was in Upper Saltings, and there Martin and Polly met Judy. Judy saw them before her carriage reached the platform, and her eyes went at once to the child. She saw a thin, anxious, intelligent little face, under a rather ugly straw hat trimmed with mauve ribbon. She saw a well-built, but too thin body marred by a clumsily made mauve cotton frock which was long and hung below the knees. She saw grey socks, held up with elastic garters, and stout, serviceable black shoes, and before the train had stopped she said to herself: "I must alter those clothes."

Judy was as nervous of meeting Polly as Polly was shy of meeting her. Judy had a retentive memory, and could well recall the horrors of different forms of grown-up meetings; the over-effusive; the people who talked down to you; the people who were boisterous and hearty. She shook Martin by the hand, and then held out her hand to Polly; her voice was polite:

"How do you do?"

Polly gravely returned the handshake.

"How do you do, Miss Griffiths?"

They said no more for the moment, but went outside where Jimson was parked and waited for the porter. Judy eyed the car and took in its oldness, and its lack of paint, and thought what a friendly, companionable car it looked. Polly pulled at her sleeve.

"It's called Jimson."

Martin smiled.

"Polly makes that sound like a compliment; actually, I'm afraid, it's called after a very noisy carrier who used to work in these villages."

The luggage arrived. Judy had four large suitcases; the porter looked consideringly at Jimson.

"If you three could manage to get in front, sir, I might get this stuff in at the back. That luggage rack of yours is that rusty I'll have to borrow a hammer if we are going to get it down."

Judy laughed.

"I don't think we need go to those lengths." She turned to Polly: "Would you mind sitting on my knee?"

It was a direct question, and Polly felt that if she said "no" her refusal would be accepted without question; even her mother and father had not used exactly Judy's voice to her. She felt that to Judy a person, even if she was only nine, had a mind of her own, and a perfect right to say "yes" or "no." It was a nice feeling to have, and made her confident and rather grand.

"I'd like to."

First impressions of places are the ones that stay most vividly in the mind. Judy could always close her eyes and recall that drive. The dusty road, cut through the chalk, with the downland rising on each side of it. The harebells, the scabious, the clouds of chalk-blue butterflies, and the strong smell of salt air mixed with thyme which belongs to the down country

Then the rise at the top of the hill, and Polly's exclamation: "Look, that's Saltings and that's our house." Judy looked down, and an involuntary "Oh!" escaped her. Den had been helping the farmers with the milking lately, and had had no time to take his scythe to the churchyard, and so he put in some sheep to graze. Martin stopped the car.

"Fine old church, isn't it? It's got a wonderful atmosphere; you can feel as you get inside the door that people have prayed there for eight hundred years."

Judy leant forward, her eyes taking in the drowsy picture.

"It's quite, quite lovely; I had forgotten there was such peace anywhere."

Martin turned his head to face her.

"Peace does not come from surroundings; there's sadness here, just as anywhere else in the world."

Judy was still studying the village.

"They look shut away, and contented; all those lovely gardens."

Martin restarted the car.

"They are contented in Saltings; they don't ask a great deal of life, and they are a thrifty quiet people, but that village down there is only one-third of the Saltings. You climb over the opposite hill and take a look at Lower Saltings; you won't use the word 'peace' then. I have as much poverty there, Miss Griffiths, and as much suffering, as ever I had in my poor dockside parish."

"Why are they so poor?"

Martin explained about the decayed brickmaking business.

"If only one could get at them so much could be done, but they've been such a long while sunk in a quagmire of depression it's hard to pull them out."

"How well I understand that," said Judy; "once your feet are really sunk in, it does take a miracle to pull you out."

Martin glanced at her, and again his eyes noted the lines of suffering on her face.

"I hope you'll find happiness here."

The expression "find happiness" made Judy conscious that perhaps she had given herself away. Why should Martin think that she needed to find happiness if she had not suggested that she had lost it. She tightened the arm that was round Polly; her voice was deliberately light and dismissing.

"Oh, I'm a very easy person; I enjoy anything."

Before Judy put a foot in the vicarage Aunt Connie disliked her. She was standing, a gaunt black figure, in the doorway when the car came up the drive. She made no effort towards friendliness, but allowed her face to express her inward feelings, and it was yellow and contracted with bitterness. She did not hold out her hand, but looked at Judy and snapped:

"So you have come, have you?"

Judy was rather taken aback, but she showed not a sign of it.

"How do you do? This is a lovely village."

Aunt Connie snorted.

"What, what! It may be lovely on the outside, but there is plenty of evil within. Martin put down those suit-cases. I don't know for what purpose you have engaged this young woman, but I suppose it was not in order that you should wait on her."

Martin gave his aunt a puzzled look; he could not believe his mother's sister could be as consciously unkind as she sounded; it must just be her unfortunate manner. He spoke gently:

"Of course, I'm carrying up the luggage."

They were spared further argument by Bertha, who came hurrying down the passage.

"I heard Jimson coming up the drive, but there was that man from the stores at my back door, and unless you go through everything he's sure to have forgotten something."

"This is Miss Griffiths, Bertha," said Martin.

Judy looked at Bertha with the pleasure she felt. After angry, angular Aunt Connie, Bertha was like sunshine following a hard winter. She held out her hand.

"How d'you do?"

Bertha rubbed her palm on her apron, and gave her broad, friendly grin.

"How d'you do, Miss? I have to wipe my hand before shaking, for that young fellow at the stores always seems to have a bit of margarine or butter get about, and it rubs on his parcels." She took the two suit-cases that Martin was carrying out of his hands. "Give those to me, sir, and I'll show the young lady her room."

Judy let the first few days at Saltings slip by without making an effort to assert herself. It was vital, she felt, that she should learn to understand the household. Particularly, she was unwilling to rush Polly. She wanted Polly to feel she was there—the final authority to appeal to if she wanted, but not that she was yet another grown-up interfering with her life. It worked well; after a day or two Polly was saying:

"Would you like to come up on the downs to pick harebells?"

"Would you like me to show you a specially odd rose tree? Half of it's red and half of it's white."

"Would you like us to go and see Mr. Peters. He's the policeman, and Bertha says he's got four puppies—quite little without their eyes open."

Judy had an early opportunity of seeing Bertha and Aunt Connie irritating each other. It was at supper on the day after she arrived. Martin had been called out to a case of illness and came in wearing his other-world look, his mind clearly nowhere near food. Bertha, seeing this, did not leave the room after serving the course, but stood over him.

"Come on, sir, I've kept these pigeons back an hour and a very nice stew they are, too, tasty in just the way you like them. Now don't think—eat." Aunt Connie's voice was like a thin, hot wire.

"That will do, Bertha, that will do."

Bertha gave Aunt Connie a withering glance.

"It'll do when he has got a bit of that pigeon down him, not before. Come on, sir, eat it up."

Martin said, mildly:

"It's all right, Bertha, I will eat it. I promise." Bertha stood her ground.

"I know your promises. Here I stand and here I mean to stay till I see those bones picked clean and not a mushroom on your plate."

Aunt Connie's face was puce colour.

"That will do, Bertha, that will do."

Bertha threw her a disparaging look.

"You leave me be. I'm used to the clergy. You should have seen the trouble I had to make Reverend Dickson eat when he had trouble with his bees, times they swarmed and that. Why, sometimes I had to take the food to the hives to him."

"What you did for the last vicar and what you do for my nephew are two totally different things," said Aunt Connie. "You'll obey me at once, Bertha, and leave the room."

Martin gave Bertha what, to Judy's amusement, she saw was a pleading look.

"I will eat it, Bertha, really, I will."

Bertha turned to Judy.

"No one wants to cause unpleasantness, nor upset the digestion, which, when one is getting on in years, is very easy," she gave Aunt Connie a dirty look, "nothing does it easier than getting angry, for it's apt to turn acid on you." Aunt Connie let out a mixed sound between what-what! and a snort, but Bertha swept on: "So it may be, Miss Griffiths, since it seems to some my being in the room is unpleasant, and there being some I don't myself care for being in a room with, that you'll keep an eye on the vicar's plate, for have him do all the work he does on an empty stomach, I will not."

Judy controlled her mouth which was twitching to turn up at the corners, and said, gravely:

"If he should leave anything, Bertha, I'll remind him."

Judy, though she saw the household as funny, had the deepest sympathy for Martin. "Poor man," she thought, "I bet he goes through it. What with me and Bertha, I shouldn't think he has a moment's peace."

Judy was only right in part. Martin did feel that perhaps Bertha took rather a lot on herself, and he could grasp that it annoyed Aunt Connie, and he was sorry, and did what he could to placate her, but where Judy was concerned, he had no qualm. He watched, without seeming to, the quiet way she handled Polly. He saw that she was letting all the approaching be done by the child, just as he himself had allowed the three Saltings to approach him, and not he them. It was too early yet to say that Polly was happier, but it was not too early to see that in Judy she had beside her just the friend she needed, and he went about with a glow of affection and gratitude to Mrs. Bramble constantly alight in his heart.

The fact that Martin was thankful to have found Judy did not stop Aunt Connie telling him what she thought about her.

"To think that I should live to see the day when I should be deliberately insulted by my own sister's son. I have no wish to speak of any sacrifices I have made, though it is not easy for a woman of my age to throw aside her little home, but don't think I grudged coming to you when you needed me. I was never one to flinch from duty. But when it comes to slipping out behind my back and engaging hussies to look after my grand-niece, I must protest. It's no good interrupting, Martin, it is my duty to speak, and speak I shall. That girl is a hussy and I know a hussy when I see one, for as you will remember I worked for many years for a society for providing laundry work for fallen girls."

Martin listened to Aunt Connie with that mixture of dismay and bewilderment with which he nearly always regarded her. He did not like to be so uncharitable as to admit, even to himself, that his mother's sister was a difficult and embittered old woman. He never admitted that a heart existed so old, or even so depraved, but that it could be softened. "If," he thought to himself, "she is in this state of mind, then I must find a way to bring her back to charity. I must not be angry with her, I must be gentle and perhaps she will learn."

"Miss Griffiths is not a hussy; apart from the fact that you can read the truth in her face, she is a very dear friend of my friend, Mrs. Bramble, and that speaks for her."

Aunt Connie snorted:

"You have brought this woman into the house, Martin, and I cannot prevent you; but I warn you now that she is a wicked, designing minx and the fact that you cannot see it makes her all the worse; it means that she is pulling wool over your eyes."

It was not Bertha's way, as she said, "to take against people unless they took against her." Aunt Connie had taken against her and that being so she returned the dislike. It was, therefore, with an open mind that she received Judy. She considered her unnecessary. "What," she asked the villagers when she heard she was coming, "did the Reverend want with getting Miss Griffiths with me, that's reared ten, in the house?" But within a few hours of Judy's arrival her viewpoint changed. Even on Judy's first night, she had spread a good report. She had slipped out officially to post a letter, but actually to let Saltings know the news. She ran into Mrs. Beam, who kept the shop and post office.

"She's all right."

Mrs. Beam had a tendency to asthma and spoke with wheezy pauses.

"How's the old lady taking her?"

Bertha's face lit as if there were a lamp behind it, and her black eyes sparkled with joy.

"You ever tasted a morello cherry?"

Mrs. Beam laughed wheezily.

"That how she is?"

"Just." Bertha moved to the door: "Well, I must be trotting, I only slipped out for a minute, but I thought you'd all like to know how we were getting along."

"And she's really all right?"

Bertha nodded.

"Haven't said much to her yet, but she's nicely spoken, and got the right sort of look; you know, you can see right away there's nothing mean about her."

By the next morning, Judy had made friends with Bertha. She learnt from Martin of Bertha's family and, thankful to know that there was someone so used to children in the house, went to her for advice. She knocked on the kitchen door.

"Good-morning, I've come to have a talk with you about Polly's food."

Bertha was willing to be pleasant, but she was not standing for interference.

"There's nothing that's served in this house but is good and well cooked."

"I'm absolutely certain of it," Judy agreed, "but you've had a family of your own Mr. Richards tells me, and I thought you might advise me about Polly. She is not strong. I gather she goes in for running temperatures, and often sick attacks, and apparently she's been used to spending quite a lot of her winters in bed with colds and bronchitis. I'm going to arrange with Mr. Richards to have her overhauled by the doctor, but there's quite a lot that I might do, isn't there? I mean, Mr. Richards says that you brought up ten healthy children, well, what did you do about them?"

Bertha was in her element. Before Judy had time to think, she was in Bertha's bedroom, being shown the wedding groups on the wall, and the snapshots of the grandchildren on the dressing-table. At the end of the exhibition Bertha plumped herself down on her bed.

"Excuse me sitting, Miss, but my thoughts come easier that way. Now you ask me how I brought mine up healthy and I don't know, but I reckon they had plenty of good air, and good food, because, though there wasn't much money, what I gave them was good. Then I'd dose them regular."

"I should think that good, simple food is what she mostly needs. Her father was an artist, and I daresay they ate odd things at odd hours. I rather think that the doctor may recommend a diet. Of course, if he does, it will be hard on you, single-handed in this house."

Bertha laughed.

"I get help in on Saturday mornings for the scrubbing and that, and if a diet is what she needs, she can have it. He's a good man, Dr. Green, though he's getting old now, but he is well liked hereabouts. But the trouble with that child, if you ask me, is having to live under the roof with that old screeching cat, Miss Matthews, she's enough to turn the milk sour, let alone a child's stomach."

Judy faced Bertha. Her eyes were understanding and amused, but her voice was firm.

"Now, look here, Bertha. My job is going to be difficult enough in this house, goodness knows, without anybody making it worse. You can see that I can't discuss Miss Matthews with you or anyone; she is my employer's aunt, and I am accepting her as just that."

Bertha flushed, then a bright smile cheered up her face and she gave Judy a wink.

"All right, mum's the word; but what you and me think in private is our concern, and if it comes to that, what me and Reverend Richards thinks in private is our concern; he don't allow her to be talked about either, but we understand each other all the same. Proper old terror, she is, but least said soonest mended."

Judy, unable to make any headway with Aunt Connie, for she had only to walk into a room for Aunt Connie, with the air of somebody who finds herself in the presence of a bad smell, to sweep out of it, was, therefore, forced to bother Martin about everything, and Martin, trying to be helpful, was inclined to hand her on to Veronica. It was natural, in a way. Judy said:

"All that mauve and grey is a little depressing for a child of that age, would you mind if I put her back in her old cotton frocks she had before her mother died?"

Martin looked worried.

"Well, my aunt had them made for her."

Judy, recalling the length of the dresses and the stoutness of the stuff used, held back her "I'm sure she did," and instead replied:

"But I think they have a depressing effect on Polly."

Martin said:

"I'll tell you, what; Lady Blacke is sure to be in some time to-day, get her on one side and ask her advice."

Another time, Judy was discussing companionship: "It's dull for Polly to be alone and see no other children, besides, she might make some friends with whom she could do lessons in the autumn. What sort of children are there hereabouts?"

Martin considered.

"Quite a lot in Upper Saltings. I don't know which would be suitable for Polly; I expect it is only a matter of starting with the right family, then she would know everybody she wanted to. I tell you what, telephone to Lady Blacke, she is sure to know which of the children are Polly's sort."

From the beginning, Judy was against this endless asking of Veronica's advice. For one thing, she very much doubted if Veronica was the right person to advise on the subject of Polly, for Polly was not easy with her. Then, too, there were things about Veronica which Judy did not like. She resented, and was ashamed of herself for resenting, for it was not her business, the way Veronica swept in and out of the vicarage as if she belonged there. She resented the frank and shameless way in which she made a fool of Aunt Connie, and toadied to the old lady. Then, too, she felt the embarrassment that any women feels at seeing another woman make a fool of her sex. She disliked Veronica's methods for holding Martin's attention. She was sorry for her, for she saw that under her glittering surface she was desperately in love, and she knew how much it must hurt to get no sign of it returned. It was, she supposed, a comfort to Veronica to realise that it was not herself only that Martin was not in love with, but that he was not a marrying man, and never considered any woman in the light of her attractions. But beyond all these feelings about her, Judy was guarded by something stronger; she felt an uneasiness when Veronica was about, it was as if something had flashed a warning to her mind, "be on your guard. Don't make a friend of this woman."

To Veronica Judy's coming to the vicarage was a blow. No woman in love likes to see another woman have more chances of being with the man she loves than she has herself. Veronica was not a fool and did not deny that Judy was attractive. She had not, she was convinced, one tenth of her own attractions, but then, Martin was such a funny man, he seemed to be unaffected by physical beauty. In any case, all men were funny, they were capable of not seeing real charm and beauty, and instead, falling for simple people, who, in comparison, had very little to offer. Not that she thought for one moment that Martin was ever likely to fall for Judy, but she did wish most sincerely that the girl had never come near the house. On the other hand, since she had come to the house, she was not going to be led into the error of making an enemy of her. Judy, just as Aunt Connie, must be bought. Judy, just as Aunt Connie, must be dependent on her for those little favours and kindnesses which would brighten a dull life. Following this scheme there was hardly a day on which she was not down at the vicarage with armloads of flowers which she handed to Judy with a charming smile, saying, "I am sure you love flowers as much as I do," or "bring Polly up to tea this afternoon, the strawberries are so splendid just now and children do so enjoy a strawberry tea, and you can pick as many as you like to take home."

"Do let me help over Polly; I know you can't use Jimson much, but you can always have my car if you want to go shopping, or to take her anywhere."

In spite of these efforts, Veronica knew she was making very little headway, though she was spared knowing that Judy was refraining from asking her opinion on many of the questions on which Martin had advised that she should be called in. She found it infuriating as the days went by to see things happening inside the vicarage in which she had no share. She learned of these happenings from Aunt Connie.

"That child," said Aunt Connie grimly, "has been put on a diet. I never knew such nonsense. A diet, indeed."

Veronica opened her eyes and asked why a diet had been planned, and learned that Martin had driven Polly and Judy in to see Dr. Green. She bit back the annoyed "Oh, why did he take them? I would have been pleased to drive them over." It was the same with other small things; Judy had taken Polly to tea with some children in Upper Saltings; Judy had decided that Polly could come out of mourning. Veronica felt increasingly things were going on in the vicarage behind her back. That she wasn't as vital to its running as she had been, and as she became conscious of this, a thought stirred in her brain. Somehow or other, it must be worked that Judy should go. Not unkindly; she would find her another job and a better one, but she must not remain at the vicarage.

It was on a Saturday afternoon that Judy first met Sterndale Adam. Sterndale knew Polly, for Martin had taken him up to see her in bed one evening, but he had not yet set eyes on Judy. Judy and Polly were walking down the village street on a very important mission. Fred Peters had said that Polly should have one of his puppies, and to-day was the day on which the choice of them was to be made. Sterndale was busy weeding his front-garden. Hearing Polly's high, excited prattle, he looked over the hedge.

"Hullo, Polly, where are you off to?"

Polly had taken to Sterndale, so she climbed the first bar of his gate and hung over.

"Mr. Peters, the policeman, has got four puppies, three boys and a girl. Their mother's a collie, but nobody quite knows who their father was, so they don't know what they're going to be like. But I'm going to have one, and to-day I'm going to choose."

Sterndale came to the gate, and smiled at Judy.

"How do you do, Miss Griffiths? This is a big occasion."

Judy nodded laughing.

"How d'you do. I should say it was; we've decided definitely on a boy, but we can't make up our minds between them. There's a black one, a fawn, and a brown one with a spot over his eye."

Sterndale was taking Judy in. He had, of course, heard an immense amount about her, but he was surprised now that he saw her. Martin had told him what a success she was, about his gratitude to Mrs. Bramble, and the splendid friend that Judy was going to be to Polly, but he had not told him how Judy would look. Now he saw her, standing in the middle of the road, in a leaf-green linen frock, no hat, and the sun bringing out all the lights on her curls. He saw her grey-green eyes and the humour in them, and he liked what he saw. He laid down his rake.

"Nobody living," he said to Polly, "is a greater authority on puppies than I am. I did, in fact, take a blue in 'puppy-spotting' at Cambridge. Would you like me to help?"

Polly was enchanted, and skipped from one barelegged, sandalled foot to the other.

"Oh please; and then you can tell me exactly what it will look like when it's bigger."

Judy looked at Sterndale over Polly's head.

"You are going to need all your skill as an old Blue to describe the future appearance of these puppies accurately."

Sterndale returned her look with gravity.

"Even an old Blue may make a mistake, but at least Polly will have the advantage of expert advice."

Fred Peters had an afternoon off, or at least, part of an afternoon. He, too, had been gardening; he was not dressed for the part, for later he would be on duty, so he was wearing his policeman's trousers, and his tunic was hung on a tree nearby. He looked up as the party came down the lane, and called to his wife.

"Rosie, Rosie; here be Miss Polly and Miss Griffiths to pick that puppy, and there's Mr. Adam with them."

Rosie had the puppies in a kennel in the backyard, but on hearing what Fred said she picked them up and put them in her apron, and carried them round to the front garden, and set them down on the lawn. Polly fell amongst them with a squeal of delight, while the rest of the party stood looking down at her. The puppies had now got their eyes open, and were waddling about in that curious blancmange fashion that comes from uncertainty of leg-power. They had pathetic, large, incapable paws, large heads, and large tummies, but in each one of the four the head was slightly different, and each one of the four was of slightly different size. Sterndale, conscious that his advice was going to be asked, drew Peters to one side.

"Got any ideas about the father?"

Fred shook his head.

"I was busy at the time, away on that burglary in Upper Saltings, and Rosie thought she had fixed up Bess secure, but she got out, so it might be one of half a dozen. Myself, I fancy 'twas that fox terrier up at Old Farm."

Sterndale looked at Fred.

"Call that a fox terrier! You don't mean that black fluffy brute that they've got on a chain in the yard?"

"He be a fox terrier," Fred retorted; "leastways, his mother was. His mother were called 'Nell,' and bit Rev. Dickson when he came round that time his bees swarmed up there. She were a fox terrier all right."

Sterndale nodded at the puppies.

"Then these are going to be collies?"

Fred was surprised.

"Yes, sir, naturally, seeing Bess be a collie."

At that moment Polly looked up from the puppies.

"Which one will grow up the nicest, Mr. Adam, and what will it look like?"

Sterndale stared at the darkest of the puppies.

"Well, I fancy that one. It will be black and fluffy, with a long, long coat. I couldn't say now for certain about its shape."

"What will its ears be like?" Polly inquired. "Will they stand up or will they hang down?"

Judy had heard the conversation between Sterndale and Fred. She looked at Sterndale, her eyes twinkling.

"Yes, what will the ears be like? We should so like to know."

Sterndale stepped forward gravely.

"The chances are, Polly, that they'll be ears of great character expressing immense personality; in fact, I wouldn't put it past him for one ear to stand straight up and the other one to hang down like a fox terrier's."

"Will that look nice?" Polly asked doubtfully.

"Charming," Sterndale said firmly. "What you want in a dog, Polly, is not common or garden everyday looks, but character. Now what we have to decide is, which of these three dogs has the most character." He gave Judy a "now-this-will-teach-you-look." "Miss Griffiths will be able to tell you about that; people like her, who bring up little girls, are tremendous judges of character."

Judy knelt down on the grass beside Polly.

"What do you think, darling? Would you like the brown one? I do think that black mark over his eye makes him very distinctive. On the other hand, the fawn one will perhaps be a very pretty dog, and then, of course, there is Mr. Adam's choice—the black one." She raised the black puppy's face in her hands. "I must say, he's got a very individual expression; but he looks a little like a dictator."

Polly lay flat on the ground on her tummy, and took each puppy's face between her hands and stared into its eyes. Then she turned to Judy:

"I think it's the black one; he does look to me a very knowing sort of dog." She glanced up at Fred. "When can I have it, please?"

Fred glanced at Rosie, and Rosie turned to Judy. "He'm won't be house-trained, Miss; will you have trouble with him with old Miss Matthews?" Judy, true to her principles of never discussing Aunt Connie, dismissed the subject.

"We'll have trouble with everybody. I can just imagine the state the house is going to be in; mess everywhere, chewed shoes, chewed furniture—still, we mustn't worry about that." She turned to Polly. "You know, I think it would be a good idea if you fetched him the first day Andrew comes for the holidays; then there will be two of you to train him, and he won't be quite so much anxiety. You see, he's a little young yet to leave his mother." Polly looked disappointed.

"It's an awful long time till August, and it will be almost August before Andrew gets back."

"Oh, the time will go like lightning; think of all the things we've got to do before then. Make him a bed, buy him a harness, find him a name, and then have his name engraved and put on the harness. It will be all we can do to be ready in time."

When Sterndale, Judy, and Polly had disappeared up the lane, Fred took his spade and leant on it.

"She be a wonderful nice lady, that Miss Griffiths. It's rarely lucky for little Miss Polly to have her." Rosie nodded.

"She has picked up wonderful, that little girl; she looked a proper sad little scrap those first Sundays in church. I reckon it was right of vicar to send for Miss Griffiths. Vicarage Bertha do say that she has made all the difference in the house. The little girl is always laughing and singing now, and mind you, Bertha do know, for she were all for taking charge of the little one herself at the beginning, but she reckoned it was more than she could do to keep that old Miss Matthews from interfering. I reckon Miss Griffiths is managing, though."

Fred chuckled.

"I hope vicar keeps Miss Griffiths; but she's a nice looking lady. Did you see the way Mr. Adam was looking at her? I reckon he was fair taken with her."

Rosie gave him a dig with her elbow.

"You get on with your gardening; you're always imagining summat."

Fred gave another chuckle.

"Maybe I'm imagining, but I'd say that Mr. Adam was looking at Miss Griffiths same way as I looked at you first time I clapped eyes on you, my girl."

Walking home, Judy, Sterndale and Polly were engrossed in the question of a suitable name for the puppy.

"Let's," said Sterndale at last, "all come into my garden and sit on the lawn; we'll each have a sheet of paper, and we'll each write down four names, and we'll put them into a hat, and Polly will draw out the one that wins."

Judy hesitated; no more than Fred had she been blind to the fact that Sterndale was looking at her with approval. She was not in the habit of thinking that men had fallen in love with her, but she did think that perhaps Sterndale was short of female companionship, and might think that a little flirtation would help to pass the week-ends when he was not at his school. But she was going to start nothing of the sort. She had not come to the Saltings to get mixed up in flirtations, however mild. The peace that she needed did not lie that way. Moreover, anything of the sort would, she considered, be most unsuitable. Vicars did not engage people to look after their nieces for those people to amuse themselves with their best friends. Her voice was as charming as usual, but firm.

"I think it's a splendid idea; but we'll do it at the vicarage. It's nearly tea-time."

Sterndale wanted a little of Judy to himself. It would not be at all the same thing to sit on the vicarage lawn and write names; he knew exactly how that would end. Judy would take Polly off to tea in the small sitting-room which she had re-christened the schoolroom, and he would be left having a dismal tea with Aunt Connie.

"I meant to ask you to have tea here," he said. Polly looked longingly at Judy, but Judy took her hand and led her firmly down the lane.

"No, Polly's on a diet, and Bertha has made her a special cake with no eggs. Come on, and don't be so lazy." She laughed down at Polly. "Take his hand, Polly; he doesn't want to come to the vicarage because he doesn't want the trouble of walking that far."

Aunt Connie, though she would have denied it, if asked, had been having an afternoon sleep. She woke with a jump to hear laughter outside. She got up and looked out of the window. A rug was spread out on the lawn, and on it sat Sterndale, Polly, and Judy. Judy held a hat, and Polly's hand was poised over it. Presently her hand darted in, and she drew it out and held up a small strip of paper; this she unfolded, while Sterndale and Judy watched her smilingly.

"S.L.O.E.," Polly spelt out. She looked up puzzled. "But he isn't going to be a slow dog; he's going to be a very fast one."

Judy laughed and put an arm round her.

"I'm sorry, darling; it's one of my suggestions. Sloes are little black fruits; you must have seen them in the hedges."

"Very good mixed with gin," Sterndale put in.

Polly suddenly remembered what sloe-berries looked like. She clasped her hands.

"I know sloe-berries; I think that's a lovely name for him." Suddenly she flung her arms round Judy, "Anyway, I'm glad it was one of yours that I picked."

Aunt Connie had never been a woman to get love. Watching that scene, seeing Polly's spontaneous gesture, and hearing what she said, she was overcome by such a blinding flash of jealousy that she felt sick, and had to stagger back into her room and sit down. Even sitting, she trembled all over. In that moment, something in her brain seemed to crack: The years of rigid restraint in which she had kept herself had not fitted her for violent emotion, and so when it came it was like waves of water flowing over a long-dried dam, breaking it down, washing it away. The woman who got up off the chair into which she had staggered, was not quite the same woman who had looked out of the window a few minutes before. There was an almost imperceptible weakness about her mouth, and the hardness of her eyes was mixed with a look of cunning. She was conscious of no change. She gave a pull to straighten her black coat, and she felt the jet brooch at her neck to see it was straight, and gave a pat to her little grey bun of hair where it showed under her hat—all actions which she had done every day for years; but her lips were moving, unconsciously she was muttering to herself: "I told him she was a hussy. He wouldn't believe me, but I was right. She's the dangerous sort; she gains people's confidence first, and then she can do what she likes. But she won't do what she likes with me, and I shall do what I can to save Martin. I expect she's after money, that sort always is. Well, that's a way I can help. I'll hide his money for him. And I can watch her—that sort always betrays themselves sooner or later. The wicked shall go to Hell; I must keep that in mind. That's where she belongs. That's where she must go."

Aunt Connie was not the only one to watch the scene on the lawn. Martin had come in, and hearing the laughter and Sterndale's voice, had gone round to the front of the house. He paused there and smiling watched, and saw Polly put her arms round Judy, and heard her honest little voice say:

"I'm glad it was one of yours that I chose."

He was intensely happy in that moment, for he knew himself for a dreamer, and one not always good at the practical things of life; but this time he had done well—he had made an effort, and was rewarded beyond belief. It was inspiring to hear that note of confidence and affection in Polly's voice. He took a step forward, meaning to join the party, and then he stopped. Sterndale looked at Judy across Polly's head, and Judy flashed him a smile. Martin went unnoticed back into the house. He felt a curiously grey lonely feeling which he could not understand. This was his Vicarage, Polly was his niece, Sterndale his friend;

if he joined them he knew he would hear welcoming voices, and yet he could not bring himself to do it. "They don't need me," was his thought, and it hurt.

Andrew was coming home for the holidays. Polly, her eyes shining, and her cheeks flaming, danced about her bedroom in a vest and a tiny pair of blue and white striped knickers, singing, "Andrew's coming! Andrew's coming!" Bertha held out the child's frock.

"Put this on now, and don't get playing up or you'll miss the train."

Polly seized the frock, and dragged it over her head.

"There's lots of time. Miss Griffiths has got to get out Jimson."

Bertha caught Polly by the arm and buttoned her frock down the back.

"If I know anything of Miss Griffiths, Jimson's at the door by now." She led Polly to the dressing-table. "Now a comb through your hair and you're off."

"Uncle Martin's put some money on his study mantelpiece," said Polly. "I'm to buy toffees and some dough-nuts for tea."

Bertha sniffed.

"It's a waste. There's nothing you children want for tea that I can't cook."

Polly skipped to the door.

"Can you make dough-nuts?"

Bertha nodded.

"Could if I had the time. Off you go now."

Polly ran to the study and met Aunt Connie in the doorway. Aunt Connie caught her by the arm.

"Don't run about so. Little ladies should be quiet and gentle."

Polly nervously tugged away from her.

"I've come for some money Uncle Martin left on the mantelpiece. It's for Miss Griffiths; we're to get dough-nuts and toffee."

Aunt Connie made a sound that bore a resemblance to a laugh.

"Indeed! For Miss Griffiths. Well, get it, my child. Get it."

Polly crossed the room. The mantelpiece was high, and she needed to stand on tip-toe to see along it. She turned a red anxious face to Aunt Connie.

"It isn't there. Do you think he forgot?"

Aunt Connie again made her strange half laughing sound.

"Perhaps. Run along, my child, and tell Miss Griffiths you couldn't find it; that there was no money lying about for anyone to pick up."

Judy was quite unmoved by Polly's tale of woe.

"It doesn't matter, darling; I've got some money. I expect Uncle Martin went out in a hurry. We'll ask him for it when we come in."

Polly settled back in the car, comforted.

"We'll have to buy an awful lot of dough-nuts; Uncle Sterndale's coming to tea, and I suppose we'll have Lady Blacke as usual."

Judy smiled, but her voice was firm.

"You mustn't grudge her tea. After all, she's very kind to you."

"I wonder why she comes to our house?" Polly marvelled. "Her own is much bigger and much grander, and she has much better things to eat than us. I don't like her, and you don't like her, and Uncle Martin never seems particularly pleased to see her. I suppose it must be her and Aunt Connie being such great friends."

Judy, her eyes twinkling, kept her face turned from Polly.

"Perhaps." She felt for her words; she was not going to lie to Polly, but all the same she could not allow the statement that she did not like Veronica to pass uncriticised.

"It's not that I don't like her; it's just that she's not my sort. People go in sorts, you know. You wouldn't expect to find a sugared almond in a bottle of peppermints, would you?"

Polly considered the question.

"She's like a rather proud geranium growing in a field where everything is wild."

Judy laughed.

"That's a very good description, and you wouldn't expect the buttercups and things to feel easy with the geranium, would you?"

Polly kicked the dash-board.

"I wouldn't. I'd expect them to ask the geranium to go back to the garden where it belonged."

Judy thought it better to change the subject.

"Well, count the geranium as coming to tea, and tell me how many dough-nuts we ought to buy."

Andrew was acutely nervous. He had been through a bad time. The boys at his school had been embarrassed at finding themselves faced with a tragedy happening to one of themselves; and feeling awkward and scared of saying the wrong thing had ostracised him. It had not been until the last few weeks that his life had got back to normal, and that had been entirely due to his own effort. He knew that if he showed any sign of being unhappy the boys would go on avoiding him, and so he had adopted a hearty who-cares manner which was foreign to his nature and a strain, considering that he was so wretched inside that he soaked his pillow with tears every night. Now that the holidays had started he was faced with new trials. He did not know Martin well; he was just Mother's brother who was a parson. He didn't know what life in a vicarage would be like, but he supposed it would mean a lot of going to church, and not doing what he liked as he had done at Rye. He looked forward to seeing Polly, but she was only a kid, and though a good companion sometimes, had a kid's way of wanting to play silly games. In her sketchy letters she had written about a Miss Griffiths, who seemed to do the same sort of job as Matron at school, and that wasn't very cheering. Matrons were all right in term time, but you didn't want them mucking about the place in the holidays.

Judy saw a small boy in a grey flannel suit, with some hair standing up in a brush on the crown of his head. He had a pale freckled face, and large grey eyes. There was something about him which caught at her heart. He looked so small, and his knees were bumpy, and he was trying so hard to give an air of being cheerful. Somehow he reminded her of a puppy that has not been wanted, and has been kicked about and got into the habit of shying away from a pat.

Polly, having hugged Andrew, pulled him towards Judy.

"This is Miss Griffiths, and we're going to have dough-nuts for tea, and afterwards you and me are going to Mr. Peters—he's the policeman—to fetch a puppy he's given us. He's mostly a collie, but because he's black like a sloe-berry, Mr. Peters thinks Sloe's father might be the black dog up at Old Farm, but me and Miss Griffiths hope he isn't, because that dog's always rather angry."

Judy, after giving Andrew a welcoming smile, left this flood of news to see that the porter was collecting Andrew's luggage. She came back with it following her on the truck to hear Andrew say:

"What's happened to all my things? My stuffed owl, and my moths?"

Judy had worried about the children's possessions. There was scarcely a day when Polly did not lament for something, but it had not seemed to her wise to take the child back to Rye yet; it would be so easy to upset her. She had asked Martin—and he had agreed at once—to hold up the sale of the contents of the house at Rye until Andrew got home.

"Children," she explained, "never treasure the things one thinks that they will. My idea is to take them over to Rye one day as soon as possible after Andrew gets home, then they can pick out everything they value, and however tiresome we'll bring them here. It would be so awful if they felt they had been done out of something they were fond of."

Judy never at any time spoke down to a child; now, because she was so desperately anxious that Andrew should feel confident, she used an even more you-are-as-good-as-me manner than usual.

"Your Uncle hasn't had a thing touched in your home. Anything you do want we are going over to fetch."

Andrew looked up at her.

"When?"

"When you like."

"To-morrow?"

Polly skipped anxiously from foot to foot.

"But Sloe will just have come; we can't leave him to-morrow."

Judy included Polly in her glance.

"If Andrew wants to go to-morrow we'll have to take Sloe with us." She turned back to Andrew. "I sympathise with you; I hate being parted from my things."

Andrew felt as though he had been very cold and was now thawing. He gave a nod as if to say, "That's all right then," and moved towards the exit.

Tea was ready in the drawing-room when Judy, Polly and Andrew arrived. Aunt Connie had pounced on the chair at the head of the tea-tray, and as Judy came in she threw her a malevolent glance as if to say, "There, you wanted this seat, didn't you, but it's too late; I've got it."

Martin had made an effort and was in to greet Andrew; he met him, Judy thought, in just the right way, with a casual:

"Hullo, old man! This is your Great Aunt Connie. It's good to have you. We've been counting the days, haven't we, Polly?" Sterndale had arrived, and Martin brought him forward. "This is Sterndale Adam—Uncle Sterndale, Polly calls him."

Sterndale, quick at summing up boys, liked the look of Andrew, and at the same time saw the sign of strain about him.

"You fond of prawning?"

Andrew's face lit up.

"Yes, but I haven't done much."

"Good! I've just started my holidays, too, and I thought one day soon—when the tide was right—you and I and Miss Griffiths, and Polly, might go over to Birling Gap; one can pick up grand prawns there."

Judy's face did not change, but she felt on her guard. She was certain Sterndale's offer was meant in all niceness, as a kind gesture to the children, but she felt, too, that she had her place in it. Before the children could answer she said briskly:

"If you take the children to Birling Gap you won't need me. It'll be a splendid chance for me to get on with some mending. You should see the pile of Polly's things I've got to patch."

Aunt Connie's lips were moving silently, now her voice rang harshly across the room:

"You are engaged, Miss Griffiths, to look after the children; not to hang about the house when they're out."

Both the children looked scared and anxious at such behaviour from a grown-up. Sterndale opened his mouth to speak, but Judy—who was beside him—gave her head a faint shake; the last thing she wanted was a row the moment Andrew arrived.

"Well, let's have tea," she said cheerfully. "We can decide about Birling Gap later on."

Martin had seen Judy's gesture to silence Sterndale, and was puzzled; they really hardly knew each other, how did they understand one another so well? He didn't grasp that Judy had relied on the fact that Sterndale was a schoolmaster, and would jump to the necessity of a quiet home-coming for Andrew. Because he was puzzled he did not move for a moment and stood staring at Judy, and Sterndale—catching his look—watched the two of them, and it was at that moment that Veronica came in.

Veronica was not particularly sensitive to atmosphere, but the expressions on the two men's faces, and some indefinable feeling in the air, rang an alarm-bell in her brain. Except that she was sufficiently feminine to dislike any male attention paid to another woman, she did not care in the slightest what Sterndale felt about Judy; but if Sterndale was a bit intrigued by her, what did it matter to Martin? Almost as soon as she felt the alarm it vanished; the two men moved, Judy was arranging a small table in the window for the children, and the feeling in the air had evaporated; only, as is the way of strong unspoken atmospheres it had left an impression which would be there to be re-felt when events gave cause.

Veronica, as usual, had arrived as a fairy godmother. She had felt really sorry for Andrew; it must be miserable coming for his holidays as a stranger, but it was not possible for her to be wholly detached in her generosity, and she had pictured how she would appear to Martin—a parcel in her arm, looking her best in a new and very lovely blue *crêpe de Chine* frock and coat. Now, after a smile all round, she swept down on Andrew, and to his horror knelt down by him and kissed him.

"How do you do, darling? We are all so very, very glad to have you with us."

Andrew with a face like a peony, wriggled and tried politely to free himself. Polly leant across the table, and said in an explanatory voice:

"Andrew doesn't like being kissed. Boy's don't, you know."

"Just on the day they come home they don't mind, do they, Andrew?" Andrew so plainly did that Veronica sat back on her haunches and held out her parcel. "A special present for a holiday boy."

Andrew looked as if he were going to be sick, but he took the parcel and unpacked it.

Veronica, meaning to be the only one who had thought of a present, had not asked anyone's advice about what Andrew would like. She had relied on a list sent front a London department store, and from it had selected a boy's carpentry outfit. She did not know that at eleven a boy uses real tools, and she could not know that Andrew was particularly handy with tools, his father having been good at it and let his son help him from babyhood to make or repair anything needed in the house. She could not see from her position anything but Andrew's cheek, and so missed his disgusted eyes examining the toys in the box, which would fall to pieces if used for proper work.

"Well," she asked, "do you like it?"

Judy marvelled at Veronica's stupidity; she knew nothing about Carpentry tools, but if anything ever was clear, it was that Andrew did not want these. It was plain too that Polly despised them. She had sprawled across the table and was peering into the box with a look on her face as if she smelt a bad smell. Judy determined to keep the atmosphere smooth, struggled in her brain for something to say which would lead Andrew to thank Veronica politely, but before she could speak Sterndale had come to the rescue. He pushed the box of tools off the table, at the same time giving Andrew's shoulder a slight school-masterish pat to call him to order.

"These'll be fine, won't they, old man."

Andrew remembered his manners, he turned an artificial smile on Veronica.

"Thanks awfully."

"As a matter of fact—" Polly started, but before she could go on Judy had pounced.

"You sit down. What's the good of our buying all those doughnuts if you don't get on and eat them."

Polly raised an accusing finger and pointed at Martin.

"You forgot about them, Uncle Martin. There wasn't any money on the mantelpiece in your study, and Miss Griffiths had to buy them."

Martin was over by Aunt Connie, waiting to hand round the teacups. He laughed.

"For once you're wrong. I may be forgetful, but I do remember that. Two half-crowns on the left-hand corner."

Polly shook her head.

"No there aren't. I stood on tip-toe, and felt every inch. There wasn't nothing."

Martin turned to Sterndale.

"Sterndale, prove this bad niece of mine is wrong. Go to my study and fetch the half-crowns off the mantelpiece."

Polly bounced up and down on her chair.

"He can look and look but he won't find them because they aren't there."

Veronica had joined Martin by Aunt Connie; she took a cup of tea. She turned to Martin.

"Did you remember? You are forgetful, you know."

He passed her some bread and butter.

"For once I did. I asked Bertha to remind me, and she saw me put them there, so I've got a witness."

Sterndale came back grinning.

"Polly wins. Not a coin on the whole mantelpiece."

"What!" Judy's face seemed to them all to have become pale. "But if Bertha saw you put them there, they must be there."

Martin crossed the room.

"I'll have another look."

While he was gone Veronica watched Judy. Why on earth should she care about two missing half-crowns? She didn't like the girl, but whatever else she might be she was convinced she was not a petty thief, she had altogether the wrong kind of face for cheap crimes. But she did care, there was no doubt of it; she stood apparently waiting on the children, but actually with a strained air, watching the door. When the study door was heard to shut and Martin's voice calling down the passage for Bertha, colour flowed back into her face, and then ebbed, leaving it whiter than before.

Martin came back, looking distressed.

"You're quite right Polly. They are gone."

"But how could they have," said Judy. "Who would have taken them?"

Aunt Connie gave a sudden chuckle.

"Anyway, they are gone, Miss Griffiths." Everybody looked in a startled shocked way at Aunt Connie, then Martin said:

"I suppose a tramp got in, though he seems to have touched nothing else. I must keep the bottom half of my window shut when I'm out."

"But how odd to take only the money," said Judy, "there must have been other valuables."

Veronica had her eyes glued to Judy's face. "How much more odd," she thought, "that you should be in such a state over it. There's something very peculiar about the whole affair. In spite of your appearance it almost seems as if there was more to you than meets the eye. I must find out." Out loud she said with a sweet smile:

"Don't worry so, Miss Griffiths. What do two half-crowns matter? And anyway, you are in no way to blame."

## CHAPTER THREE

THE children were fetching their puppy, so Judy went upstairs to unpack Andrew's things. Bertha followed her and offered to help.

"Let me give you a hand, miss?"

Judy smiled gratefully, but shook her head.

"Goodness no, you do the work of ten as it is."

Bertha leant against the door.

"I keep well on it. Does me good."

Judy paused, her arms full of shirts and pants.

"What d'you suppose happened to that money?"

Bertha shrugged her shoulders.

"Couldn't say I'm sure. Never knew anyone to get in here, Reverend Dickson never missed anything."

Judy laid the clothes in the drawer, her voice was bitter.

"I hate that sort of thing. It's loathsome."

Bertha opened her eyes.

"Whatever for d'you want to take on like that. You're not to blame, and I'm not to blame. You can't spend your time worrying about other people's consciences."

"No, I suppose not, but one can't help wishing that sort of thing didn't have to happen. Who could it have been?"

Bertha shook her head.

"A boy or a tramp, anyone could have got in."

Judy turned to her.

"You really think that. Oh, I'm so glad. It would be so awful if it was someone in the house."

Bertha chuckled.

"Well, it may have been, I wouldn't put anything past Miss Matthews, but you and me aren't discussing her so mum's the word. Is that right what Polly was saying that you're fetching their things from Rye to-morrow?"

Judy was kneeling by the box, now she sat on the floor, and faced Bertha.

"Yes. They want their own toys and books." She looked up, "With what you know about children would you say that seeing the house again would upset them?"

Bertha pleated her apron while she considered.

"No, likely it won't. Children are funny that way. I shouldn't wonder if being pleased to see all their own stuff again put it out of their minds. Reverend going?"

Judy sighed.

"No. I don't suppose he could get away, but I wish he could. It would be nice for Andrew, his first day home."

Bertha came a step or two into the room.

"He could. Nobody's dying, unless you count that old scoundrel in Lower Saltings, who sends for the Reverend once a week, and is no nearer dying than me, and no one's being buried. A day out would do him good. Beside," Bertha's black eyes twinkled, "it would be a good slap in the face for a certain titled lady, though we won't mention no names. Do her good to find out we can sometimes move without her."

Judy would not discuss Veronica with Bertha, so she turned back to the box.

"Well, I might ask him."

"Never put off till later what you can do now," said Bertha, "He's in his study. Tell him I want to know. Say I'm seeing to a picnic lunch, and is four going or three."

Martin was at his desk writing when Judy knocked. He gave a hopeless pat to a pile of cards beside him.

"How fine it must be, Miss Griffiths, to be a doctor or a scientist, and be able to say, I've made him well, or I've discovered this fact. A parson's work is never finished, the best I can say of my work is that perhaps I have made an impression."

Judy came over to the desk.

"What's the trouble? The people all look models of good behaviour to me, and the church is always packed."

Martin sighed.

"But that's Saltings and Upper Saltings, and even there I fail. Why is it, Miss Griffiths, that charity is so rare a quality? 'Though I speak with the tongues of men and of angels, and have not charity, I am become as sounding brass, or a tinkling cymbal.'"

"Why indeed," said Judy bitterly. "If people knew the suffering they caused. If they could just read the epistle on charity once a year they might remember that 'Charity thinketh no evil.'"

Martin was stirred by her tone, and had a priest's longing to heal, and his intuitive gifts told him that for all her gaiety of manner there was a lot in Judy that needed healing. But he knew too that forcing a confidence was a mistake, and that if his help were needed it was better it should be asked for. So he merely said gently.

"'For we know in part; but when that which is perfect is come, that which is in part shall be done away.'" There was a moment's silence, and then he gave his cards another pat. "If there were sufficient charity in Saltings and Upper Saltings, these cards could be burnt."

Judy leant on the desk.

"What are they?"

"Family histories, one for each of the families in Lower Saltings." He took one up. "The Browns can't come to church because their shoes are worn out, and Mr. Brown is in Wormwood Scrubs doing eight months, and the parish nurse reports that the little Browns are filthy, and she isn't sure that it isn't a case for the S.P.C.C." He laid back the card sadly. "It isn't a case for the S.P.C.C., it's a case for charity from some person in Saltings or Upper Saltings. The Browns need money and an occasional parcel of food and clothes; they want a friend who comes in and sits and talks to Mrs. Brown over the kitchen table. A friend who wants to hear all the worries and is prepared to work out how to get round them all, and will set the Brown's on their feet, and when they are on them will go on being a friend, and see that they stay on them."

"And can't you get anyone to adopt them?" Martin banged a despairing fist on his desk.

"The Browns are one of dozens. They all want adopting and nobody will help. Lady Blacke is wonderfully generous, but she isn't quite the person I mean."

Judy considered a moment.

"Why don't we adopt the Browns? Myself and Bertha, and Polly, and when he's home, Andrew. Perhaps we'll start a fashion."

Martin raised his eyes that were suddenly alight with hope.

"Could you? I mean have you the time?"

"I'll make time. I won't take the children there till the Browns are cleaned up a bit. But it will be very good for Polly, all children ought to take a personal interest in others poorer than themselves."

Martin's face seemed to Judy to shine as if lit from inside.

"That's splendid of you, and you'll get your reward, it's a fine feeling pulling the helpless out of the mud."

Judy smiled.

"That's settled then. The Browns are ours. Now look, I came in to ask you to do something. Could you take a day off to-morrow and come with the children and myself to Rye? I think it may be rather a straining day for them, and you would be a help."

Martin opened his engagement book, and ran through its crowded hours.

"There's nothing at the moment that can't wait. I could come if you really think the children want me."

"I do think they want you, and I think that you ought to come. They are parishioners of yours, too, you know, just as much as any of your people in Lower Saltings."

Martin's voice was humble.

"You mean I don't see enough of them?"

Judy's voice was frank.

"Yes, it's particularly important now Andrew is home. You are in the place of his father. Yon ought to see a lot of him."

Martin looked like somebody learning something new.

"Ought I? Yes, I suppose I ought. Very well, I'll take to-morrow off."

Judy went to the door, then she turned.

"And to-morrow is only the first day, of I hope a good many. I'm going up to London one day soon, I want to get materials for Polly and I must order some new things for Andrew. On that day I thought you might get Mr. Adam to help, and take the children for a picnic or something."

"A picnic!"

"Yes. Don't you ever do anything but work? All work even for a parson isn't a good thing you know."

Martin was plainly staggering under a new idea.

"Oh! Well perhaps it isn't."

Judy opened the door.

"Of course it isn't, but it's never too late to mend, you know."

Some days stand out in a lifetime because of a glow which hangs over them which has nothing whatsoever to do with what was said, or what was done. Such a day was the visit to Rye. The weather was perfect, the country seen through a shimmer of heat and a cloud of chalk dust was exquisite, the air scented with the tang of the sea, mixed with thyme. Judy sat at the back with Andrew, and between them they had Sloe in a basket. Polly was officially in front beside Martin, but she divided her attention equally with those at the back, hanging over now to talk to Judy, now to look at Sloe, and now to discuss what was in the lunch basket.

Judy was surprised at how happy she felt. Here she was rattling through Sussex in an old tin can of a car, with two children and a parson. Of course the day was lovely, but what was there to cause this gaiety of heart which made her find every-thing fun? And why was she so glad that the day was only in its beginning, that ahead of her stretched such a lot of hours?

Martin never took days off, his nearest approach to such a thing were the various parish outings, and he felt like a boy with an unexpected holiday. He had taken very much to heart what Judy had said about the children, that they too were his parish-ioners, and was charmed to find how easy and natural they were with him. He listened to Polly's chatter and answered her ques-tions, but as well he had half an ear for the conversation at the back, and he was full of admiration for Judy, who was drawing Andrew out with sympathy and understanding. She could not really care about the cricket matches he had played in, or what the school had said when somebody called Pincher had missed a catch. It couldn't mean a thing to her that the maths master was going to get married, and everybody had subscribed sixpence and bought a clock as a wedding present. Nor, although she laughed, could she really have found the long story about a cater-pillar in somebody's bed funny. But there was so much interest in her voice over all these things that they might have been her own pet subjects for conversation. Then Martin heard the talk change, Judy was gently leading to things she wanted to know. What Andrew liked doing, what he read, what he wanted to be. "Nobody," thought Martin, "can take a mother's place, but that young woman comes wonderfully near it. It will be a sin if she doesn't some day have children of her own."

Judy, still uncertain how the sight of their old home would affect the children, had decided they would have lunch before they got to Rye. They had it on the beach just outside Hastings. They sat in the shade of some rocks, the tide was going out, but an occasional ripple bigger than the rest flowed to their feet. Sloe was seeing the sea for the first time and was extremely doubtful of it, and showed his disapproval by bouncing just out of reach of the waves, making noises which would one day be a bark. While they ate Martin told the children about the Browns.

He tried to tell the story in such a way as to stir their interest, and he succeeded, but not in the manner he intended. He had a feeling that Judy did not want the Browns discussed, but in the end he caught her eye, and now and then they silently shared the joke of the children's reaction to his story together, and felt something different from employer and employee, for friendship had come into it.

"Miss Griffiths," said Martin, "has suggested that she and both of you adopt a very poor family called Brown, who live in Lower Saltings."

"And Bertha," Judy added, "we must have Bertha in on the adopting."

Polly took a sandwich.

"Why are they poor?"

Martin's voice was sad.

"Their father is in prison:"

Polly and Andrew stopped eating, Andrew's face was pink.

"I say! Prison! Which one?"

Polly bounced up and down.

"What did he do? What did he do? Was it a murder?"

Judy's face was strained. She had to turn the conversation.

"Who wants a plate?"

But Polly was not to be put off.

"What did he do? Was it murder?"

"No, Polly, nothing so terrible. He stole," said Martin.

The children spoke together.

"What?"

Martin shook his head.

"I don't know. I didn't ask."

Polly's voice was full of pity for such inefficiency. "Always ask. It makes it much more interesting."

"I wonder," Andrew's voice was hopeful, "if it was robbery with violence."

Judy was not eating, and her face was white, but the other three were not looking at her.

"We must pray not," Martin said decidedly.

"But you see, with a father in prison—"

"Which?" Andrew interrupted.

Judy suddenly caught Martin's eye, and it was twinkling. She pulled herself together and attempted a smile.

"Wormwood Scrubs," said Martin. "But as I was saying, with a father in prison and not able to earn money, they are very poor, and need help, and presently if you like, you can go and see the children and give them some of your books and things." Andrew took another sandwich and a lettuce leaf.

"When's he coming out of prison?"

Martin and Judy exchanged glances, and this time Judy was really amused.

"In seven months I believe," Martin said. "A long time, poor things."

Andrew sighed.

"Gosh, it is a long time. I wish I could have seen him these holidays. Nobody in my school knows a man in prison."

Polly suddenly looked at Judy, and her voice was a squeak.

"Look at Miss Griffiths. She hasn't eaten nothing at all, and her face is all yellow."

Judy took two sandwiches.

"My face is yellow from the reflections of my hat, and as for eating I'm a slow starter, but I'll get more than you in the end."

The house at Rye was a bungalow lying outside the town. It had the sad look that houses get even if they are unlived in for a short time. Judy watched the children's faces as Martin unlocked the door, and saw they had both grown serious and Andrew a little white.

"What are we going to do with Sloe?" she asked. "He can't go in. He isn't nearly house-trained enough for a house that hasn't a Bertha to mop up after him."

The question distracted the children as she had hoped.

"Would he be all right in the garden?" Andrew suggested.

Judy appeared to consider, then shook her head.

"No. Better have his basket. Run to the car both of you. You bring the basket, Andrew, and Polly you bring his little blanket. We'll see if we can make him go to sleep, he must be tired after all that trying to bark." As the children ran off she touched Martin's arm. "We must make this quick, and try and be very cheerful over it."

Martin had the door open. Inside in the passage were signs of who had lived in the house. There was an easel, and a case of canvases, and on the hall table a novel and some dark glasses. He felt a lump in his throat at these things which had so recently been used, but this was no time to think of himself, he stiffened against emotion.

"All right. We'll do what we can."

Judy was not deceived.

"It's awful for you too, don't think I don't feel that, but the children must come first, so if I get them to make a lot of noise you'll understand."

The children were coming back so there was not time for more, but Martin was comforted, he felt that he as well as the children was to be helped through the ordeal.

The collecting of the children's treasures was a task that took all Judy's energy and ingenuity to carry through without a breakdown. She saw with tugs at her heart-strings the children's parents' night things still on the beds, and those pathetic make-shifts which are so moving when the people who contrived them are gone. The wedge to make a cupboard shut, the plasticine foot modelled to take the place of a broken one on a porcelain figure, the flower embroidered on the curtain to hide a burn. But because she, who had never known John and Sylvia, was moved, it galvanised Judy into action which would help the others.

"Now," she said cheerfully, "we can't spend all day over this. We must think of a quick way of getting the stuff out. Andrew, find some strong string and a basket, and you can make a pulley so you can lower the things to your uncle from the window." The making of a pulley proved so absorbing that it looked for a time as if Andrew would do nothing but lower Polly's games and toys to Martin, and forget his own things, so Judy invented a new distraction.

"I shall use this rug as a kind of stretcher, and pull all these things to the gate."

"Let me help," Andrew called.

"Well get your things down first," said Judy. "I want to see how much there is, whether Jimson can take it or not." She saw Polly looking in a rather woe-begone way at an old teddy bear. "Come on, Polly. You and I'll be Volga Boatmen."

For the next few minutes the air was rent with "Yo heave ho's," then Andrew's head appeared at the window again.

"I say, Polly, do you want your doll's house? It's out at the back, the outside's all done." There was a pause. "We were going to do the inside decorations these holidays."

Polly's face turned pink and puckered. Judy sprang to the rescue.

"Of course we want it. It can go in the attic, and we can all work at it on wet days. But that settles it, Jimson can't take all this stuff. Get a move on, Andrew, and come down and say what you want to take to-day, and the rest can come by carrier."

When at last, with a car crammed with books, cases of moths, and boxes of what seemed to be rubbish but which was cherished by the children, they left Rye behind, Judy relaxed and felt as if she had been in a race, but a race which she had won. The children were all right, they were a little flushed and above themselves, but they were not upset. They had insisted on sitting together in the back where they could be near Sloe and were noisily engaged in dressing the poor little fellow in a kilt off one doll, and a small straw hat off another. Judy was thankful to see the children happy, but sorry for Sloe. She settled back in her seat and then glanced at Martin and realised that she still had work to do. His profile was towards her, his eyes on the road ahead, but in the line of his jaw she saw suffering. She opened her bag.

"I should like a cigarette after that; I know you're a pipe-smoker, but will you have a cigarette for a change?"

He turned to her, and the pain lines softened on his face.

"Perhaps I will. Thank you."

She lit both cigarettes, and passed one to him.

"If you believe in another world," she said, "you must have been proud to-day. If your sister and her husband can see the children from where they are, they must be happy about them."

Martin smoked a moment in silence.

"If they can see us—and I believe they can—then the greatest share of their gratitude is for you."

Judy flushed, and her eyes unexpectedly smarted with tears. For so long she had felt an outcast, such sincere praise was like balm on a festering sore. Polly leant forward.

"What are you two talking about?"

Judy swung round with a smile.

"Nothing important; but what is important is where are we going to have tea? I want a real farm-house tea with masses of butter, home-made jam, and a new loaf, and I'll give sixpence to whichever of you spots the right place first."

Bertha was having a field-day. It was, she told herself, no more than her duty to give the house a good turn-out with the Reverend, Miss Griffiths and the children away, but apart from her duty she was delighted; it was a superb opportunity to get a little of her own back on Aunt Connie.

"It's lunch on a tray in your room or in the garden, whichever you fancy," she announced as soon as she saw Jimson safely out of the gate.

Aunt Connie was at the time fiddling round her bedroom. Now her eyes snapped and her lips twitched.

"Lunch will be in the dining-room as usual."

"No, 'm, it won't. Dining-room's being turned out. It isn't often Reverend's out, and I can't let the chance slip. It hasn't had a proper doing since he was away for the choir outing, and that was early June."

Aunt Connie turned her back on Bertha, and pretended to be doing something to the things on her dressing-table.

"Why has Miss Griffiths gone with him?"

Bertha was shocked at the venom in Aunt Connie's voice.

"It's her place to go. Isn't she engaged to look after the children? And wonderfully she does it. It's the talk of Saltings how much better Polly looks."

Aunt Connie's eyes slid round so that she could watch Bertha's face in the looking-glass.

"And who suggested that my nephew should go, too? His place is here, with his parish."

Bertha strained forward to try and see Aunt Connie's face. She wondered if the old lady was feeling the heat. It wasn't natural to speak in such a nasty way. She considered her a sour old cat and never stopped saying so, but she had never known her as bad as this.

"It's hot in here, 'm," she suggested. "Why don't you let me put you a nice chair in the garden?"

Aunt Connie stiffened, and gave a tug to her coat.

"Certainly not. If others neglect their duty, that is no reason why I should. I shall take round the parish magazines."

Bertha stood aside and let Aunt Connie pass. She watched out of the window her gaunt black figure with a bundle of magazines under one arm go down the drive and out of the gate, and she shook her head.

"If she doesn't get a heat stroke, marching about in that stuffy coat and skirt, she never will. Still, no good pretending I should cry." She went back to her work, singing truculently, "Sweeping through the gates of new Jerusalem."

Veronica drove up to the vicarage at four o'clock. In the back of the car was a large thermos of ice-cream. She had come to give all in the vicarage a treat.

Bertha, who was still at her cleaning, leant out of the window and watched the car arrive, and her eyes danced. "You've got a surprise coming, my lady. I'd go down and tell you myself, only you may as well hear it from your dear friend Miss Matthews."

She watched Veronica carrying the thermos go in at the front door, then she whistled softly to the chauffeur who was doing something to the bonnet of the Rolls Royce. The chauffeur looked up, and Bertha leant further out and lowered her voice:

"Hullo, Mr. Perkins! You've come for nothing this afternoon. We're out."

Perkins grinned.

"Isn't he coming in?"

Bertha shook her head.

"Gone off for the day with Miss Griffiths and the children."

Perkins left the car and stood under the window. "She's a good looker, Miss Griffiths. Shouldn't wonder if our nose was a bit out of joint."

Bertha's eyes twinkled, but her voice was severe.

"There's no need why it should be. Miss Griffiths is here for the children, and knows her place and keeps it, what is more'n I can say for some people. Besides the Reverend isn't the marrying kind." Perkins took a packet of cigarettes out of his pocket and lit one before he spoke.

"Every man's the marrying kind if he gets caught, and we've"— he nodded towards the house to indicate his mistress—"a lot to offer."

Bertha sniffed.

"Nothing that we want, thank you."

"That's what you think."

Bertha flushed.

"It's what I know." She was annoyed with Perkins because he made her feel uneasy, so she withdrew her head. "Well, I must be getting on with my work. I've no time for gossip, if others have."

Aunt Connie, hot and exhausted from her round of delivering parish magazines, was sitting, when Veronica arrived, at the dining-room table, checking her list. She looked up.

"Good afternoon, dear. Some people have no gratitude. If they think it's any pleasure to me to walk about in the heat, they are wrong. At Rose Cottage that Mrs. Ellis actually had the impertinence to lean out of a window and to tell me to put it on the doorstep as she was washing herself, and couldn't come down. Very annoying, for I especially wished to speak to her about that youngest boy of hers in the choir. I distinctly saw him eat a sweet during the sermon on Sunday."

Veronica put down the thermos.

"Where is everybody?"

Aunt Connie let out a shrill nasal sound which had a dim resemblance to a laugh.

"You may well ask. It's that hussy. My dear nephew never took a day off until she came to this house, and now he's out picnicking, and I don't know what."

Veronica's legs felt suddenly weak. She sat down abruptly.

"Picnicking! Martin!"

The fact that she had used Martin's Christian name for the first time was missed by both of them.

"Yes." Aunt Connie's eyes flickered restlessly. "It's that hussy. They've gone to Rye to fetch the children's things. She went into the study and persuaded him. She doesn't know that I saw her, but I did. Probably making him spend money." She turned to Veronica, and had Veronica not been so absorbed in her own feelings she would have noticed the wild look in her eyes, and the looseness of the mouth. "She thinks she can do what she likes, but she can't. I'm watching. 'The wicked shall go to Hell.'"

Veronica had not known that jealousy could hurt physically. There was a pain round her heart, and she had difficulty with her breathing, but there were things she must know. She wanted to cry, but that would have to wait. She got control of herself, her voice was calm.

"Do you say this trip to Rye was Miss Griffiths' idea?"

"Yes. It was after you had gone yesterday. She sent the children out with Mr. Adam to fetch that nasty little dog, and pretended that she was going to unpack Andrew's things. But she didn't. She slipped downstairs again, and into my nephew's Study. She was there for quite a while. I didn't hear what they said; you can't hear anything outside the study door. Not that I would listen, but sometimes it is a duty. Then the next thing I knew was when Bertha told me this morning that they were gone."

"Do you mean to say they didn't tell you they were going?"

Aunt Connie held back the fact that Martin had been speaking at a meeting and had not been in to supper, and that Judy had been engrossed with Andrew.

"Not a word. Slipped out. I'm sorry to speak so of my nephew, but there's no other term for it."

Veronica knew she must be alone. She got up, her voice in spite of herself trembled.

"There's ice-cream in that thermos. Give it to the children."

Aunt Connie was glad of someone to talk to, and saw no reason why Veronica should go.

"But you'll stay for tea?"

Veronica shook her head.

"No. The heat's upset me a little. I'm going home to lie down."

Aunt Connie peered at her.

"I must say you do look white. Come and lie on my bed, and I'll give you some sal volatile."

Veronica made a blind kind of gesture, as if to physically push Aunt Connie from her.

"No. No. I must go."

Perkins sprang to attention as his mistress came out of the house. Neither he nor any of her staff cared for Veronica, but something about her now touched all the chivalry in him. He opened the car door and would have liked to arrange a cushion, but Veronica dismissed him with a gesture.

"Straight home, Perkins, and please hurry. I don't feel very well."

It's hard in a house full of servants to be absolutely alone, so that you can let yourself go and not be heard, and let your face get into a mess and it not be noticed, but this afternoon Veronica didn't care. The car had no sooner stopped at her door than she was out of it, up the stairs, had locked her bedroom door and was face downwards on her bed. It was half an hour before her sobs died down, and giddy and with an aching head, she went to her bathroom to do what she could for her face. Jealousy had torn and rent her. In her easy control of the vicarage she had never dreamed that such news as this could reach her. The trip to Rye was the sort of thing that a few weeks back would have been hers almost without question. Jimson was small and rattling, and it would have been taken for granted that the Rolls was more suitable. If they were really fetching the children's things there was no room for them in Jimson; they must have known that. Besides, if there was any lifting or packing to be done, Perkins would have been such a help. No, it was no good running away from the truth, this was a deliberate attempt to cut her out. Judy, for all her open honest face, must be sly. At tea-time yesterday there had been no mention of taking Martin to Rye; Judy was too clever for that—she had waited until she, Veronica, was out of the house and could not offer the Rolls, before she had talked Martin into it.

Wearily Veronica worked on her face, washing out her eyes, putting some soothing lotion on her skin; but her mind was not on what she was doing. She was engrossed with Judy. She had thought before that she wanted the girl out of the vicarage, and now she was determined on it. But how?

Judy waited until Andrew and Sloe had more or less settled down before she arranged her day in London. As far as she herself was concerned, London was the last place she wanted to see. She had been so wretched there that the thought of it could still cause a cold feeling in her inside. Besides, few people could want to leave the peace of Saltings to go to a city in the middle of August during a perfect patch of weather. But Judy was not considering herself; there was a lot of shopping to be done for the children, and she could not pretend it could be done as well in Lewes or Eastbourne. Regretfully she fixed a day.

As she had warned him that she would, Judy refused to fix her day in London until Martin had found a day that he could spare to take the children for a picnic.

"If the tide's right," she said, "why not get Mr. Adam to take you all to Birling Gap for prawning."

Martin still remembering Judy's words about the children being his parishioners, was humbly anxious to fall in with any arrangement which she suggested; the stumbling block to the scheme was Sterndale. He had come in to smoke a pipe with Martin after dinner when the idea was put to him. Judy was in the hall when he arrived, and she snatched the opportunity to get things settled.

"I've got to go to London next Wednesday; would the tide be right for you to take the children and Mr. Richards prawning?"

Before Sterndale could answer Martin came to his study door, and Judy could hear Aunt Connie, who hated to miss anything, opening the door of the dining-room. It did not seem to her to matter who heard what she was saying, but she had misjudged Sterndale. His voice had the sullen tone of a small boy who has missed a treat.

"I thought you'd promised to come to Birling Gap."

Judy could have slapped him, but her voice was casual.

"I never heard such nonsense. It's a day for the children, and whether I come or not has nothing to do with it."

Sterndale refused to be snubbed.

"That may be your idea, but it isn't mine."

Judy, cursing the tiresomeness of men, called Martin in to help.

"You talk to him, Mr. Richards. The heat's made him cross."

She was turning away on that, but Martin's voice stopped her. It was not his usual tone at all, but had a detached, lonely sound.

"That's all right, Sterndale, old man. We won't bother you. I'll take the children somewhere else."

Judy was horrified. Martin and Sterndale were such tremendous friends, it was ludicrous that Sterndale—because he was feeling flirtatious over her, whom he hardly knew—should spoil one of Martin's few holidays by a fit of the sulks. She turned to him, her eyes flashing.

"It isn't often Mr. Richards gets a day off."

Sterndale grasped that he was behaving badly, and was losing such friendship as Judy might feel for him. He pulled himself together.

"Sorry. It's the heat. I've had a foul headache all day. Of course, Wednesday's all right. I'll have to look up the tides, but we can picnic, anyway."

Judy, relieved, was again moving off, and again Martin's voice stopped her.

"I don't want to force you. If you'd rather wait and go later when Miss Griffiths is free, it'll be all right, old man."

Judy could have knocked both the men's heads together.

"Do go and smoke, you two, and stop talking as if I had anything to do with it. We are discussing a treat for the children."

The two men obediently went into the study, and Judy heaved a sigh. How difficult life was. Why must that stupid Sterndale behave like a donkey; didn't he know his friend Martin well enough to grasp how unselfish he was, and how at the faintest hint of forcing someone against their will to do a thing to please himself, he would gently withdraw the suggestion. "However," she thought, "I suppose they'll settle down over a pipe. Only I do hope Mr. Richards doesn't think I've anything to do with his friend Sterndale's lunacy."

Aunt Connie made her jump; she had come up softly behind her, and suddenly gripped her arm. Her voice was a whisper.

"Women like you break men as if they were toys."

Aunt Connie was as startled as her foolishness could allow at the effect of her words on Judy. The girl turned green and clutched hold of the wall.

"It's not true. Why did you say that?"

Aunt Connie sniggered.

"I know you and your sort. You break men—but God will punish you."

Judy opened her mouth to answer, then suddenly she turned and ran up the stairs, tears pouring down her cheeks.


Veronica drove Judy to London. She made the offer in her usual gracious way.

"It will be so much nicer for you. It's such a tiring day by train."

Actually there was strong purpose behind her offer. Judy must go. In the vicarage she was a danger. It was true that Martin was apparently uninterested in her except in regard to her job, that in fact gossip said it was Sterndale who was fond of her, but that did not alter the fact that Judy's influence was too great. Beside, if a man like Sterndale—who had so far shown no excitement about any woman—could apparently fall in love at sight, Judy must have a lot of appeal that did not appear on the surface. Was Aunt Connie right? Was Judy what she called a hussy? If it was true, what could be better than a long motor drive for finding out about her. In intimate conversation she would be sure to give herself away—women always did.

Quite likely there was something queer about her; Veronica remembered how strongly she had felt that the afternoon Andrew had come home, and there had been that fuss about the missing half-crowns. On the other hand, if she could find nothing wrong about Judy that she could use to get her dismissed, there was always the chance that she could talk her into taking another job. Probably a nice-looking and intelligent girl like that had ambitions; she couldn't really want to be a companion to children, and if she had any ambitions how easy to put up the money, and start her on a new career. It would look kind and generous, and be a good way of getting rid of her for good.

Judy had been exceedingly unwilling to accept Veronica's offer of driving her to town. She did not like Veronica, and had no wish to be beholden to her, and thought regretfully how bored she would be during a long *tête-à-tête* with her. Such a waste when, in the train, she could have sat comfortably reading a novel. However, hers not to argue; the car would save Martin's purse. With a nicely acted air of gratitude she accepted politely.

The drive to London was an aggravation to Veronica. Judy, looking charming, was on the doorstep of the vicarage when the Rolls Royce arrived; as she got into the car the two children and Martin came out to see her off. Polly flung her arms round Judy.

"Good-bye, dear darling Miss Griffiths. Please come back quickly."

"I wish you were coming with us for our picnic," said Andrew. "It won't be half as much fun without you."

Judy put an arm round each child.

"Where are your manners? Say 'Good morning' to Lady Blacke."

Martin came to the car door, and after greeting Veronica turned to Judy.

"We'll hope to have some prawns for you, to welcome you back."

"If Uncle Sterndale buys the prawning nets we will," said Andrew; "but he mightn't—he's cross because you can't come."

Judy flushed, and Veronica saw a look she could not place pass across Martin's face.

Bertha, who was leaning out of an upstairs window, caused a diversion.

"Don't forget to try and pop into Woolworth's, Miss Griffiths. You've got the list of what I want, haven't you?"

Judy was grateful for the interruption. She hung out of the open window of the car.

"Yes. If I have time I'll get everything."

As the car moved off Veronica said, in what was meant to sound like a friendly voice:

"Wonderful how at home you've got in a short time."

Judy had had a rushed morning, helping to pack the picnic lunch, seeing to the children, and getting herself ready. She had a headache, and she was worried. Andrew's remark about Sterndale had reawoken the nagging fear at the back of her mind. Were Sterndale and Martin as good friends as ever? Surely she hadn't come between them? If so, why? Martin cared nothing for her; was it just that he didn't like what perhaps he thought was a silly flirtation? Was there truth in what Aunt Connie had said? Was there something evil about her that made her effect bad on the men she came in contact with? She answered Veronica vaguely.

"It's nice to feel wanted."

"Have you ever felt anything else?"

Judy, her mind on Sterndale and Martin, hardly heard her.

"I'm fond of children, but these are the first I've had full charge of." She suddenly realised that she was only giving half her attention to her hostess; she pulled herself together: Veronica enjoyed giving advice—well, then, she should give it. Judy brought out the shopping list. "Now you help me, Lady Blacke. I've all these things to buy. Where shall I go for them?"

For the rest of the journey Veronica struggled in vain to get the conversation where she wanted it. Judy at no time was given to womanly heart-to-heart talks, and certainly had no intention of having one with Veronica. She was perfectly polite, but the moment the talk became personal she was vague and monosyllabic.

Part of Veronica's invitation to Judy had been to lunch at her club.

"Goodness," thought Judy, following Veronica down long carpeted passages to the green and gold cocktail bar, "she is being good to me. It's awful I can't feel more grateful."

Veronica seemed well-known in her club; the barman came to her with a deferential smile.

"Good morning, Milady. Will you have the club special?"

Veronica took up a list of cocktails and passed it to Judy. She nodded to indicate the barman.

"He was barman in a bar in Honolulu, so there's nothing he doesn't know about mixing drinks."

Judy passed the card back.

"Just a tomato juice, thank you. I never drink at lunch time."

Just as the drinks arrived a friend of Veronica's appeared—a smart, foolish-looking, exquisitely-dressed woman.

"Veronica, darling, how divine ! You must have a drink with me."

Veronica patted the stool beside her.

"Gloria! No, have one with me." She turned to Judy. "Do you two know each other: Mrs. Meridian—Miss Griffiths."

Gloria looked at Judy with a puzzled expression.

"Yes, we do, don't we? I'm sure I've met you somewhere. I know, it was at Mrs. Bramble's."

Judy tried to seem at ease, but her fingers on her glass had turned sticky.

"Was it? How clever of you to remember."

Gloria still seemed puzzled.

"Matter of fact," she said candidly, "I'm not often so good at remembering people. But I do remember you, but you've changed. You looked most terribly ill."

Judy gave a nervous laugh.

"Oh, I'm sure I didn't. I'm never ill." She put down her glass. "Would you think me most awfully rude, Lady Blacke, if I asked if we could have lunch? I ought to be getting on if I'm to get my shopping done."

Veronica, her eyes darting over Judy's face, nodded. She turned to her friend.

"You're lunching here, Gloria?"

Gloria sipped her cocktail.

"Yes."

Veronica paid for the drinks.

"Good! Will you meet me for coffee in the lounge?"

Gloria lit a cigarette.

"Yes."

The meeting with Gloria had for some reason so plainly upset Judy that Veronica let luncheon pass without bothering her with questions. "She'll only lie," she thought, "and Gloria will tell me what it's all about." She noticed with interest that Judy couldn't eat, and that though she tried to hide it her hands were shaking.

"You are tired after the drive," she suggested. "You ought to have had a cocktail."

Judy managed a smile.

"No, it's just the heat."

Veronica, feeling sure she was on to something interesting and, anxious to get Judy out of the way, barely waited to finish her own lunch before she got up.

"Well, my dear, I mustn't keep you. I'll meet you here for tea, as near five as you can make it." She hardly waited to see Judy down the club steps before she was off in search of Gloria.

Gloria was sitting alone in the smaller of the two dining-rooms. She seemed pleased to see Veronica.

"Sit down, do. How I hate London in August. Nothing bores me more than eating food alone."

Veronica sat.

"Fancy you knowing Judy Griffiths."

Gloria ate a mouthful of salad.

"Not so odd, really. My husband adores good-works-women, and Mrs. Bramble is the queen bee of them."

Veronica lit a cigarette.

"Mrs. Bramble got Judy Griffiths the job of being governess to my Vicar's wards."

"She would," agreed Gloria. "She spends her life getting jobs for the needy."

Veronica opened her eyes.

"Is Judy Griffiths needy?"

Gloria beckoned a waiter, and ordered an ice.

"I don't know anything about her money, but she was certainly in a nasty state when I met her. That's why I remember her. She looked awful, and everybody was talking about her."

"Why?"

Gloria shook her head.

"That's just what I can't remember. She was the centre-piece of some scandal or other."

"What!" Veronica leant forward. "Look, my dear, I've been a bit worried about Judy Griffiths. Our Vicar's a vague sort of man, and he took the girl with no references. Do you think you could find out about her for me?"

Gloria waited while her ice was put in front of her.

"I'll be pleased to. Nothing annoys me more than to know I know a bit of dirt about somebody, and not be able to remember what it is. Give me your telephone number. I'm going to stay with people who were at that same do at Mrs. Bramble's; I expect they'll know all about her, and I'll pass it on."

## CHAPTER FOUR

AUGUST went by, and as day followed day Judy was surprised at the happiness she was finding. Nothing much seemed to go on, and yet she woke up with a singing heart, and went to sleep wrapt in contentment.

The children were an ever-growing pleasure. She was proud to see Polly getting sturdier day by day, and to hear her laughing. She loved the way she would suddenly jump on to her knee and fling her arms round her neck. She liked the way she would dash into the house shouting for her when she had seen or heard something which appeared interesting. Judy got, too, an infinity of pleasure from her friendship with Andrew. He was a funny little boy, and he still suffered from the shock of his parents' death, and he wanted the most sensitive handling. Judy was exactly what he needed. She had a horror of interference; she had an almost morbid dread of seeming to push in where she was not wanted, she knew how easily the wrong words could cut like a knife. She attempted nothing with Andrew; she made no overtures, she simply laid all her heart open for him to walk into if he wanted to. Andrew took his time; after his harrowing term of pretending he didn't care about the death of his parents he needed a long spell of quiet, with nothing to disturb his nerves. But by degrees he turned to Judy. He had from the beginning liked having her about, but presently he took her into his confidence. It was one evening after Polly had gone to bed that he first began to talk. He and Judy were sitting on the lawn, waiting for the gong for supper.

"It's only three weeks and two days to term," Andrew said.

Judy lay back in her deck chair.

"Do you mind?"

Andrew examined a scar on one of his knees.

"No, not really. I mean I know I have to go to school. But these have been awfully good holidays, and I expected they'd be foul."

"Yes, I suppose you did."

Andrew went on fidgeting with his scab.

"I don't mean I don't wish that Dad and Mum were—well, you know."

"Of course I know. You mean that things haven't been so bad, allowing for their not being here."

"Yes." Andrew hesitated. "There's two things I wanted to ask you. Do you mind?"

"No, of course not."

"Well, first, must we call you Miss Griffiths. It seems awfully stuffy."

Judy laughed.

"I hate being called Miss Griffiths. I'd much rather you and Polly called me Judy."

Andrew glanced at her.

"You never said so."

"Why should I? You and Polly have tongues. You can ask for what you want."

Andrew nodded.

"Yes, that's what I like about you. That's where the other thing comes in. Would you write to me every week when I'm back at school? Mum or Dad wrote nearly always; now, except Uncle Martin and Polly sometimes, nobody does much."

Judy turned her head away, so that he should not see the tears in her eyes.

"Of course. What day do you like getting them?"

"Well, the middle of the week's best, because then I've got it in time to answer on Sundays."

The gong boomed out. They both got up. Andrew looked a little sheepish, feeling perhaps he had said rather more than he meant. Judy was conscious of embarrassment.

"Oh, dear," she pointed to some broken night-scented stocks under the drawing-room window, "I'm afraid Sloe must have done that. Remind me to come out afterwards and pick them up and put them in water before your Aunt Connie sees them."

"All right." Andrew paused. "Judy!"

There were, of course, flaws in Judy's happiness. There was Aunt Connie, with her bitter tongue. Judy tried hard not to mind her.

"Poor old thing," she told herself; "she's lost all her money, and she hates being in somebody else's house. I expect you'd be just as difficult if you were her." But another part of her mind disagreed. "No, you wouldn't. She's not nice, and she hates you. If you aren't very careful, she'll manage to get you sent away." When Judy thought this it was as if a cloud blew across the sun, and she shivered.

There was Veronica, too; but Veronica, Judy considered a very minor tiresomeness. She didn't like the woman, and wished she wasn't always around the house, but she considered she was unreasonable to mind her. She meant, after all, to be kind. "The trouble is," Judy told herself, "you don't trust her somehow, and that's just your own nasty suspicious nature. She's very good to you, and if you had a spark of decency you'd be grateful." But for all her tough talks to herself Judy couldn't change her mind, and Veronica went on being a flaw in her happiness.

Judy's worst trouble, though, was neither Veronica nor Aunt Connie—it was Sterndale. Sterndale had come right out in the open in the matter of loving her. Nobody in the three Saltings could have failed to hear about it, though only Bertha actually mentioned it. Bertha never minced her words.

"Are you having him?" she asked Judy one day, while they were making the beds.

Judy turned red.

"Having who?"

Bertha was delighted.

"Oh, there's more than one, is there? I meant Mr. Adam."

Judy tucked in a sheet savagely.

"I can't think why he wants to be such an idiot, mooning about. I've never pretended I liked it."

Bertha laughed.

"That's men all over. The less we seem to like it the more they carry on."

"Silly idiots."

Bertha's eyes twinkled, but there was a world of affection behind them.

"Don't you fancy him? He's good looking."

Judy gave her shoulders a nervous shake.

"I don't fancy anybody. I want to be left alone."

Bertha leant on the bed and patted Judy's hand.

"I don't know what you've been through, Miss Griffiths, and I don't want to know, but I've lived my life, and I'll tell you this— whatever it was, don't let it turn you against men. People can say what they like about marriage, but it's the only real happiness. There's nothing like having your own man, and your children."

Judy said nothing for a moment, and the two women finished making the bed. Then, as Judy was straightening the cover, she asked abruptly:

"Do you suppose some women aren't meant to marry? I mean, do you think there are some who, without meaning to, bring out the worst in the men they know?"

Bertha gave a final pat to the coverlet.

"It's not my place to say anything to you, Miss Griffiths, but I don't mind telling you, if you were one of my own daughters and got a silly notion like that, I'd take a strap to you. Not meant to marry indeed! If ever a woman was born to make some man happy, you are. So give over with foolish thinking, and get yourself ready for when Mr. Right comes along."

The beds were finished, so Judy moved to the door. She looked at Bertha over her shoulder.

"I think it's a pity I'm not your daughter; I dare say a strap would do me good, now and again."

In spite of the light way Judy spoke, Bertha watched her go with a worried sigh. Whatever had happened to Miss Griffiths before she came to the Saltings? There she was so nice and so straightforward, and yet there was something queer about her.

"Oh well," she told herself, "no good fretting. Speak as you find, as my old mother always said, and I find Miss Griffiths a bit of all right."

Bertha was not the only person to worry over Judy. Martin found himself spending a lot of his thoughts on her. He wanted most desperately to help her, and he was convinced she needed help. True to his principle of letting those who wanted help seek it, he never made an effort to get her to talk, but it struck him that in some ways she confided less than any person with whom he had come in contact. She was, according to herself, twenty-four. She had been at school, she said, in the West country, where her parents lived. She had said on one occasion that her father was dead. She had not, she said, ever looked after children before. She had not apparently done work, for she had no references.

What had she done between leaving school and coming to the Saltings? Then there was the matter of letters. Surely most nice young women had some friends who wrote to them, but Judy hadn't. Except for a letter or two from Mrs. Bramble—most of the contents of which she retailed to him—he could not help noticing that she had no letters at all. It looked as if she had given nobody her address, as if she wanted to cut herself off from her past. If that was so, thought Martin, there must be a great sorrow somewhere, and she must be very lonely. Perhaps, he puzzled, Sterndale is more the person to help than I am. It might be an unhappy love affair which has made those lines of suffering on her face, and if that's so a decent man like Sterndale in love with her, and perhaps she with him, may bring her contentment. Martin when he reached this point in his thoughts—and he readied it after that summer—tried to hope that that would he the solution. But somehow, though he told himself it would be a splendid thing, his heart and mind did not agree. He puzzled over this; both his heart and his mind ought to feel what a good sensible marriage it would be. Why didn't they?

Often Martin wanted to talk to Sterndale about Judy. He and Sterndale had been such close friends for years that it seemed queer that there should be a subject on which they couldn't speak. But somehow, neither of them mentioned her. In fact, Martin saw with grief that Sterndale being in love seemed to have built up a barrier between them. Their evenings together seemed to have dropped, and when they did meet the old easy intimacy was lacking. Martin still told Sterndale about his problems with his poor in Lower Saltings, and Sterndale still argued on his theories for modern education, but it was as if they were both making conversation, and they avoided those long friendly silences which had been such a part of the time they spent together.

Before the end of Andrew's holidays Judy, true to her promise to Martin had, with the children and Bertha, what she called "taken over" the Browns. The Browns needed a lot of taking over. Mrs. Brown was scraggy and careworn, so tired by her ever-losing fight with existence that she had given up trying. She had a quantity of things wrong with her which added to her misery, but neither the money nor the energy to put them right. There were six little Browns, ranging from eight months to eleven—the dirtiest collection, in miserably ragged clothes, suffering alternately from nits and impetigo, and often both.

Judy went alone to pay her visit to Mrs. Brown. Martin had said the Browns were not a case for the S.P.C.C., but a case for charity: "They want a friend who comes and sits and talks to Mrs. Brown over the kitchen table." So across the kitchen table Judy sat and talked.

Mrs. Brown's kitchen was not an inviting place that afternoon. It was a stuffy overcast day, with thunder in the air. Between Judy and Mrs. Brown were a pile of unwashed dinner plates smelling strongly of cabbage, and on the end of the table was a bowl of inky water, with an unspeakable dish cloth hanging out of it. Judy as she sat down felt that she was going to retch. To avoid this for a second she took her mind out of the house, and in memory caught the tone of Martin's voice: "Though I speak with the tongues of men and of angels, and have not charity ..." When she looked back at Mrs. Brown she had lost the feeling that she might be sick, and interest and friendship shone in her face. Forgetting the greasy table she put her arms on it, and leant forward smiling.

In the talk that followed the whole wells of Judy's sympathy were brought to the top. The story dragged out bit by bit was such a hopeless one.

"You see, Miss," Mrs. Brown finished, "it isn't just the once Mr. Brown is put away. It's off and on, as you might say, and recent he's been more in than out. Not that I'm saying anything against Mr. Brown, for he's a good husband when he's home. But you lose heart. There's times when it hardly seems worth going on."

Judy, by this time unconscious of her surroundings, laid a hand on Mrs. Brown's dirty work-stained one.

"You must never feel that. There's one thing none of us must ever lose, and that's our courage."

Mrs. Brown shook her head.

"It's easy for you to talk, Miss; you don't know how it is to wake with hardly the heart to get out of bed."

Judy held Mrs. Brown's hand more warmly.

"You're wrong there. I do know, and because I know how dreadful that feeling is, and because when it had nearly got me down a woman came and pulled me together and asked me what I had done with my courage, I'm going to help you. Will you let me try?"

Mrs. Brown raised tired watery eyes, and smiled showing a mouth of missing or decayed teeth.

"Yes, Miss. And thank you."

Judy took the beginnings of the Brown problem to Bertha. Bertha had all Saltings' scorn of Lower Saltings; the people there in her opinion were trash, and always would be trash, and Reverend was wearing himself out for nothing wasting time on them, and so was Judy. All the same, if help was needed no one should say that she, Bertha, was unwilling to give a helping hand.

"What we have to do, Miss Griffiths," she said, "is get them out of the way. Nobody could clear up any house with a thriftless woman and six children in it."

It was Bertha who had the inspiration that got the Browns away.

"Hopping," she suggested. "Good open-air life, and they'll earn some money, and while they're gone what can be done with a scrubbing brush and Lysol shall be done."

It took a lot more than a scrubbing brush and Lysol to get the Brown house decent. Almost all the furniture and most of the bedding had to go. Bertha, once she had put her hand to the work, was ruthless.

"No good spoiling the ship for a ha'porth of tar," she said truculently, as she threw the Brown possessions into a heap on the lawn. "What can't be boiled must be burned."

Judy had hoped that she and Bertha, and the children, could have managed the Browns alone, but when the question of furniture and bedding—let alone clothes—turned up, she was forced to ask for help. She was surprised at the fervour with which she tried not to ask for that help from Veronica.

"I must be a cad," she thought. "She'd love to be nice. Why won't I let her?"

But in spite of her thoughts, Judy got her help elsewhere. In this she was enormously helped by Bertha, who not only seemed to know what spare furniture there was in every house and cottage in Upper Saltings and Saltings, but also what there was hanging unworn in the wardrobes; and Bertha, too, was against asking Veronica.

"Whatever we do," she said, "let's not go bleating to Lady Blacke. She's not the only kipper on our barrow."

The children found the refurnishing for the Browns the greatest fun. Bertha's instructions turned the job into a game.

"Now you ask the Reverend for Jimson," she said, "and pop down to the 'Cedars' in Upper Saltings. In their attic there's a lovely roll of linoleum that's near as good as new. They only had it down a short time. You just pitch the tale of how there's nothing on the Browns' floor.

"You slip along to Mrs. Berridge's. She must have got some lovely things those children of hers have out-grown, and if she has another baby all that stuff will have the moth in it before it's big enough to wear it.

"You go along to Rosie Peters. She's got all those clothes that belonged to her baby. Fred told me that the looking at them kept Rosie back, he reckoned, and when she starts another baby, she won't let it have them. She'll think it unlucky. They'll do fine for that little misery of Mrs. Brown's.

"You children run across to the post office. Don't let on to Mrs. Beam what you've come about, but just tell her what you're doing for the Browns. If you're lucky you'll get that bed in her outhouse. It's no good to her and in her way really, and she has a terrible job keeping the damp from the mattress. She'll be glad to see it go, really, but she'll make a shocking favour of it. But who cares so long as we get the bed."

The result of all this effort reached its height on the last Saturday before Andrew went back to school. The Browns were returning from their hopping the next day, and their home was ready for them. It was really a triumph. The walls and ceiling were freshly distempered. There was linoleum on the floors, and an almost new carpet in the front room. Judy had worked half the night on a borrowed sewing machine, and there were gay curtains fluttering in every window. There was a clean, and quite grand, wardrobe in the cupboard and the chests of drawers, for every Brown. The children had added presents; there were books, and dolls, and a clockwork train. As a final touch Judy bought a vase and filled it with roses and stood it on the table in the front room.

"There, that's all we can do, I think."

Bertha sniffed.

"All we can do until to-morrow, you mean. But if you think I'm going to let those dirty, thriftless Browns come into this clean house in the clothes they've worn hopping, you're all wrong. They're letting me know from the station what time they're likely to get in, and I'll be here to meet them. Not a rag on them crosses that doorstep until I've boiled it. And not one of them sleeps on these beds until I've scrubbed them and had a good go at their hair."

Judy felt sorry for the Browns.

"You won't spoil their home-coming, will you?"

Bertha laughed.

"Not me. You can come along, too. I dare say a smile from you will get the washing over easier."

Polly and Andrew looked anxiously at Judy.

"We can come, too, can't we?"

Judy shook her head.

"Not to-morrow. Not until after the bathing, and the boiling of the clothes are over." She saw their disappointed faces: "You put yourselves in the Browns' place. I want them to meet you feeling pleased with themselves, not shabby and dirty as they're bound to be after hopping."

Because Judy did not want Martin to know of their combined labour for the Browns until it was finished, and because she did not want the children's enthusiasm snubbed by Aunt Connie, Judy had persuaded Andrew and Polly to keep what they were doing a secret in the vicarage. But that Saturday, because the work was finished, the children could hold themselves in no longer. Judy had gone upstairs to finish a letter as soon as they got in, so Andrew and Polly dashed off to find Martin. They found him in his study. He had been trying to finish his sermon for the next morning, but first Veronica had come to see him, then Sterndale—hoping for a glimpse of Judy—had appeared, and lastly Aunt Connie, because she hated to be out of anything. Martin had resignedly put the blotting paper over his notes, and tried to give them his attention. Veronica said she wanted to talk to him about the village nurse, but she thought she would wait until she had him to herself, and could he lunch on Monday; she would send the car. Sterndale had no very good excuse for turning up at that hour, and because, as is the way of those in love, he supposed nobody noticed the state he was in, he tried to disguise the reason for his presence by saying he had come about some plants which he could let Martin have in the autumn.

"It isn't like Sterndale to make untrue excuses," thought Martin sadly, and though he tried to fight against it he felt irritated with him. "Judy was probably busy. Sterndale had no right to pester her."

"If only that girl would marry Sterndale," thought Veronica, as she watched Sterndale's dog-like expression of listening for every footfall. "He's an excellent match for somebody like her; too good for her, probably."

Aunt Connie's eyes slid slyly from face to face, and then she started to chuckle.

"You're all thinking of that hussy."

The other three jumped and looked at Aunt Connie in dismay. The fact that she was right in her statement, though only Veronica agreed that Judy was a hussy, made each of them self-conscious. They were thankful to hear a scratch on the door, which was Andrew's and Polly's way of announcing themselves. In answer to Martin's *"Come in!"* the children and Sloe leapt into the room, talking as they came.

"The house is finished, Uncle Martin."

"And I've given the littlest but one my baby doll, not the new one, but the one whose arm is broken."

"And I helped distemper. Bertha's done all the roofs, and Miss Griffiths and I did the walls. Gosh, it was fun!"

"And we've put roses on the table, lovely ones out of our own garden."

Martin caught the children and put an arm round each.

"What are you talking about. Whose house have you been distempering, and who has Polly given her baby doll to?"

Both children started again, and Sterndale came to the rescue.

"I'll be time-keeper in this. Let's have the story from one of you at a time—ladies first. You start, Polly, and when I stop you Andrew goes on, and neither of you is to interrupt the other, or you miss a turn."

Judy, holding her letter, came in just as the children's combined story was drawing to an end. The door was ajar, so nobody heard her. She stood watching the scene. Sterndale with his watch in his hand. What a way he had with children. Aunt Connie's face was turned away from her, but Judy could see Veronica's, and the expression on it made her feel warmer to her than she ever had before. Martin was sitting in the chair at his desk, and he had a child leaning against each of his shoulders. Veronica's attention was on this group, and the expression on her face was pitiful for those with eyes to see. Judy had eyes to see, and she thought, *"Oh, my goodness, how she loves him, and he hasn't any idea of it. Poor Lady Blacke."* But while the thought was still in her mind something else took its place—something that made Judy's breath shorten. She wanted, so badly that it hurt, to be part of that group at the desk, to be able to kneel down by Martin, and put her arms round him, and it be her proper place to be there.

The violence of this emotion so flooded over Judy that she couldn't move for a moment, but her mind worked and rang alarm bells. "Don't be a fool. You, of all women, ought to be safe against feeling like this; you aren't fit to black his boots, and you know it. Besides, use your wits, he doesn't care for you, and if you let yourself fall in love, it'll be good-bye to your contentment and peace."

The children came to the end of the recital, and Polly wriggling around saw Judy. She pulled herself out of Martin's arm and flung herself on her.

"We've told Uncle Martin. We can, can't we, now it's done?"

Judy, thankful to be dragged from her personal feelings, laughed.

"I don't know how I can stop you now you've told him." She turned to Martin. "We wanted it to be a surprise for you. We've really started to put the Browns on their feet."

Martin's face shone.

"How splendid. You must tell me all about it."

Aunt Connie, Veronica and Sterndale reacted at once.

"Spending money like water, I suppose," said Aunt Connie.

Andrew stuck his nose in the air.

"We didn't. So there! Everything was given us."

Martin and Judy spoke together.

"That's not the way to speak to your Aunt, old man."

"Andrew! Don't spoil a good afternoon by being cross."

Martin and Judy over Andrew's head exchanged a look which said, "We've got to speak like that, but he had provocation." The intimacy of that look hurt Veronica and Sterndale. Sterndale said:

"You might have asked me to help."

His voice was so like any small boy's who feels he has been done out of something, that Judy had to smile.

"But Andrew likes distempering, and he does it beautifully. We were asked to look after the Browns, but there are plenty of other families if you want to help."

Veronica's eyes were hard as diamonds.

"You seem to me to have gone to quite unnecessary labour. You know perfectly well that I would have given you all you needed, and sent down people to do the work."

Judy quite saw why Veronica spoke so bitterly, she must be resenting Martin's appreciation for a job well done. Her voice was gentle.

"It was more fun doing it ourselves, and if you really do want to help, there's still a lot of things we can't manage. For instance, Mrs. Brown will have to have new teeth."

Sterndale was not going to be left out.

"And what can I do?"

Martin's face was glowing.

"But this is splendid. You said that if you set an example others would follow didn't you Miss Griffiths?" He opened a drawer and took out the Lower Saltings cards, and looked at Sterndale and Veronica. "You leave the Browns to us. We'll manage. But you take on one of my other families. You might adopt one between you."

Sterndale's checks flamed.

"I don't get time, you know that. But I'll do any odd job Miss Griffiths orders."

Veronica gave Martin what was intended as a sweet smile.

"I don't think I need adopt a family. You know you have only to ask me for anything you need."

Martin's face fell, and he put the cards back in their drawer.

"Of course. I was just carried away by enthusiasm. You see my poor in Lower Saltings need personal contact, they need in fact, to paraphrase the words of the sermon on the Mount, to see our light so shining before them, that they may glorify our Father which is in Heaven. It's easy to give material things, but in the work of Miss Griffiths, and Bertha, and these children, not only the Browns, but their neighbours can see selfless labour, devotion, and friendship, just in the way that Christ Himself would have given it."

There was a pregnant silence. Martin was always totally unaware when he had made an effect, and calmly continued putting away his cards.

Judy stared at the carpet, her heart throbbing. "How grand he is. Oh, why aren't I more like him?"

Sterndale fumbled in his pocket for his pipe.

"Dear old Martin," he thought, "he's too good for this world. I'm a surly devil, who doesn't deserve his friendship."

Veronica was furious. So that was how Martin felt was it? It was easy to give money was it? She'd a good mind to let him try how he got on with nothing but labour and devotion and friend-ship. They wouldn't go far. But another part of her was sore as if it had been whipped. He had said "You leave the Browns to us." "Us!" Oh, God, how that word hurt.

The children created a diversion.

"Gosh," said Andrew, "it's raining." He looked anxiously at Judy, "Did we leave any of their windows open?"

Judy shook her head.

"Nothing to matter. It looked like rain, so I remembered."

Polly picked up Sloe.

"As it's raining and we can't go in the garden, will you play Happy Families?"

Judy nodded.

"Yes. Go and put the card table in the drawing-room, I shan't be a second, I'm just running to the post box."

Sterndale held out his hand.

"Give it to me. I'll take it across for you."

"No." Judy moved to the door. "Why should you get wet?"

Sterndale ran after her and held her arm.

"Give me the letter. It's raining cats and dogs."

Judy held her letter firmly, her face was white.

"No, please. I'd rather post it myself."

Veronica, watching Judy, broke in:

"Let Perkins take it. He's on the doorstep, doing nothing."

Judy appeared to lose her temper.

"Please let me alone all of you. I'm going to post my own letter."

There was silence as the door shut on her. The fact that for some reason Judy did not want any of them to know to whom she wrote was the obvious interpretation of her behaviour.

"She's quite right," said Sterndale truculently, "It's her letter and she can do what she likes with it."

Veronica said nothing, but she eyed Judy, who could be seen from the window hurrying down the drive, her head down to the sheeting rain, and her expression was calculating.

Aunt Connie gave her neighing sound.

"You see. You see. Sly, that's what she is."

Martin's eyes were also on Judy, and his heart was warm with pity. What trouble had she? That there was something he was certain. He prayed silently that he might be allowed to help.

Polly felt that Judy had behaved oddly, and at once took up her defence.

"We like walking in the rain, don't we Andrew? And so does Miss Griffiths. It's only fussy people who mind."

Andrew looked from face to face, and felt the curiosity in the air. His voice was loud, because he was scared, he hated grown-ups being mysterious.

"Come on Polly. Let's put the table up."

Outside the gate Judy stood by the post-box. Her heart was beating with fright. She raised her face to the sky, and the rain slashed against it, but she did not notice. "Oh, what did they think? What did they think?" was the cry in her head. Then her thought changed. "What did he think?"

*

It was evening when the Browns came home. Mrs. Brown was as tired as any woman would be, who has cleaned and tidied a hut, overseen the packing of the belongings of herself and six children, walked herself and those six children through the driving rain to the railway station, and travelled home wet and uncomfortable, in an overcrowded railway carriage. The train came in at an awkward hour for catching a bus, and seeing they were all wet anyhow, Mrs. Brown decided they would save the money and walk from the station at Upper Saltings, to Lower Saltings. It was quite a walk for the fresh in fine weather, for the wet and tired it was a devastating trek. It was when the family reached the crown of the downland road and saw Lower Saltings that Marge, the eldest, gave a scream.

"Look, Mum, there's smoke coming out of our chimney. Somebody's lit our fire."

Mrs. Brown was pushing the pram, and it was hard work, loaded as it was, and she was in no mood to listen to foolish talk from her children.

"Give over, Marge. You're looking at the wrong house."

But by now the children had stopped, and all those old enough to have a sense of direction were pointing, and the others were conscious of excitement and were shouting.

"'Tis our house."

"I can see it's our house because there's Mr. Harris's rabbit hutches next door."

"'Tis ours Mum. Have a look."

Thus urged Mrs. Brown stopped and raised her drooping head. Below lay the main street of Lower Saltings. To those unfamiliar with it each of the jerry-built cottages which clung to its neighbour, looked so alike that nobody from above could possibly have picked out one home from another. But that was not how the inhabitants of Lower Saltings saw the district. To Mrs. Brown her house, No. 16, was as clear as if it had a ring round it. Let alone the rabbit hutches next door; there was the privet hedge of No. 12, and the out-house behind No. 13, and above all, the distinguishing features of her own place. The subtle differences, so insignificant in themselves, but so vital to Mrs. Brown, which spelt home.

"Somebody has lit our fire," she whispered, and then added, looking round at her wet bedraggled children, "God bless them, whoever thought of it." Mrs. Brown was so unused to kindness and friendship that she lived the next hour in a dazed state. Dimly she realised that her children were being stripped, and given hot baths, and that their wet things were put into sacks and put in the Vicar's car outside. Dimly she took in Judy and heard her say, "Get your wet things off, and sit in this dressing-gown until your bath is ready." She first began to focus on things a little when she found herself in the hot bath. It was seldom she had a bath, for it was work boiling the water, and there was nothing to bath in big enough for her to sit in. But to-night there was a large rubber bath set out in the kitchen, and sitting in the hot water it was as if the tiredness was running out of her. Afterwards, once more in the dressing-gown, she heard Bertha say, "Pity to have all that hot water about, and not let me give your hair a nice wash." Mrs. Brown would have argued at that, but her head was in the basin before she had time. It was after the head washing that her wits completely returned. She had heard excited screams from the children ever since they got home, and now she took in what the excitement was about. With goggling eyes she walked from the kitchen to the front room, and then up the stairs to the bedrooms. She came down and found Judy who was bringing a bowl of soup into the front room where the table was laid for supper.

"You done all this Miss?"

Judy put down the soup and fixed the towel back in place round Mrs. Brown's wet head.

"You ought to have stayed by the fire drying that. Will you promise to do it after supper? We'll stay and put the children to bed, and wash up."

Mrs. Brown laid a hand on Judy's arm.

"You done all this?"

Judy saw she really wanted to know.

"Not me only. The Vicar's little nephew and niece, and his maid Bertha, out there in the kitchen." Mrs. Brown looked at her clean, distempered walls and ceiling. At the new coat of cheerful green paint on her woodwork. At the crisp flowered curtains in her window. At the bowl of roses on her table. At the rich smelling dish of good soup, and she began to cry.

"I can't help it," she sobbed. "Nobody hasn't helped us like this. It's as if I'd started new."

Judy put her arm round her.

"That's what you have done, and with us to help you things are going to be different." She gave Mrs. Brown's shoulder a squeeze of sympathy and to be sure she was attending. "Don't slide back. It isn't often one gets a chance to start new. I've just had one myself, so I know what it means. Let's make a promise, you and I, that as we both know what it is like to get stuck in the mud, we'll keep on dry land now we've found it." Judy was uncertain how much of her words Mrs. Brown had taken in, so she said no more, and instead called out:

"Come along, children. Your supper's ready."

Sterndale was in a mess. In his life he had liked girls, and sometimes thought he was fond of them, but until he met Judy he had no idea what it was like to be in love. He had no idea that one person could be so important that they could fill a whole horizon. He had no idea that he could get in such a state that his entire days were spent inventing excuses to go to the vicarage. He could not have imagined that he could have sunk to such feeble excuses as he had, but there it was, he had sunk to them, any and every excuse he could invent that would give him even a "hullo," or a nod from Judy. And now the holidays were coming to an end, and even those occasional glimpses of her would be lost to him. Of course he could always go up to the vicarage after supper for a smoke with Martin, but that didn't mean he would see Judy, and there was something different about Martin these days. Sterndale could not see, often as he puzzled over it, why he and Martin's friendship was falling apart. But equally he could not deny even to himself that in a way it was; of course they were still friends, but that easy communion which had been the essence of their friendship was gone. It was as if now they had to keep talking when they met, as if they wanted no time for the other to read their minds.

It was just before the Autumn term started, and a moment when Sterndale was feeling at his most despairing at the thought of the blank Judy-less days ahead, that his mother rang up. She was, she said, in a fix; she had agreed to go and spend the autumn nursing a friend who was ill, but Chloe was on her hands.

Sterndale, who knew his mother's breathless, long-winded way of getting to the heart of any trouble, stopped her there. Chloe was his sister and a lot younger than himself, and as his father had died when he was at Cambridge, he had felt almost paternally responsible for her ever since.

"Stop a moment dear. First tell me why you and Chloe are back from France, and why you didn't wire me to meet you? You were stopping until Christmas."

"Yes, we were, Sterndale, but then poor Gladys said she was ill and had no one to nurse her, so we came straight home and—"

"But why Chloe?"

"Well, dear, I couldn't leave her."

Sterndale bit back his criticism that Chloe's future as a French speaking private secretary should have come before Gladys's illness, and instead made the best of the situation.

"Well, can't Chloe start her secretarial training, and then go back to France later?"

There was a burble of sound over the telephone, out of which Sterndale gathered that his mother thought Chloe was run down and needed a rest, and would dear Sterndale take her until Christmas. Sterndale gasped.

"But my dear mother, I'm out all day, and Chloe's only seventeen, and—" and there he stopped. A sudden vision came to him of what having Chloe in the cottage might mean. A nice person like Judy would never leave a child like that alone all day. She would be sure to take her under her wing. And surely she wouldn't only invite Chloe to the vicarage. Surely if Chloe were in his cottage, Judy would visit her. At last he had found a means of getting Judy under his roof, away from the glaring eye of Aunt Connie, away from constant interruptions from Veronica, away, though that was a thought of which he was ashamed, from Martin. He changed his tone of voice. Yes, it would be perfectly all right to send Chloe. The people in the village would help to amuse her. Yes, she could come to-morrow, he would meet her at Upper Saltings.

The news that Sterndale was expecting his little sister the next day flew round the Saltings. The information came from Mrs. Reynolds, who "did" for Sterndale. She had no sooner had orders to get Chloe's room ready than she managed to slip out to the post office, to tell Mrs. Beam. Mrs. Beam was enthralled, she had not had news like that to broadcast in weeks.

"Do him good," she wheezed to Mrs. Reynolds. "Take his mind off Miss Griffiths a bit. He's getting quite thin."

Mrs. Reynolds sighed romantically.

"That's the truth. Terrible what love does. Well, I must be slipping back. This makes extra work for me."

Mrs. Beam spoke between wheezes.

"Coming on the 2.40 you say?"

Mrs. Reynolds was going out, she paused so that her words would not be masked by the jangling ring that would occur as she opened the door.

"That's right, and she's staying till Christmas."

A child came into the shop a few minutes later for a penn'orth of sweets. Mrs. Beam held out an additional handful.

"You can have these if you run up to Vicarage Bertha, and tell her if she's the time I'd like a word with her. And tell your mother when you get home as she might inquire about extra laundry at Mr. Adam's. He's got his sister coming."

Mrs. Beam heard the shop bell clang behind the child with the smug contentment of one who is doing well. She knew there was no flaw in the news system she had set working.

Polly and Judy were gardening when Sterndale brought Chloe to meet them. Judy had of course heard from all sides that Chloe was expected, but she had not heard the news from Sterndale and so was not prepared for how Chloe would look. She had vaguely visualised a female edition of Sterndale, and had hoped she was the sensible sort, who would keep her brother in order. The real Chloe was so ridiculously unlike this that she laughed as she greeted her, and instead of shaking hands gave her a kiss.

Chloe was a little thing, with enormous brown eyes, and a sleek dark shingled head. She had a heart-shaped face, which was as pretty as a flower. She was wearing a yellow silk frock, and had bare legs and sandals. She did not really look a great deal older than Polly.

"My dear," said Judy, "I'm sorry to laugh, but I was expecting somebody so much older."

Chloe had a low soft voice.

"I'm seventeen."

"Well you don't look it." Judy pulled Polly forward. "This is Polly."

Polly raised a face with a smudge of earth across the check, to be kissed, and then drew back with a fixed, interested stare. She approved of what she saw, for she dashed under a bush and brought out Sloe, and led him up to Chloe.

"This is Sloe. He's partly mine, and partly Andrew's, only now that Andrew's back at school he's all mine."

Chloe was fond of puppies, she knelt down by Sloe and hugged him.

"Isn't he lovely."

"Chloe will be on her own all day, while I'm in Lewes," said Sterndale to Judy, "I thought perhaps you'd keep an eye on her."

Judy looked down at Chloe's childish head.

"Of course, Polly and I will love that, won't we, Polly? I hope you won't be dull," she added to Chloe, "We do very simple things, gardening and blackberrying, and so on."

Chloe might have heard a list of fantastic gaieties; she raised glowing eyes.

"Oh, that will be lovely."

"And in the mornings I shall be taking Polly in the car to Upper Saltings for her lessons, perhaps you'll make some friends there you can play tennis with; if so we can always take you, and fetch you back."

Chloe's eyes shone even more fervently.

"Oh, that will be lovely."

Judy looked at the child with a mixture of exasperation and amusement. Was everything lovely to her?

They heard Jimson rattling in at the gate. Sterndale unwillingly took his eyes off Judy.

"That'll be Martin, come along Chloe."

Martin was climbing out of Jimson as the party came out on to the drive. He was tired, but his face lit with a smile as he saw them. Sterndale pulled Chloe forward.

"D'you know who this is?"

Martin considered.

"You can't be Chloe can you?"

Sterndale laughed.

"There's a good memory. You haven't seen her since she was five."

Martin shook hands.

"You won't remember, but I spent a holiday with you at Bexhill."

Chloe's large glistening eyes were fixed in a wrapt way on Martin.

"But I do remember. I thought you were Saint George, out of 'Where the Rainbow Ends.'" Sterndale put his arm round Chloe.

"Chloe's staying with me until Christmas. Miss Griffiths says that she and Polly will keep an eye on her for me while I'm away."

Chloe's soft little voice broke in.

"I'd like to be useful. Perhaps I could help in your parish, Uncle Martin." They all laughed, and Chloe flushed. "I always used to call you that." Martin, who had not reckoned up the years, supposed Chloe to be still a schoolgirl.

"Of course I'm still Uncle Martin, and I'm sure you can be a great help." With one of his kind vague smiles he went into the house.

As Martin disappeared Chloe turned to her brother. "Of course I remember him, but I hadn't remembered he was so good looking. He's a little like Robert Montgomery."

Sterndale laughed.

"Well don't tell him that, I don't think he'd like to know he looked like a film star."

Chloe swung round to Judy.

"Don't you think he's good looking?"

The question startled Judy. Full of her secret knowledge of her love, the last thing she wanted to do was to discuss Martin. Even at Chloe's artless query she felt her checks begin to burn. She moved away.

"I suppose he is."

Her voice was emotionless, so emotionless that Sterndale, who by now knew and loved Judy's every inflection, gazed at her with a scared expression behind his eyes.

Chloe, Judy discovered, was no more grown-up than her appearance. She was the simplest and most unaffected child. Just like Polly, she spoke out the first thoughts which came into her head; and one of the first thoughts that she expressed to Judy was that she was in love with Martin. Judy was gardening at the time, and Chloe came and sat on the grass and turned her enormous eyes up at her.

"Have you ever been in love, Miss Griffiths?"

Judy paused in the act of tying up a Michaelmas daisy. "Why?"

"Because I think I am, and I wanted to be sure. When you're in love do you feel as if your heart had got bigger, and then sometimes when you see the person you love does it feel as if it had stopped beating?"

Judy fiddled with the bass in her hand, and looked at Chloe in dismay. She was too direct not to guess who the child supposed herself in love with.

"D'you mean that you think you've fallen in love with Mr. Richards?"

Chloe nodded.

"Yes. I'm sure I have."

Judy came and sat on the grass by her.

"I wouldn't be too sure. You see he's so much older than you are, and I don't think he's looking at you in that sort of way."

"No," Chloe agreed. "He isn't. He thinks I'm still a child, but I'll show him. I'm going to work and work and then he'll know what a good wife I'll make for a clergyman."

Judy could not help her eyes twinkling. Chloe was so serious, and looked such a baby.

"Well, I shouldn't start the work just yet," she suggested. "I've seen a letter the doctor in France wrote to your mother about you. You're very anaemic, you know, and you want a holiday."

Chloe shook her head.

"No, I don't. What would do me good would be to work for him."

Judy went back to the Michaelmas daisies.

"What sort of work?"

"Oh, I don't know. I thought I could teach in Sunday School, and run a Mothers' Meeting, and perhaps I could be a Guide, and clean the brass in the church, and . . ."

Judy tied up a plant and moved on to another.

"I should do one at a time."

Chloe nodded.

"I'm going to do just what he thinks. I'm waiting for him now to come in, so I can talk to him about it." There was the sound of a car in the drive; Chloe got up. "There he is."

Judy jumped off the bed and laid her hand on Chloe's arm. "No. That's Lady Blacke's Rolls." She fidgeted for words: "Listen, darling! Don't tell Lady Blacke what you've just told me."

"Why not? I don't mind everybody knowing."

"Just don't. Please promise."

Chloe looked worried.

"I'll try not to, but I always do tell everybody everything, and I expect she'd be pleased. They say everybody loves a lover."

Judy saw Veronica coming round the house; she increased her pressure on Chloe's arm.

"I'm not sure that Lady Blacke does. Anyways darling, do please try not to tell her."

Chloe became as violently busy as she had said she would be. There was practically no activity in the parish in which she did not help; from morning to night she was working, and could be seen at all hours careering to and fro on the bicycle that Sterndale had hired for her. Judy had got fond of Chloe; her artlessness and her lack of self-consciousness brought out all the protective mothering instinct in her. It distressed her to see Chloe's large eyes fixed adoringly on Martin, regardless of who was there to watch. Why didn't the poor pet realise that all three Saltings must be watching what was going on with breathless interest. That the fact that Chloe had entered the field against Veronica would be giving unbounded satisfaction. That probably in practically every cottage bets were being laid on the chances of "little filly," or "T'old filly." Judy tried to get an idea of what the gossip was like from Bertha, but for once Bertha, usually so forth-coming, was uncommunicative.

"Oh, there's talk. There always has been about her ladyship, and there's more now that little Miss Adam has fallen for the Reverend, too. But it's a lot of gabble, gabble. Proper set of geese they are. If they wouldn't talk so much and would give their eyes and ears a chance they'd see and hear something one day."

Judy, who knew Bertha to be the first clearing house for gossip, was surprised.

"What would they see and hear?"

Bertha shrugged her shoulders.

"Never mind what. We shall see what we shall see."

Judy saw that for some reason Bertha wanted to be mysterious, and dropped the subject.

"But I'm worried about Miss Chloe. She's wearing herself out with all that work; she isn't nearly strong enough for it."

"She's a proper skinny Lizzie," Bertha agreed.

"And she's such a dear little thing. I don't like people talking about her. You think how you'd hate it if she was a daughter of yours."

Bertha nodded.

"I should, too. But you needn't worry about the talk; nobody says anything unkind that I've heard, for she's no more than a child. It's the thought of her ladyship, with, her buying this, and paying for that, and her sheep's eyes that makes everybody mad."

They were talking in the kitchen. Judy wandered to the wall, and idly played with the flour box.

"Do you think Mr. Richards has noticed? Do you think he could care for . . . ?"

Bertha fetched a bowl out of the cupboard behind her, and slammed it on the table.

"I don't know. Unless he's got less sense than I've given him credit for. Of course he'd never think of Miss Adam, for to him she's just one with Miss Polly."

"And Lady Blacke?"

Bertha got out another bowl. Her voice was almost angry.

"In a world where people can't see happiness when it's right under their noses anything can happen, if you ask me." Judy's heart thumped; she hated to hear Bertha say that. "And as for Miss Adam," Bertha went on, "if she was one of mine, I'd put her in the way of meeting some boys near her own age, and end all that. She's in love with being in love. Lots of girls get taken that way to start with."

Since Chloe had been living in Saltings Sterndale had succeeded in his wish, and Judy went to his cottage. It happened quite naturally, and became a habit. On those days when Sterndale was working Chloe had tea in the vicarage, and when he was home Polly and Judy were invited to tea in the cottage. It had become a habit before Judy realised what was happening, and once it was an established custom it was hard to break. For one thing, Polly enjoyed herself so much. At the vicarage, when she could, she had her tea with Bertha, but more often Aunt Connie expected her in the drawing-room, and then a dreary, constrained meal followed. At the cottage, especially as it became autumn, there were teas which were Polly's idea of perfection.

Toast made at the open fire, scones in a large plate right in the fireplace, and Polly herself allowed to sit on the floor. Then the conversation was so entertaining. Sterndale might be in love, but that did not make him forget that Polly was in the room. He kept them all in fits of laughter by a kind of serial story of a Sussex sheep called Susan whom, according to him, he met and spoke to daily on his way in to Lewes.

Judy, who liked Sterndale better every time she saw him, was very puzzled as to what was the right line to take. It was glaringly obvious that Sterndale was not getting less—but rather more—fond of her. Did it help him not to see her? Or was it better to see a person, even if there was no hope? Judging by herself she thought that seeing a person, however hopeless the situation, was something. She knew what a difference it made to her to even know she was under the same roof as Martin. Then there was Chloe. Because on Sterndale's afternoons at home she and Polly came to tea, Chloe kept those afternoons fairly free, and it must do her good, Judy thought, to relax even once or twice a week. Finally, and most important, there was Polly. Polly flushed and laughing, Polly boldly calling Sloe and finding him a toasted scone. Toasted scones were not good for Sloe, but it was good for Polly to be perfectly natural, and not speak with that lowered voice, and not have that scared manner that were hers too often in the presence of Aunt Connie. Taking all these facts together, Judy thought the afternoons in Sterndale's cottage a good thing, and they should go on.

It was on a wet Saturday afternoon, in October, that Martin, after a wearying round of visits, was suddenly conscious of how often he had his tea alone with Aunt Connie, or with Aunt Connie and Veronica. He had been subconsciously aware for some time that he was being left out of things a bit, but it took that Saturday afternoon to bring it to the front of his mind. He was cold and he was tired, and he would have been wet, only Bertha had waylaid him in the hall, and insisted on feeling his trouser bottoms, and had made him change. He wanted to relax, and to play with Polly, and to watch Polly with Judy. Instead he found Aunt Connie behind the tea-tray, with Veronica facing him. He gave both women a charming smile, but as he sat down he felt dispirited. Of course Veronica was a very good woman, and he was always glad to see her, but at this moment he did wish she was not there. Her eyes were always so eagerly fixed on his face as if she expected to hear worth-while words at any moment. And she was so anxious to discuss parish affairs, and to break in with offers of monetary help. As for Aunt Connie, Martin was gradually reaching the view about her that everybody had crosses they were intended to bear, and she was one of his. He took the cup of tea handed him and asked, more wistfully than he knew, where Polly and Miss Griffiths were. The two women stiffened resentfully. Aunt Connie's face was pink.

"Where d'you think? She must always have a man, that young woman. She's with your friend."

Veronica watched Martin's face. Was he jealous? Did he care? But for all her careful watching she learnt nothing. Martin only seemed to look more tired than he had before.

"Polly enjoys going out to tea," he said gently.

Aunt Connie's withered lips twitched.

"You can't be such a fool as that, nephew. It's not Polly she thinks of."

Martin looked at his Aunt with sorrow. His voice was stern.

"I will not have that kind of vulgar tittle-tattle spoken in my house."

Aunt Connie gave him an angry darting look, but she was sufficiently awed to confine herself to an unintelligible mutter. Veronica was startled; she had heard Martin reprove his Aunt before, but not quite in that tone. Was it just that he hated gossip? Or was it because the gossip was about Judy? Trained as she was to a social life, she quietly filled what might have been an awkward pause by a query about repairs to the organ, but while she chatted her mind was working. She wished Judy was safely out of the Saltings. Whatever had happened to Gloria? Why didn't she answer letters?

When Polly and Judy came back to the vicarage that afternoon Martin was in his study, working. He opened the door when he heard their voices.

"Had a good time?"

Polly burst into an account of Susan the sheep, and toast and a chocolate cake, and Judy stood quietly by, watching Martin. Had she been mistaken, or had he asked them if they'd had a good time, not in exactly a resentful tone, but rather a hurt one? She had never supposed he noticed if they were in to tea or not; could it be that he thought she was playing with Sterndale? In the first break in Polly's flow of talk, she said:

"Why don't you sometimes come to tea at the cottage?"

Polly was enchanted, and skipped from foot to foot.

"Yes, please do, Uncle Martin; please do. That would make tea absolutely perfect."

Martin was touched. He stroked Polly's hair.

"I should like to. Will you let me know the next time you are going?"

It was Polly who hugged him and said "Yes," but the question had been asked of Judy.

# CHAPTER FIVE

CHLOE'S spirit proved greater than her strength. She came in one day to tea at the vicarage after a round of good works with flushed checks, and too bright eyes. She said she was not hungry as she had a headache, but she was terribly thirsty. Judy gave her a glass of milk, and went upstairs for a thermometer. She was not surprised to find that Chloe's temperature was 101 degrees, and as soon as Martin drove Jimson home, she put Chloe into it and took her back to the cottage and put her to bed.

Often in his imagination Sterndale had pictured what it would be like to come home one day and find Judy alone, waiting for him. That evening, when he found that his dream had come true, he could hardly believe it. There was a staircase from his sitting-room to the bedrooms, and Judy was coming down it as if, as he thought longingly, she belonged.

Judy, in her anxiety about Chloe, forgot the position of herself and Sterndale, and sat down easily on the arm of an arm-chair.

"Chloe's got a feverish chill. I sent for Doctor Green for you, but he says a day or two in bed is all she needs; she's been over-doing it, and bicycling about in wet things, and she's run down and got no resistance."

Sterndale was sorry about Chloe, but he could not fail to enjoy the enchantment of the moment.

"Poor kid!"

Judy's voice was urgent.

"No, don't pity her; it's a good thing in a way. Going on as she's been doing she might have been really ill. You must put a stop to this limitless good works; she isn't strong enough for it."

Sterndale smiled.

"You tell me how to stop her."

Judy joined in the smile.

"You know, and I know—in fact, everybody knows—that she thinks she is in love with Mr. Richards."

"Don't you think she is?"

Judy considered before she answered.

"Bertha says she is in love with being in love; I think that's more like it."

Sterndale, with Judy so near, found it hard to focus on anything but her.

"Is that possible? I find—I mean, in my experience that's not a mistake you could make."

The conversation had slipped out of Judy's control. She flushed and struggled to lead it back to Chloe.

"Of course it is," she said briskly. "At least, it is at seventeen. Bertha says that what Chloe needs is to meet boys of her own age. Haven't you any young masters you could bring over to entertain her?"

Sterndale watched Judy's face, the colour coming and going, and the eagerness in her eyes. He was trying to attend to what she was saying.

"Not as young as she is."

"I don't think that matters. See what you can do. If she's better you might get them over this weekend." She got up: "I'll just take one more look at her, and then I must be off. I'll be round to see how she is in the morning."

Sterndale held out a protesting hand.

"Don't go—Judy."

She looked him straight in the eyes.

"I must. You forget I'm here to look after Polly."

He seemed not to know she had spoken.

"I love you. Do you think you could ever love me?"

Judy raised her eyes; they looked at him honestly.

"I'm afraid not. I'm glad you've asked me because I've known you were getting fond of me, and I wanted to tell you it was no good."

"Why? I dare say you don't now; in fact, God knows why you should, but perhaps later on."

"No, Sterndale, don't imagine that. I like you awfully, but I don't love you. Please get that into your head."

"Is there somebody else?"

She had been afraid of that question, and she wouldn't lie, so she turned it.

"There are things in my life which I don't want to talk about." She laid her hand on his arm. "Please try to believe that it's no good. I can't tell you how glad I'd be if I did love you; there's nobody who would make a nicer husband, but I don't, and that's all there is to it. We must just arrange things so that you don't see much of me, and that'll make it easier for you."

Sterndale refused to accept defeat. He'd had a nasty knock, but there was the future; she might change.

"Please don't say that. I can get over what I want to in my own way, but Chloe needs you, and Polly enjoys coming here. I don't want to mess things up. I won't bother you."

She eyed him questioningly.

"Truthfully?"

"Swear."

She patted his arm.

"All right. And now I'll go up to Chloe, and don't forget about collecting some men to amuse her."

Sterndale was where she had left him when Judy came down. He turned as he heard her. He had himself in hand, and his voice was casual.

"How is she?"

"All right, asking for you." She moved to the door, and then stopped. "I didn't say how proud I was that you could love me. But I am. Good night."

Judy, because she had cleared the situation with Sterndale felt even happier, and more secure in the Saltings than ever. The autumn to a person in need of warmth, ties, and affection, proved a very heartening time. Because soon bleak winds would make the downside cold, the villages turned their eyes to home amusements. The buses would run all the winter through, but a bus on a fine summer day was one thing; on a day of rain and mud it was quite another. So as old man's beard whitened the hedges, and the scarlet of berries shone through the grey of misty mornings, committees that had been dormant in the summer months met again, and whist drives, choral evenings, and a play from the dramatic club were planned. Then there were the children. There were evening amusements for them—folk dancing, health exercises, classes at which they could learn to make their own Christmas presents. Because they had learned to like her, and it was a good idea to have a representative from the vicarage—and nobody wanted Aunt Connie—Judy was invited to sit on quite a lot of these committees. Before she accepted she, of course, asked Martin if she might. He was delighted.

"Nothing could be better. Perhaps you can persuade the ladies that we have got a Lower Saltings, and that every person who is drawn in from there is worth three attending from Saltings or Upper Saltings."

Judy had to laugh.

"I can't put it quite like that, or I'll be thrown out of the committees before I'm on them. But I will try and delicately lead them to that way of thinking."

Martin was at his desk; he turned to her with a face which glowed. Judy's heart seemed to contract; she never loved Martin more than at these moments when enthusiasm for a cause—backed by his belief in miracles—made his whole being light up as if by a lamp from inside.

"This year I am confident we shall see a change. Look at the Browns."

Judy's face was rueful.

"Yes, look at them. The paint is being scraped off everywhere, and the walls are nearly as dirty as they were before."

The light in Martin glowed even more brightly.

"That's ingratitude to God, through Whom what you have done has been done. The school reports that the change in the Brown children is most marked. They are dirty sometimes, but often they come to school clean. They are being properly fed, and above all they come regularly to church and Sunday school."

Judy was ashamed.

"Yes, I'm an ungrateful creature. Besides, they have done me so much good." She flushed, and her words tumbled over each other. "I very much needed to be brought in contact with people more wretched than myself. I was inclined, when I came to you, to indulge in self pity."

This was the nearest Judy had ever come to speaking freely of herself. Martin, trained to hear confessions, knew how fatal the too eager delving into another's life could be: he spoke gently, but with no undue interest.

"That doesn't sound like you. It's the sin of a weak person, and I should not have thought you were that."

"It's a very easy sin to fall into. Especially if you feel cut off and friendless, and you think—perhaps wrongly—that you've been uncharitably treated."

"Every sin is easy to fall into if you let your faith weaken."

Judy was almost unconscious of the fact that she was talking so personally, so wrapt was she in the spirituality of Martin.

"It isn't given to everybody to have yours."

He rose to that, flashing like a salmon taking a spinner.

"I don't know how a person can lack faith. I am as sure of the love of God as I am that the sun will rise to-morrow."

Judy's tone was humble.

"I know that's true, and being here is increasing my faith." There was a pause, and in it she felt Martin was waiting for more, and she shied like a frightened horse. "As for the Browns, I'll get them to go to the classes and things, and perhaps they'll set a fashion in Lower Saltings."

After this talk with Martin, Judy felt a difference in her love for him. It was as if she gave up fighting against it, and let it flow over her. "There can't be anything wrong in loving a person like him," she reasoned; "in fact, it must be good for one. The only thing is to teach oneself not to let anybody know that one cares. That would be wrong, because then I'd have to go, and I must never risk that: another change now would be so bad for Polly and Andrew."

It was when she reached this point in her reasoning and allowed herself to accept her love, that a peace rather like the peace of childhood came to her. It was not that she had any idea that Martin would care for her—that she knew to be hopeless; he cared for nothing but his work, but just loving without any possible return was uplifting. It was a lovely pleasure and pain that she was glad to have.

Because she had shut her secret inside herself, Judy supposed that it was just there, and made no difference to her daily life, but she was wrong. Being in love changes the substance of every action, and every thought. It is also blinding. It focuses the mind's eye one way, and dims interest in other people. Because of this, Judy did not bother to notice how Veronica was looking or feeling.

Since the day when Martin had said that she and Polly were often out to tea, Martin had taken to joining them—on the afternoons when Sterndale was home—at the cottage. If Sterndale felt that he would rather be the only man at these tea parties, he beat the feeling down and managed to disguise it. After the day when he had told Judy that he loved her he was honestly glad to see Martin, because he guessed his being there made it easier for Judy.

It was late on one of these afternoons that Veronica came in to the vicarage, and found nobody at home but Aunt Connie, who greeted her with:

"They're all out. She knows that I watch her here, so she gets him to meet her in Mr. Adam's cottage."

It was cold, and Veronica had on a mink coat; she fumbled with the fastening at her throat.

"Do they often go there?"

Aunt Connie was delighted to air her bitterness; she pulled a chair up to the fire for Veronica.

"Quite often. She makes the excuse that they go to see that silly girl, Chloe. But she doesn't deceive me. She's the sort that must have the men round her. She's already got that poor Mr. Adam behaving like a fool, but now she's after my nephew." Veronica turned her face from Aunt Connie; her voice was level and unemotional.

"What makes you think that?"

Aunt Connie was like a kettle boiling over; she had to spill out her imaginings.

"There's something very wrong about her. Where does she come from? You ask her about herself, but you'll learn nothing. I've warned Martin over and over again to be on his guard. I should not be surprised to find if I were to go to Scotland Yard that they knew all about her."

"What makes you think that?"

"She's in hiding here. She gets no letters. It's my belief that that friend of Martin's, Mrs. Bramble, runs some kind of rescue home. I used to work for one; laundry work ours did. But sometimes we found them places, and when we did we were very careful that only one person knew their history. So as to give them a fresh start."

"But wouldn't Martin know?"

"He should; we always told the employer, but I think this girl has got round Mrs. Bramble to keep her secret. I'm sure Martin knows nothing, and because he's easily taken in by her talk and her fussing over that Brown family, he suspects nothing. But I'm watching; I know from experience that the sort who's gone wrong will do it again."

"What sort of wrong do you suspect?"

Aunt Connie tugged, with fingers that trembled from excitement, at the jet ornament at her throat.

"I don't know. It may be that men are her trouble. That was what it was with most of our girls. Or she may be dishonest. Or it might be both. We can only wait and see. In time she'll give herself away. They always do."

Veronica's hands, in spite of her nearness to the fire, were cold. She held them out to the flames.

"If you are right about her—and it wouldn't surprise me—we oughtn't just to wait and see. She should be got rid of before she can do any harm." Aunt Connie twitched with excitement.

"Of course. But how?"

Veronica mentally considered Gloria. She had promised to let her know what she found out. Why hadn't she? Why didn't she answer letters? Then suddenly she remembered something that had up to then escaped her. Gloria's mother had a place somewhere in Kent. She could easily be found in a country telephone directory. She would ring her up. She would know where her daughter was.

Having remembered Gloria's mother, Veronica could not get out of the house quick enough. In any case, though, she bore with Aunt Connie because it suited her to keep in with her; she disliked being with the old lady intensely. Though she got a lot of gossip from her, she was uncomfortable with her; irritated by her twitchings and mouthings. She thought Martin was a saint to keep her; if she was her Aunt she would have put her into a home weeks ago.

Aunt Connie was surprised and hurt to see Veronica going so soon.

"But you've only just come." She took on a whining tone, which went badly with her gaunt appearance, and masculine coat and skirt. "I'm so much alone. They all have secrets in this house, and they tell everybody but me."

In the hall Veronica was just going to call Bertha to fetch Perkins when a thought struck her. She would like to have a look at the tea-party. It was dark outside, nobody would see her; she would like to watch them all without their knowing she was there. Their faces would be off guard; she would have a chance to find out if she was really up against anything.

In Sterndale's cottage tea was over, and the party were sitting round the fire. Sterndale had kept his promise to Judy, and had brought over his fellow masters to meet Chloe. There was one there that afternoon, and Sterndale noted by far the most successful. He was a good-looking man, called Michael Evans—a double blue and obviously an athlete; he was well over six foot, and towered over little Chloe. For the first time since she had come to the Saltings, Chloe seemed interested in someone but Martin. All through tea she plied Michael with food, and now and then gave him a quick interested look out of the corners of her eyes. As for Michael, he couldn't take his eyes on Chloe; he felt about her as Polly felt about Sloe—a need to pet and to stroke. Not that, of course, he could pet and stroke her at this first meeting, but that he would like to was clearly written on his face. Sterndale, seeing all this, wanted to share what was going on with Judy; after all, bringing over rival attractions had been her idea. But Judy wouldn't look at him. In fact, Judy wasn't looking at anybody; from the moment Michael walked in she had become the retiring governess, sitting quietly in a corner, scarcely saying a word. It hurt Sterndale; he quite saw Judy felt she had to avoid *tête-à-têtes* with him, but it was carrying things a bit far for her to refuse to exchange a look even about Chloe.

Martin was lying back in an arm-chair smoking, with Sloe on his knees. He was enjoying himself. He had led a life so consecrated to his work that these afternoons—when there was only the lightest talk and a lot of laughter—did him a world of good. He enjoyed helping to make the toast for tea; he enjoyed that day's excerpt of Sterndale's conversation with Susan the sheep. Above all, he enjoyed the easy friendly atmosphere, in which he was not there as a parson, deferred to and giving advice, but just one of the gathering, treated no differently from anyone else.

Because he did not himself talk much, Martin watched them all, and he found his eyes most constantly on Judy. Always he was sure that she had suffered, but this afternoon there was something about her which wrung his heart. She was sitting exactly opposite to him, with her back to the window. There was a lamp on the table beside her, and it threw up the moulding of her face. It seemed to him that the lines of suffering were more clearly marked than usual. She was not often silent, but she was to-day, sitting quietly, her hands locked together; she had an interested expression on her face, but it seemed to him it was only a surface look, and that her thoughts were a long way off, and they were anything but happy.

It was getting on for half-past five, and Martin was regretfully thinking that he must be getting on, as he had a lot of work to do, when once more glancing at Judy, his eye was caught by the window behind her. It was dark outside, but the curtains had not been drawn, and against the pane he thought he saw a face. Even as he looked it was gone. He didn't want to frighten Polly, so he put Sloe under his arm and strolled over to the window.

"What are you looking at, old man?" Sterndale asked.

Martin had peered all over the garden, but he could see nothing. But he would never tell even a white lie. He turned smiling to Polly.

"This is the time to look out for witches and bogeys, isn't it Pollikins?" He glanced at his watch: "I must be going. I've got to see Fred Peters about the Men's Society."

Martin, still convinced he had seen a face at the window, paused on the garden path and looked round, but there was nothing to be seen, and not a sound.

"I must have imagined it, I suppose," he thought. "And even if anybody was there, what harm could they do?"

Veronica waited behind a bush at the edge of the little lawn until she heard Martin's feet disappear up the street, then very quietly she slipped out of the gate. Back at the vicarage she rang the bell for Perkins and got into her car. There she shut her eyes and let herself re-picture what she had seen. Judy had had her back to her; she had no idea how her face had looked, but she had seen Martin's. The number of times he had looked at Judy, the troubled loving expression he had worn. She shivered. There had been nothing on Martin's face to suggest that Judy was exchanging glances with him. If Martin could look at Judy like that when he got no response, how would he look when she was returning glance for glance? Veronica was not given to prayers at odd moments, but she prayed then: "Oh God, let me find a way to get rid of her before I lose him. Please help me; I love him so terribly."

At the cottage Judy got up.

"Come on, Polly darling! It's bed-time."

"Oh, goodness!" Polly scrambled unwillingly off the floor. "It's always bed-time."

Sterndale also got up. He didn't see why he shouldn't take advantage of the situation between Michael and Chloe; it was so much what Judy wanted that it was only reasonable to suppose she would like them left alone.

"I'll walk with you as far as the gate. I'd like a breath of air."

Judy shook her head and gave Sterndale a look which seemed to him asking for help.

"No." She turned politely to Michael. "I want Mr. Evans to walk with us. He must know how to find his way to the vicarage."

Judy had not appeared to take any interest in Michael until that moment, and the excuse about the vicarage was so feeble that both Sterndale and Chloe stared at her. But Michael took her suggestion calmly.

"That's a good idea." He uncoiled himself from his chair, and stood up with his head and shoulders bent to avoid hitting the beams of the ceiling. He smiled down at Chloe. "And then, can I come back and have that supper you offered me?"

Chloe looked like a small child who has started a game with a big dog and found it too strong for her. She knew she would be awfully disappointed if Michael didn't come back to supper, and yet she couldn't think why she wanted him to. She couldn't think why she cared if she saw him again or not; after all, the only man she cared about was Martin. She felt she ought to say "Do as you like," instead, she said in a voice which she couldn't stop sounding eager:

"Oh, please do."

Outside in the street Michael took Polly's hand.

"Is the village shop still open?"

Polly skipped beside him.

"Yes, there it is. It doesn't really shut ever, not even on Sundays if you ring the back door bell; only when it's shut Mrs. Beam calls it 'obliging,' and you pay next time."

Michael felt in his pocket and found a shilling.

"Well, go and buy some sweets."

Polly caught hold of Judy.

"May I? I'll walk close to the side in case anything comes."

Judy gave permission. After the child had run off there was silence a moment, then she said:

"I had to speak to you. It was nice of you not to seem to recognise me. They none of them know here."

"How is he?"

Judy's voice was distressed.

"I write whenever I'm allowed to, but he won't answer, and it's too far off for me to go to see him. I heard about him once before I came down here; it wasn't a very good report."

"You should stop worrying."

"I do try to. It's easier here where nobody knows. I want all that part of my life to be dead." They were level with the village shop. Michael awkwardly put out a hand and squeezed her arm.

"As far as I'm concerned it is. Don't worry that any of them will learn anything from me."

Up at the Manor House Veronica had found the telephone number of Gloria's mother. She had asked for it, and hardly able to contain her impatience was waiting to be connected. At last she heard the dialling tone at the other end. A maid answered. Mrs. Talbot was at home. Who was it? Lady Blacke? Yes, she would fetch her.

Mrs. Talbot had never heard of Veronica, but she was used to calls from unknown members of the village institutes. Her voice came over the wire brisk and efficient. "Who? What? Oh, it's not about the jam-making competition? Gloria? Oh, but she's here. Yes, I'll call her."

Gloria spoke almost before she reached the telephone.

"Veronica, darling. What must you think of me. But I went to stay at a villa at Sidi Bou Said. Most divine place; absolutely nobody there but Arabs. My dear, I'm so brown. Real mahogany. I'm going to have treatment so I don't go all yellow stripes when it wears off."

Veronica at last got a word in.

"Did you find out about Judy Griffiths?"

"My dear, did I! I meant to write only I went off in such a hurry. Besides, it's a long story."

"What is it?"

"I can't tell you now. It'll take ages, and Mother gets livid if I'm long on the 'phone; but I'm going to Town on Friday, can you lunch?"

"You lunch with me. Will Claridges do you, at one o'clock?"

"Perfect. Good night."

"One moment." Veronica's hand on the receiver was sticky. "Was it a scandal like you thought?" Gloria laughed.

"I'll say it was. I'll tell you this: if ever there was a dirty little skunk walking free who should be behind bars and having the 'cat' thrown in, it's Judy Griffiths."

News of even the least interest was never a secret in the three Saltings. Veronica had to attend a meeting in the Parish Hall the next afternoon, and while she was there Perkins went into the shop for some stamps and tobacco. Mrs. Beam liked Perkins, for he had an aunt who suffered from asthma, and the difference between the way it took the aunt and Mrs. Beam formed a bond.

"Good afternoon, Mrs. Beam," Perkins said cheerfully. "How's the wheezles?"

Mrs. Beam sighed.

"Bad! It's this damp foggy weather we've been having, Mr. Perkins. I'll just have to give in to it now till the spring comes again. That is, if I live to see it."

Perkins appreciated that Mrs. Hearn enjoyed believing that she might be carried off at any moment, so he sighed in sympathy before saying cheerfully:

"My Aunt always says that her doctor says that she need never worry; whatever she dies of it won't be her asthma."

Mrs. Beam gave a deep breath full of wheezes, to show how little chance there was of this prophecy being true in her case.

"Ah, it takes all sorts to make a world." This statement seemed to take her mind to Veronica. "She at the committee?"

Perkins grinned.

"You bet. They want to act that bit of a play after Christmas for new curtains for the Parish Hall, and she wants to give them."

Mrs. Beam nodded.

"Set on it they are. And what's the harm. Can't get settled between that 'Henry the Eighth' and 'The Ghost Train.' 'Henry the Eighth' being Shakespeare there's them as favours it, being good for education, only people won't go to see it much. They say that 'The Ghost Train' is beautiful; makes you come over cold to read it."

"Well, her Ladyship don't want them to do either. She says it's more expense in the end than giving the money right away."

"That's true, too, but it's the pleasure you have to think of. They don't half enjoy themselves at those rehearsals. Still, her Ladyship isn't one to think of that."

Perkins nodded at the tobacco shelf.

"Give me a packet of my usual. Pity they didn't fix the committee for Friday; we're going to Town that day."

Mrs. Beam turned a shocked face to him.

"What, the day after to-morrow! It's the first I've heard of it. What you going for?"

"Only knew myself this morning. We're lunching. Claridge's at one o'clock. I'll take a two shilling book of stamps."

Mrs. Beam was comforted. If Perkins hadn't known the news till that morning, then her system was keeping its end up. She passed him his book of stamps.

"I've a kettle on, Mr. Perkins. You'll take a cup of tea. It's cold work hanging about this weather."

Judy had missed the meeting at the Parish Hall as she had Polly in bed with a little cold. To Mrs. Beam's delight, she came into the shop about three minutes after Perkins had left it.

"Have you got any of those flower transfers, Mrs. Beam?"

Mrs. Beam climbed on to a stool, wheezing violently with the effort.

"Just one sheet left, I think. But there's some of birds if Miss Polly isn't up to-morrow."

Judy was by now so used to the ways of the Saltings that she was not even surprised that Mrs. Beam should know that Polly was in bed.

"I'd better take the birds. The weather's so nasty I think she'll be better where she is for the next forty-eight hours."

Mrs. Beam climbed laboriously on her stool and came back to the counter.

"How's Master Andrew? I noticed when I was sorting the letters that he'd written to you this morning."

Judy, in the manner the Saltings found so friendly and endearing, leant on the counter and took Mrs. Beam into her confidence.

"He's all right, I think, but his parents' death was a terrible shock, poor little boy. I worry sometimes that he gets moments when he feels lonely and miserable, and perhaps has no one to confide in."

"It's like enough," Mrs. Beam agreed. "You could see the difference being at the vicarage made to him. Looked quite a different boy by the end of his holidays, didn't he?"

Judy smiled.

"Yes, thank goodness. I think one day soon I'll ask Mr. Richards if I can go over and see him."

Mrs. Beam's face grew eager; this was one of her better moments when her news service could be put to practical use.

"You ought to go Friday. Her Ladyship's going to London in the car. She's lunching at one. If she gave you a lift it would save the Reverend a lot. The school's only just outside London, isn't it?"

Judy paid for the transfers and put the parcel under her arm. Her mind weighed Mrs. Beam's suggestion. If Veronica would give her a lift it would be a good idea; the only drawback was her unwillingness to ask favours of Veronica. Then she thought of Andrew, and threw aside her own feelings.

"That's a good suggestion. Mr. Richards is in; I'll go and ask him if I may ask her. Is she at the committee, do you know?"

Mrs. Beam made an expressive face.

"You may be sure she is."

Judy was not going to be led into even a hinted discussion on Veronica, so she gave Mrs. Beam a friendly nod and left the shop.

Judy fixed Polly up with a tray, a pair of scissors, an empty drawing book, and a saucer of water.

"D'you think you could be very careful, darling, and not upset that water if I leave it with you while I go and have a word with your Uncle?"

Polly looked up from her sheets of transfers.

"I shall start on a flower. What d'you want to talk to Uncle Martin about?"

Judy ruffled her hair.

"Curiosity killed the cat. But, as a matter of fact, I hear Lady Blacke is going to London on Friday, and I thought I'd ask her for a lift and go and see Andrew."

"Am I going?"

"No, if you haven't got that cold you'll be doing your lessons."

Polly carefully cut out the transfer of a daisy.

"Well, I don't mind; even to see Andrew I wouldn't want to go in her car. I'd rather be in Jimson."

Judy laughed.

"You're a bad girl." She looked under the bed at Sloe. "Now you're not to get on the bed, old man. If you do both you and Polly will get whipped."

Polly squealed with laughter.

"Sloe and me would laugh and laugh. I wouldn't think you could whip anyone; you'd be so miserable at having to do it."

Judy was at the door; her face behind her smile was sad.

"That's all you know."

Martin was writing when Judy came in; he pulled a chair forward for her. He was conscious that he was glad to have her in the room, and that surprised him. He supposed he never wanted to be interrupted in his working hours.

Judy opened Andrew's letter.

"This came this morning." She read:

*"Dear Judy, thank you for the cake and the sweets. I am glad Sloe is well, I expect it was eating that piece of bad bird like you thought that made him sick last week. We had a man to talk to us about darkest Africa, with pictures of snakes it was not bad but the man had a cold and talked through his nose so every time he meant to say snakes he said snaigs and nobody could help laughing. I wish it was nearly Christmas it seems such a long time off and never gets any nearer, perhaps this is because it is winter which is always worse than summer and there's no one much to talk to here so it would be nice to see you again much love. Andrew."*

She refolded the letter. "I don't like that end part. I'd like to go and have a talk with his head master, unless of course you'd go."

Martin considered.

"I think you'd be better than I would. I thought last summer that you were more what he needed than myself. I think he's still a bit reserved with me, probably because I'm a parson."

"I don't think that, but I think that a woman is what a child needs when he's ill, and in a way Andrew's ill. He's suffering from shock."

"When shall you go?"

Judy explained about Veronica.

"If she'd take me there's most of the fare saved."

"She's always so kind, I'm sure she will," said Martin. "Will you telephone her?"

Judy pointed in the direction of the Parish Hall.

"She's at the committee; she's sure to come here to tea."

Martin nodded. Then with a gesture he stopped her getting up.

"There's something else I wanted to talk about." Judy lowered her head so that he shouldn't see her face. His voice was so grave. What had he heard? What did he know?

"Yes?"

Martin was unwilling to speak for a moment, then he blurted out:

"It's my Aunt. Has it struck you that she's not quite herself? Do you think she ought to see a doctor?"

Judy had always thought Aunt Connie a case for the doctor, but she had noticed lately that she was more difficult, and she had thought that her habit of whispering and muttering must be a bad sign. As well, Bertha had spoken her mind. "Breaking up, that's what she is, and she can't do it too quickly for me."

"Ought to be in a loony bin; she gets more missing on the top storey every day."

"Well," Judy said cautiously, "I think perhaps if you could get Doctor Green to come in casually, not as if he had come to see her, it might be a good idea. She"—she hesitated, looking for tactful words—"she might need a sedative or something."

Aunt Connie had been on Martin's mind for some time; he was glad he had confided in Judy. His voice was easier.

"I'd better drive down and see Green and tell him how the land lies."

"You might get him up here to-morrow to see Polly; she doesn't need a doctor, but her cold is a good excuse. Perhaps he could come in the morning and stop to lunch."

Martin smiled at her gratefully.

"That's a very good idea; I'll fix that."

Judy saw Veronica coming up the drive.

"There's Lady Blacke. You will come in to tea, won't you? You hurt her feelings when you don't."

Martin looked shamefaced.

"Of course I will. I'm afraid I'm rather slack about these social things, but sometimes when I'm busy it's easier to have just a cup of tea in here."

Judy could not keep her eyes from twinkling.

"And it's nothing to do with not wanting to hear parish chat, is it?"

Martin grew even more shamefaced.

"If I don't have to hear parish tittle-tattle I can forget it. Petty quarrels, unkind gossip, and small snobbisms are only clouds; but they can, for a time, dim the glory of God."

Judy went to the door to tell Bertha they were ready for tea.

"If the gossip is unkind enough it's not only for a time. It can dim it for ever."

Martin lit up with his inward light.

"If you have faith, nothing can do that."

Judy paused, marvelling why he who had so many daily pricks to try him should remain with so blazing a faith. It was on the tip of her tongue to ask him why his belief was so strong, and hers so wavering; then she thought of Veronica, who would at any moment come in, and she went out with her question unasked.

Nothing was more becoming to Veronica than to be a little annoyed. It suited her English rose beauty to have a spark behind her eyes and a flush on her cheek-bones. She had both that afternoon, and she poured out her grievances over her tea.

"The people here are enough to drive anybody mad. I quite agreed we must have those new curtains for the Parish Hall, and I'm quite willing to pay for them. But I don't see the necessity for getting patterns and having the stuff selected by a committee; it's obviously more sensible for me to buy up some line that's cheap in the January sales. As I told the committee, I'm such a good customer that practically all the London shops eat out of my hand; they'll let me know if they've any bargains going."

Judy looked up from the teapot.

"They want to get something pretty so the room will look nice when there's a dance or social." Veronica took a sandwich.

"So they said, but I pointed out that beggars couldn't be choosers."

Martin raised his eyebrows.

"But I thought they were going to earn the money? Aren't they doing a play?"

Veronica made a despairing gesture.

"They want to, but it's such lunacy. It means endless work, and puts us all to a lot of trouble. I shall never forget that time they did 'Julius Caesar.' The sheets they wanted, and half of them got torn."

Judy made her voice polite, though she didn't feel a bit like it.

"If they do 'The Ghost Train,' they wear their own clothes."

Veronica gave an angry bite at her sandwich.

"They are doing 'The Ghost Train,' but I'll only believe they're wearing their own clothes when I hear of it." She turned to Aunt Connie, "Already Mrs. Reynolds, who is to play an old lady, said she wondered if you'd got a hat she could borrow."

Aunt Connie was not interested in the curtains for the Parish Hall, her mind had been on Martin and Judy. What had they been saying to each other in the study? Her lips twitched, and her hands shook. Instead of answering Veronica, she suddenly spat at Judy.

"O, thou daughter dwelling in Egypt, furnish thyself to go into captivity."

Judy, who was about to swallow some tea, was so startled at this attack that she choked. Veronica watched her gulping behind her handkerchief and wondered if, for all her oddness, Aunt Connie was not a bit of a prophet. She would be very surprised if in no time Judy was not in captivity, or something very like it. Martin, after a sad, worried look at his Aunt, changed the subject.

"Miss Griffiths tells me you are going to London on Friday—" Veronica interrupted him.

"Really, the way news gets about. One would think you had an ear to my key-hole, Miss Griffiths. I only decided last night that I'd go to London, and I haven't told a soul."

Judy had recovered from her choke. She was not going to let Veronica get away with that sort of rudeness.

"I expect you told Perkins. It was Mrs. Beam who told me. We were wondering if you'd be so kind as to give me a lift. I want to go and see Andrew."

Veronica was annoyed, she did not want Judy with her on Friday. She had nothing to get out of her now—all the news she needed she could get from Gloria, and the drive back might be a little awkward. In fact the whole journey would be tiresome. She knew she would feel ill at ease making small talk to a woman she intended, if not to ruin, at least push somewhere where she could do no harm. However, she had built up her life in Saltings on the "Lady Blacke is so kind" principle, and she couldn't shatter it in front of Martin. She forced her mouth to smile.

"That'll be lovely. Though I'm not quite sure I can bring you back. I rather thought of looking up some friends on the way home."

"That's very good of you," said Martin sincerely, "the journey home doesn't matter half so much, does it, Miss Griffiths? It's getting into Upper Saltings and then the slow journey to the Junction."

Judy said nothing but gave a nod of acceptance, but mentally she thought, "Blast, it won't save much money if I've got to take a single ticket home, and she obviously doesn't want me for all her smiles, and goodness knows I don't want to drive with her. Never mind, I'll have a nice time with Andrew, and I'll have a peaceful trip home. I must be thankful for small mercies."

Doctor Green was interested in Polly, interested in fact in the whole running of the Vicarage. Since his visit was supposed to be on Polly's behalf he did just look at her tongue, take her temperature and sound her chest, then he looked up at Judy, his eyes twinkling.

"I don't think we need fear complications." He sat down by Polly. "What do you do with yourself in bed? Do you read?"

Polly liked Doctor Green; she wriggled back comfortably against her pillows.

"I can, of course, but I like being read out loud to best. Judy reads to me a lot."

"We belong to the county library," Judy explained.

Polly hugged her knees.

"It's very easy to get books for me because before I came here nobody had read to me much, so there's heaps to choose from. In the holidays we have books about the sea and adventures because Andrew likes them."

Doctor Green, without appearing too interested, drew her out.

"Andrew likes being read to too, does he? So did I at his age. But I expect Miss Griffiths gets tired of it, doesn't she?"

Polly shook her head violently.

"She's often more interested than us. When we were reading about pirates last holidays, we got to a place where the people were being made to walk the plank, and though it was nearly ten minutes after my bedtime Judy said we couldn't leave them there, and she'd rather I was even an hour late in bed if only we found out just how they were rescued."

The eyes Doctor Green turned on Judy were full of kindliness. He had long thought she was the most remarkable find.

He marvelled that a dreamy creature like Martin could have picked with such wisdom.

"And were they rescued?" he asked.

Polly answered:

"Yes, by a British gun boat. The pirates were Chinese. We're reading a book now about some very poor children. But they aren't nearly as poor as the Browns."

Doctor Green had the Browns on his panel and knew them well.

"I hear you've adopted them."

Polly sighed.

"We have, but they're a great worry to us. Judy and me saw them last week and it was a terribly cold day, and do you know the baby wasn't wearing the lovely little clothes Judy had knitted him."

"She'd only thought they were too good for ordinary wear." Judy explained.

Polly bounced about the bed.

"Mrs. Brown was awfully funny when Judy asked why he wasn't wearing them. What do you think she said?"

Doctor Green shook his head.

"I couldn't guess."

"She said, 'You think I've taken them to Uncle's, don't you, Miss, but you're wrong.' And then she opened a drawer and there they were in the paper they came in. But Judy never had thought she'd taken them to an uncle because she didn't know the Browns had one."

Judy and the Doctor laughed, and Judy got up and pulled Polly's dressing gown straight.

"We're going down to lunch now, and Bertha's going to give you yours, and don't talk so much that you forget to eat."

Out in the passage Doctor Green touched Judy's shoulder.

"You ought to be a proud young woman. It isn't given to many of us to carry out such a good piece of work as you've done for that child and her brother. If all my mothers would give their children such a healthy, happy, wise upbringing as you are achieving, my work would be halved."

Judy had a lump in her throat, her cheeks were scarlet.

"That's terribly kind of you," she said at last, "but you shouldn't be so nice, or I'll ruin any good opinion you have of me by bursting into tears."

Aunt Connie was glad to see Doctor Green at the luncheon table. He was, for all his foolishness in putting Polly on a diet, a sensible looking man. He might, she felt, be a great help in protecting Martin, when the time came that Judy was caught out in open sin, and had to be sent away. Because she felt like this about him she made what was for her an effort to be sociable, and instead of behaving like most patients, who are being, unknown to themselves, observed, and giving little help to the doctor, she gave Doctor Green a grand opportunity to study her. He noticed that one side of her mouth behaved a little differently to the other. He heard her voice now loud coming like a gust of wind and now in a whisper. He tried to focus her eyes and found it impossible; at a direct look they slid away from him as if he were a light that hurt. He drew her into conversation—Martin and Judy were so used to Aunt Connie's irrelevances, and text quotings, that they had come not to notice them.

But Doctor Green noticed, and the moment lunch was over he suggested a pipe with Martin in his study.

"I suspect your Aunt has had a slight stroke. And either through that or perhaps some other cause her brain is not functioning normally."

Martin was filling his pipe, he stopped and looked up, his face distressed.

"You don't mean that she's becoming insane?"

"That's a strong term, but I think the old lady needs care. I should say she was jealous of Miss Griffiths, and that seeing her constantly about is aggravating her state of mind. In fact I should make some other arrangement."

Martin seemed almost winded by this suggestion. When he spoke it was in a dazed way.

"But there's the children to think of. She's made all the difference to both of them."

Doctor Green pushed the tobacco into his pipe and looked up to give Martin a shrewd glance.

"Good heavens, I wasn't suggesting Miss Griffiths should be moved. She's first rate. No, it's your aunt."

"Oh, Aunt Connie!"

Martin's unconscious tone of relief made the Doctor smile.

"Yes. She's used to a place of her own I gather, and watching a young woman giving orders, however tactfully it's done, aggravates her condition. Of course, if you could find an excuse for me to have a real look at her I could tell you more—"

"I'm afraid that's difficult. She doesn't know we are anxious about her."

"Quite. She's no other relations?"

"No."

"Difficult." The Doctor smoked thoughtfully for a time, then he said, "Well, you must think of something. She can't stop here. For one thing, anyone in her state is bad for a sensitive child like Polly."

Martin accepted that, but he was worried.

"I couldn't force her to do anything. She's my mother's sister, and I'm all she's got."

Doctor Green nodded.

"I know. You're not the first person to be faced with a crisis of this sort and you won't be the last. But you have to take an entirely unsentimental view. First of all, ask yourself: is your Aunt really happy here?"

Martin thought of Aunt Connie's gaunt figure trudging angrily from cottage to cottage, now with magazines, now with tickets for a parish affair, never welcomed, perhaps always conscious that she was unwanted. He thought of her behind the tea table at meals, eyeing everybody with distrust, fearful of an encroachment on those things she took to be her rights. He thought of the hours she spent alone in her bedroom, he doubted if she read or amused herself, more likely she was at the mercy of her disordered thoughts. Was any of this happiness?

"No, I daresay she's not, but she would I think be more unhappy anywhere else, except in a place of her own, and I can't afford that."

The Doctor got up.

"We must work out a plan. In the meantime you can help by sounding the old lady; see if she's got a pet scheme hidden away."

"Pet schemes cost money," said Martin sadly.

The Doctor moved to the door.

"Not always. You've got a lot of good friends. I should be surprised if you couldn't lay hands on help if you wanted it." He paused. "That Miss Griffiths is a very fine young woman, and she'll do better work still if she has a freer hand. She'd do wonders for you all if she had this vicarage to herself."

Martin, who had been following the doctor to the door, stopped dead.

"But if my aunt were to go she couldn't stop here—I mean—"

The doctor laughed.

"I should take one fence at a time. I shouldn't be surprised if a plan could be made about that too."

## CHAPTER SIX

THE drive to London the next morning was as tiresome as Judy had expected. Because Veronica, however hard she told herself she was only doing her duty, was conscious that the be all and end all of her journey was to get Judy out of the Saltings—she felt awkward. Awkwardness, especially when there is no apparent reason why a person should be suffering from it, takes various forms. Veronica tried to hide hers by excessive chattiness. She could not face a silence, and so, from the moment Judy got in to the car to the moment she was dropped at Paddington, Veronica babbled. She had nothing on earth she wanted to say and her conversation sounded like it. Judy eyed her with amazement.

"What on earth's the matter with her," she thought. "She's not usually like this. She sounds nervous."

Then as the chatter flowed on she became convinced that it was nervousness, and turning over in her mind what Veronica had to be nervous about. She decided that the trip to London was to see either a doctor or a dentist, and that Veronica was dreading it.

"Poor thing," she thought, "I don't like her, but if that's her trouble I wish I could help her."

In order to give what she supposed was necessary consolation, she tried to get Veronica to confide in her.

"Whereabouts are you going?" she asked when she could get a word in.

Veronica felt more uncomfortable than ever, and explained it was Claridges, and then dashed off on another subject.

"Shopping in the afternoon, or what?" Judy persisted.

Veronica felt hot, but she agreed she might do a little shopping, and then turned the conversation again.

"I really ought to come up and see my dentist some time," said Judy, hoping to give Veronica a lead. "Do you dread going to yours?"

Veronica's mind was so many miles from her dentist that she really hardly heard Judy's question, and only answered her by a brief "No," and then scurried back to the subject of septic tanks, which she had been on when Judy had introduced teeth.

It was with a sigh of relief that Judy got into her train at Paddington. There was nobody in the carriage and she put her feet up on the opposite seat and relaxed.

"Oh, that woman!" she thought, "I do hope that she'll be an object lesson to me, and when I've nothing to say I'll remember to keep my mouth shut."

Andrew had been given leave to meet Judy at the station. She saw him as the train drew in, looking very small and thin inside his blue overcoat.

His knees above the turnover stockings in the school colours were blue and lumpy, and to Judy very endearing.

Although there were several people on the platform, including another boy from his school, Andrew was so pleased to see Judy that his pleasure swamped his natural shyness, and with a muffled ecstatic cry of "Judy" he flung himself on her.

There was something about the warmth of that hug and the tone of Andrew's voice that made Judy more than ever convinced that the boy was, if not actually unhappy, at least feeling rather lost. As they walked up the platform she moved forward so that she could see his face.

"You've got thinner, darling!"

Andrew clung to her arm.

"You'd get thinner if you ate our awful food. D'you know we've had cod's eyes, you know, tapioca pudding, twice last week."

Judy had made careful enquiry into the school food and knew it to be on the whole excellent, so she accepted the statement with a smile.

"Poor starved boy." She looked at her watch. "It's only a quarter past twelve, could we go somewhere and get coffee?"

Andrew had always had this in mind.

"Yes, we'll go to the Cosy Corner. They've got ginger snaps curled up full of cream."

Judy weighed the bad effect on Andrew's lunch of eating cream cakes at such an hour, against a chance to talk to him comfortably, where they would be alone and warm, and decided in favour of the Cosy Corner.

Over a frightening number of cream filled horrors Judy tried to draw Andrew out, but he was unusually reticent. It was not until they had left the tea-shop and were walking up the hill to the school that he gave his first hint of where his troubles lay.

"I say, Judy, if Mr. Bindon says anything about me don't get fussed."

"I don't get fussed about what other people, even head masters, say about my friends," Judy retorted. "I've learnt by experience that what people say is usually wrong, and so if I hear anything about them I ask my friends to their faces if it's true."

Andrew kicked a stone up the hill.

"Sometimes it's awfully difficult to explain. And sometimes both sides think you've been skunkish."

Judy looked at her watch and was thankful to see they still had plenty of time before luncheon. She slowed her steps.

"I'm not either side; couldn't you tell me what it's all about?"

Andrew scowled and shuffled his feet.

"It's all rot, really. You see when Alford's sister got married he went to the wedding, and he brought a lot of stuff back, and gave a do in the dormitory at midnight."

"Yes," said Judy encouragingly.

Andrew looked red about the ears.

"Well, Mr. Bindon came snooping round and found me in the passage, and he thought I was keeping cave, which I wasn't, because we hadn't bothered to keep cave, because nobody ever does snoop about in the middle of the night."

Judy's voice was interested.

"I see, and what happened?"

"Oh, well, he went in and saw the wedding cake and stuff, and there was a bit of a row, not bad, but the others had their half stopped, but he got into a real flap with me because he said I told a lie when I said I wasn't keeping cave."

Judy felt her way carefully.

"Perhaps you explained badly."

"I didn't explain at all. Alford and all the other boys were there, and anyhow, though they didn't exactly say so, I think they thought I was outside the dormitory to split on them."

Judy looked down at his worried little face.

"So that's why you say both sides think you've been skunkish?"

Andrew nodded.

"They still do, but I don't care. Only I didn't want Mr. Bindon telling you about it. You see you'll sit next to him at lunch, but he won't say anything then because I'll be the other side of you, but after lunch he'll take you into the study for a jaw."

"What about Mrs. Bindon? Don't I see her?"

"She's got a newish baby, at least it was new last term, and she feeds it or something."

They were nearly at the top of the hill, and Judy knew the school was on the crest. She walked more slowly than ever.

"I'm sorry you've had a row with Mr. Bindon, because you used to like him, didn't you."

"Do still." Andrew hunched his shoulders. "Matter of fact, I'd have told him only he fell over me, and I woke with such a jump I didn't have time to say a thing."

Judy had never seen the school, but she pictured a door at the end of the corridor, and somewhere in that corridor Andrew lying asleep. Andrew was a sensible boy, he wouldn't sleep in a cold corridor without what he thought was a good reason. She racked her brains for this motive, or something she could say which would lead to his motive.

"It was unlucky you were there the night of the party. I suppose it did look suspicious. Besides, it doesn't seem the sort of thing you would do. You aren't usually idiotic, and it must have seemed pretty idiotic lying in a cold corridor when you'd got a bed."

"I take my pillow and my eiderdown."

Judy gave him an anxious glance. She knew very little about claustrophobia—was Andrew suffering from it?

"Can't you tell me what this is all about? You know I wouldn't take any action without talking it over with you."

Andrew hunched his shoulders more than ever.

"You'll think me such an ass."

Judy, increasingly certain that claustrophobia was the trouble, spoke lightly.

"Not more of a fool than usual."

Andrew hesitated, then he spoke in a little torrent as if the words had been wedged behind a dam which had broken.

"'Tisn't as if it was me, but you can't help what you do when you're asleep, and though sometimes I manage to stop anybody hearing, often they do, and then the boys laugh because they don't know I do it in my sleep."

Judy remembered her own troubled past. Dropping asleep, and waking with a cry as the fears of the living world pressed through to her consciousness.

"You've been crying out in your sleep?"

Andrew looked more morose and red about the ears than ever.

"I cry. You know, properly blubbing. Not that I want to, but I wake up and I'm doing it."

Judy decided that she must probe straight to the heart of Andrew's worries.

"Have you been doing that since your father and mother were killed?"

"Yes. Not much in the holidays, but quite a lot at school."

"How often do you go and sleep in the passage?"

"Most nights, or I did till Mr. Bindon took to snooping, and now I sleep with my bedclothes over my head, so if it happens nobody will hear."

"You ought to have told me this before," said Judy briskly.

"What was the good. I wouldn't now only I don't want Mr. Bindon telling you I'm a liar."

Judy's voice was coldly matter-of-fact.

"Of course there was some good. To begin with, any doctor could give you some stuff so it didn't happen, and secondly, there's probably a room on your own you could have."

"Only in the San."

"Well, that wouldn't hurt for a bit. It's easily fixed up, the doctor can say you're run down and move you there."

Andrew turned trusting but anxious eyes to hers.

"Are you going to tell Mr. Bindon?"

"Not if you don't want me to, but I think you'll be an ass if you don't let me. Why should he think you a liar when you're not."

"He'll think I'm pretty soft."

"Why should he. I had a time in my life when I used to wake up like that. I went to a doctor and got cured and nobody thought I was soft."

They were at the school gates. Andrew seemed suddenly to throw off his cares.

"All right." He gave Judy a quick critical glance. "You look posh. I'm awfully glad, Dibble's aunt came to lunch last week and she looked simply frightful, and though she was quite old she had bright gold hair, and we told Dibble we thought it was dyed."

It was after lunch. Judy was sitting in a chair in Mr. Bindon's study. Her eyes were looking out across the garden, where through a gate small boys in football shorts and jerseys were pushing and ragging. But Judy did not see either the garden or the small boys.

"I think it's a dangerous point in his life," she explained. "If he's misunderstood and muddled now he might get out of gear"—her voice was tense—"and then anything can happen."

Mr. Bindon had brought his wife in to hear the discussion. When it was a question of the boys' health he liked her in on it; he felt that where children's health was concerned a woman was worth half a dozen men. Gladys Bindon was a plump maternal looking girl. She now turned absorbed eyes on to Judy's face.

"Andrew's an awfully sensible little boy," she suggested. "I shouldn't think anything would throw him out for long."

Judy shook her head.

"You can't tell. I knew a boy who lost his mother at about Andrew's age. He didn't seem to have been very sympathetically handled at the time and it seemed to leave him weak. She had been a marvellous mother and saw him through everything, and when she was gone he was lost without her."

"What happened to him?" Gladys asked.

Judy seemed not to hear the question at first, then she jumped.

"Happened? Oh, it's a long, wretched story. I won't bother you with it."

Mr. Bindon lit his pipe.

"What d'you want me to do about Andrew?"

Judy locked her hands together to hide the fact that they were shaking.

"I think he ought to sleep alone, where he can make as much noise as he needs to, and I think he ought to be able to talk over his crying attacks with somebody who's awfully matter-of-fact about them. You know, takes them as things that happen, without making him feel peculiar or interesting."

"Was the other boy you knew made to feel peculiar and interesting?" Gladys inquired.

"Not made to. You see, nobody knew that he was in the state he was in, and so he turned in on himself, and worked out what was the matter with him. It made him full of self-pity, and almost anything he did seemed to him understandable."

Mr. Bindon drove Judy to the station. He came back to find his wife still sitting in his study.

"That's an awfully nice person," she said.

"Nice looking, too," he agreed. "She's got a face you can trust. Surprising to find a young woman like that without kids or a husband so psychological about Andrew."

She looked up at him.

"I've been busy over baby, but it strikes me that you and Matron haven't a great deal to pride yourselves on over the handling of him."

He nodded.

"I've been a fool. It was that damned midnight feast put me off. I really thought the kid was keeping cave." He stood at his desk fumbling with some papers, a puzzled expression on his face. "How does a girl with no experience put her finger on the spot like that?"

Gladys got up and slipped her arm through his and gave him a shake.

"No experience! Where are your eyes, you old idiot? I should hate to think by what suffering she gained her experience."

In Sterndale's cottage breakfast was over and Mrs. Reynolds came in with a large black japanned tray to clear the things. She looked out of the window at Sterndale's back hurrying down the drive, and with a meaning sigh turned to Chloe, who was finishing her last cup of coffee.

"This is the day her ladyship is driving Miss Griffiths to London. I said to myself, when I heard they were going, 'Pity it isn't Mr. Adam that is driving her up, he wouldn't half enjoy himself, poor young man.'"

Chloe swallowed her coffee.

"I can't think why Miss Griffiths doesn't like him. I should think he'd make an awfully nice husband, wouldn't you?"

Mrs. Reynolds leant across the table and picked up a jam dish.

"Miss Griffiths likes him well enough, but just liking wouldn't do for her, she's one to fall into love like a ferret going down a rabbit hole, as you might say. But it's sad for your brother though, he's fallen away shocking these last weeks."

Chloe got up and helped to clear the plates.

"Has he? He doesn't look any thinner to me."

Mrs. Reynolds gave a breathy sigh.

"Ah, that's because you're young. It's only when you've had troubles yourself you can see it in others."

Chloe put the plates on the tray.

"I don't think I should call being in love a trouble. I think it's a kind of nice, lift-you-feeling, even when you know it's hopeless."

Mrs. Reynolds paused with the teapot in her hand and chuckled.

"You're nothing but a child, Miss Chloe, you don't know what love is."

Chloe flushed. She was confused about her angle of mind to Martin and didn't like to hear herself called a child. If she was going to fall out of love with Martin, and regard him more in the nature of a god, which she suspected was what was happening to her, perhaps it was rather a pity she had made her feelings about him so clear, so that all the village knew about them. She changed the conversation.

"Tell me about the play."

This was a certain bait for Mrs. Reynolds. She gave up all pretence of clearing the table, and leant comfortably on it instead.

"You were spoken of, Miss Chloe, at the meeting, as the young lady in it. Nothing wasn't finally settled on account of it being thought better to have a word with Mr. Adam. You see the part of the young man with whom you'd have to carry on with and that, was spoke of for Mr. Perkins, and it wasn't known how Mr. Adam would feel for you acting up with her ladyship's chauffeur. Then her ladyship was difficult; she said as how she didn't know if she could spare Mr. Perkins for rehearsals, on account she might want him to drive her at night, but nobody took much account of that, because her ladyship didn't want the play done at all."

Chloe lolled on a chair back, her eyes bright with an idea.

"I suppose there isn't another part Mr. Perkins could play, because there was a man came over here, the other day, you know, that Mr. Michael Evans, who teaches at the same school as my brother. I should think he's an awfully good actor."

Mrs. Reynolds, who was not slow in the uptake, jumped at once to the suggestion.

"And a very nice young gentleman, too. Has he any money, would you think, Miss Chloe?" Chloe looked surprised.

"He wouldn't want any to act in the play, would he? I mean nothing but his own suits."

"There's other things in life besides acting in plays." Mrs. Reynolds went back to clearing the table. "School-mastering's all right, but he might fall ill or that. Has he got a bit of money, private-like, would you say, Miss Chloe?"

Chloe had been thinking quite a lot about Michael Evans since she had met him, and had no difficulty in concentrating on him now.

"I believe he must have, he's got a motor car, and a boat, not exactly a yacht, but something you can sleep on, and he's got lovely clothes, at least I thought the suit he wore the other day lovely." Mrs. Reynolds nodded approvingly.

"He sounds as though he had a bit behind him, and that's what you want. My husband always used to say, 'You can put your feet under your table as long as you're working, but it's the bit buried in the garden that'll stand by you when you're sick." She swept the two cups on to the tray, and remarked without apparent consecutive thought, "As soon as I can slip up to Rose Collage I'll have a word with Mrs. Ellis, she being secretary of the Curtains Fund Committee, and I'll put forward what you say about Mr. Evans. I shouldn't wonder if the committee wasn't to think it a very good idea."

Mrs. Reynolds was never one to let household duties interfere with any slipping out that she might want to do. She knew her Saltings, anti that whatever tradesman might call would learn her whereabouts by merely shouting across the village street, so before she got down to what she called "My beds and that," she slipped up to see Mrs. Beam. She hurried in at the shop door, causing the bell to make such a jangle that she was leaning across the counter before she could make herself heard.

"I've only popped in for a minute, Mrs. Beam, dear, I'm on my way up to Rose Cottage to see Mrs. Ellis, and what do you think?"

Mrs. Beam let out a wheezy and hopeful sound. "Whatever?"

"It's Miss Chloe. I was telling her how there was thought to ask her to take a part in the play acting, and how it was thought Mr. Perkins might play her opposite, so to speak."

Mrs. Beam let out a deep breath, which gave the effect that there was a basket of kittens kept under the counter.

"That wouldn't never do, and so I said, directly I heard what the committee had suggested. Miss Chloe has her place, and Mr. Perkins has his, I said, and no good won't come of mixing."

"Well, that wasn't what Miss Chloe was thinking; you know what a nice simple little thing she is, and not one to stand on her dignity. No, what she said, flushing up very pretty as she spoke, was, how would it be if the committee was to pick Mr. Michael Evans to play her opposite."

Mrs. Beam breathed more quickly.

"Him from Mr. Adam's school, that came over in the smart little red car?"

"That's him," Mrs. Reynolds agreed, "and if you ask me, Miss Chloe's struck all of a heap." Mrs. Beam let her mind run over her telegraph system. If she let Mrs. Reynolds get to Rose Cottage with this story the news was mined, and the efficiency of her system wrecked. She leant across the counter and dropped her voice to a confidential whisper.

"You've done very right to come to me, Mrs. Reynolds. That sort of thing wants encouraging. A very nice match it would make and give pleasure all round, and very much better than Miss Chloe hanging around the Reverend, which never could do any good, him not having an eye for the women, or if he has," she paused meaningly, "it's not for Miss Chloe. But don't you go and see Mrs. Ellis, Mrs. Reynolds, it's better I should speak. I've got some lovely patterns in a book with stuff for the curtains, and if I was to drop a word in the right place I could get it wholesale, and that'll mean there's a piece of money over towards that new clock the village institute's always speaking about. I'll get Mrs. Ellis down here, seemingly about the pattern book, and I'll throw in the bit about Mr. Evans at the same time."

Mrs. Reynolds was disappointed; the news about Chloe was hers, and she would have liked to have handed it on herself, but Mrs. Beam was too valuable an ally to be quarrelled with, what with the gossip she heard in the shop, and the telegrams and postcards she read, she could be relied on to be first with the news to such people as were her friends, and Mrs. Reynolds did not intend to come off that list.

"Very well. In any case I ought to be getting back to my beds and that." Mrs. Reynolds had her hand on the door, but just before she started the bell jingling, she turned to Mrs. Hearn with a grin. "I wouldn't mind being a fly inside her ladyship's car to hear what she says to Miss Griffiths. I should think rancid butter's sweet to what she'd have to say."

Mrs. Beam took an immense breath, which was followed by a wheeze, like the whistle of a kettle.

"That shouldn't worry Miss Griffiths. Sit still and say nothing, that's what I would do if I was her."

"Shouldn't wonder if that isn't what she is doing." Mrs. Reynolds agreed, and added with deep satisfaction, "I reckon her ladyship's fair riled."

Mrs. Beam had not only Mrs. Ellis to see. She wanted some first hand information of Judy and Veronica's start to London. The children were all in school, so she waddled out into the street to look for someone to send with the message. Fred Peters was passing on his bicycle.

"Good morning, Fred," said Mrs. Beam, "How's Rosie?"

Fred got off his bicycle and leant it against the wall of the shop.

"Of course it's early days to talk, but the doctor thinks it'll be in May."

Mrs. Beam felt this really was being a day of days.

"Well that is good hearing, Fred. How's she keeping?"

"Fine, bit of sickness, but nothing to count."

"She pleased?"

Fred nodded.

"Wonderful pleased. She had carried on as you know, saying she didn't never want another to take the place of the little one that's gone."

"The vicar was a wonderful help to her, I reckon."

Fred nodded.

"Wonderful, but it's Miss Griffiths that we've really got to thank. Vicarage Bertha sent her and Miss Polly down to ask Rosie for our baby's bits of things for that Brown baby in Lower Saltings. Maybe Miss Griffiths looked at Rosie's face, when she was packing the things up, and maybe she noticed the way she carried on about that litter of puppies; you know Vicarage Sloe came from us. At any rate, she didn't just take the clothes and do no more about it, for after she'd fitted the Brown baby out she often stepped in to see Rosie, talked to her about the Brown baby, and asked her advice, and then from that got to wishing Rosie would have another, because, she said, they could have such fun making it a set of clothes and all that. Anyway, talking to Miss Griffiths seemed to get Rosie wishing for a baby, and because she was wishful for it she got peacefuler minded."

Mrs. Beam wheezed approval.

"Ah, that's the time."

"That's right," Fred agreed simply. "Then I slipped up to the Reverend and asked if maybe he'd say a prayer for us, not meaning Rosie and me wouldn't pray for ourselves, but thinking he'd get more hearing maybe." His face suddenly was alight with happiness. "Anyway, the prayers was heard."

"Does the Reverend know?"

"Yes. 'Course I didn't like to tell everybody until it was certain, but I let him and Miss Griffiths know it was likely. And, if you'll believe it, Miss Griffiths was down next day with a knitting book, and sitting there with Rosie planning six of this and twelve of that." He grinned reminiscently at the foibles of women. "Reckon they had that baby born and dressed and out in a pram." Fred took up his bicycle again, "Well, I must be off." He paused, one foot on the ground. "She's a fine lady, Miss Griffiths. Hope we keep her in the Saltings."

Mrs. Beam opened her mouth to answer, and then shut it again. Little and often was her view of gossip.

"Ah, well, you never know. As you pass the Vicarage you might ask Vicarage Bertha if she's got a minute to pop in, and as you go by Rose Cottage call over the hedge to Mrs. Ellis and say I've got some patterns I want to show her."

It was half an hour later when Bertha ran into the shop.

"I can't stop, not above a minute, and I wouldn't have come out now only I thought Sloe'd be the better for a run, and there's no one to take him seeing Miss Griffiths is away."

Mrs. Beam looked over the counter at Sloe.

"Open that tin on your left and give him a Petit-Beurre. I heard something this morning that I thought you'd like to know, you being interested in her as it were."

Bertha raised her head from the biscuit tin, her tone was on the defensive.

"About Miss Griffiths?"

Mrs. Beam registered the defensive note in Bertha's voice but showed no sign that she'd noticed it, and instead told the story of Chloe's suggestion that Michael Evans should act in the play. Bertha, clean forgetting that she could only stay for a minute, sat down on some boxes of oranges.

"And very nice, too. I haven't seen the young gentleman, but Polly came home full of him. Seems he walked back as far as the Vicarage with her and Miss Griffiths."

Mrs. Beam wheezed a moment thoughtfully.

"Now why did he do that?"

"How'd I know?" said Bertha. "Maybe the night was dark, and they needed seeing home."

"But why didn't Mr. Adam? You'd think he'd jump at the chance."

Bertha remembered Polly's conversation after that tea-party. "Such an awfully nice man, Bertha, and he said, 'is the village shop still open?' and when he heard it was he gave me a whole shilling to buy some sweets." And then Polly had turned to Miss Griffiths. "Had he known you before, Judy? Because you said 'Good night, Michael.'" Miss Griffiths hadn't answered directly, but had said, "Grown-up people call everybody by their Christian names." It had all been nothing and absolutely harmless, but it was part of those strangenesses about Miss Griffiths, the little things that made her seem to have something to hide. Bertha got up and called Sloe, and her voice dismissed the subject.

"I'm sure I don't know why it wasn't Mr. Adam, maybe she didn't want him." Then feeling that she had left a feeling of uneasiness in the air, she said, "Her ladyship looked like a Morello cherry tastes this morning; she was acting as pretty as you please, but you could see she didn't want Miss Griffiths in the car with her."

"That's right," Mrs. Beam wheezed. "Like the two halves of a Seidlitz powder, those two. Not that I'd like to describe Miss Griffiths as anything of the sort, I was just speaking in a manner of mixing."

Polly's cold had recovered sufficiently for her to go to school, so in Judy's absence Martin drove to Upper Saltings to fetch her home. Polly raced out when she saw Jimson, and climbed into the seat beside Martin, talking as she came.

"Oh, you have brought Sloe. I was dreadfully afraid you'd forget."

He felt in his pocket and handed her a paper.

"So was Miss Griffiths. She left me this."

Polly opened the sheet and read out.

"Twelve-fifteen, start off in Jimson to fetch Polly. P.S. Be punctual or Polly may stand about outside and she shouldn't with her cold. P.P.S. Bring Sloe," Polly turned an indignant face to her uncle. "I wouldn't have stood outside."

Martin smiled.

"You are like me, Polly. We don't mean to do things that are bad for us, like standing about in the cold, but we forget and need people like Miss Griffiths to keep us in order."

Polly gave his knee a friendly pat.

"You're improving. I heard Bertha say to Judy that you were eating twice what you did."

Martin considered his past meals.

"Am I?"

Polly wriggled into her seat.

"Yes, I've noticed it. I think it's because you've Judy to talk to. When I first came to live with you and there was only Aunt Connie, it was simply awful, and both you and me used to eat as fast as we could to get eating over."

Martin thought back to that dismal past. It must have been depressing when he and Aunt Connie ate alone. He ought to reprove Polly for saying so, but she had put her finger on an undeniable truth.

"Aunt Connie's an old lady," he suggested.

Polly knew that for grown-up prevarication.

"I don't believe she was very nice when she was young. I mean not like Judy. Judy will be nice for ever and ever, even when she's a hundred. Don't you think so?"

Martin never answered questions casually. Now he tried to picture an old Judy. A Judy with white hair, and wrinkles, and he found that as far as he could imagine, what Polly said was true. He couldn't see an age when Judy was not Judy, and therefore a person he would always be glad was in his house.

"She has a very fine character," he said, speaking more out loud than to Polly, "and age doesn't dim her kind."

Polly looked up at him curiously.

"You said that just as you say the Blessing at the end of Church. As if it was a lovely thing to say, that you liked saying."

Martin gave her a quick startled glance.

"Did I?" and then after a pause he repeated, "Did I?" and added in puzzlement, "I wonder why?"

Veronica and Gloria sat over their lunch. Gloria, who had enjoyed her holiday on the African coast, could not at first be got off it. She had to have her tan admired, and describe who had made up her party, what they had done with every minute of their days, and the more intimate details of life among an Arab population, and how disgusting the English weather was to come back to. But at last she put an olive into her mouth and Veronica was able to get a word in.

"Tell me about Miss Griffiths."

Gloria swallowed her olive.

"Wait till we've ordered something to eat. It's a terrific story, and I must get my teeth into it." She considered the menu. "The one redeeming feature of this time of year in England is oysters. I'm not sure I won't eat twelve and nothing else."

Veronica was for all so simple a choice, but she remembered her duty as a hostess.

"Have something before them."

Gloria screwed up her face and took another look at the menu.

"Well, perhaps I'll have a fish day." She looked up at the waiter. "Just a wee scrap of caviare and some very hot toast."

Veronica gave her own order and then leant forward.

"Well?"

Gloria leant forward also. The two women's hats almost touched.

"You remember I told you I'd met her at a do at Mrs. Bramble's, and that she looked simply awful, and that I thought she was mixed up in some scandal. Well, I was absolutely right. I couldn't run it to ground at first. I was staying with the Alfords and Popsy Alford was at that same party, but she's such a nit-wit she never remembers anything about anybody except what they wore. Then by luck her cousin Avis came down. Avis was at the party too, she's got eyes like a hawk and never misses anything. She remembered your Judy Griffiths, and what's more, she'd wangled her way in to hear the case."

Veronica contained herself while she and Gloria were served with caviare, then she said:

"What case?"

Gloria took a piece of toast and buttered it and spread some caviare on it before she answered.

"Don't bustle me and I'll tell you all the dirt."

"What'll you drink?" said Veronica, hoping wine of some sort might hurry Gloria's tongue Gloria raised shocked eyes.

"Darling! nothing. Do you think I got as slim as this in the summer to put it all on again in the winter." She swallowed a mouthful of caviare.

"Your Judy Griffiths was the daughter of a doctor somewhere in Buckinghamshire, or Essex, or one of those odd counties, and her father had a partner called Edwards, who was his great friend. Well the partner died and left a little boy called Dennis, who was about four years older than she was. There wasn't a mother, so the boy spent his holidays with the Griffiths. Well then the Griffiths father died, and the Griffiths mother, with the girl Judy, who was then I think sixteen or seventeen, came up to London for the girl to be trained as a secretary or mother's help or manicurist, or whatever it is. By that time the boy Dennis was grown up and had got a job in a bank, in the North."

Gloria paused and finished her caviare. Veronica watched her in fury. Gloria, she thought, was the slowest eater she had ever met. As Gloria's last mouthful of toast and caviare disappeared Veronica beckoned to the waiter.

"The oysters, please."

Gloria was one of those women who take an unconscionable time dolling up their oysters, drips of lemon, drops of red pepper, it seemed it would never be finished, but at last she looked at her twelve in satisfaction, and turned to Veronica.

"After the Griffiths had been in London quite a time Mrs. Griffiths went to live somewhere in the country, and the girl Judy moved into some drab kind of hostel, run by Mrs. Bramble— you know the sort, that smells of cabbages and is a home from home with a latch-key, with nasty reproductions of old masters in the front hall. As you know, she is pretty, and of course she was bored, and that was when Dennis reappeared on the scene. He got moved to a London branch of his bank."

Gloria stopped and folded a piece of brown bread and butter and dug her fork into an oyster. Veronica, seeing that the whole story was obviously going to be told her in bits, swallowed one of the six she had ordered for herself, but when she saw Gloria's fork poised over a second oyster she broke in:

"Yes?"

Regretfully, Gloria laid down her fork.

"Well, the moment that Dennis saw Judy again he fell in love with her. I daresay there'll been a bit of goings on before, you know one of those boy and girl fun-in-the-shrubbery affairs, but anyhow it flared up when he saw her again, and I suppose there was nobody else about and so she decided to cash in on him. Anyway, she started going out with him. It began with cheap flicks and meals in Soho, but that wouldn't do for Judy, and before long it was the Berkeley, the Savoy, this hole and any night club or bottle party that happened to be going, and as well—" Gloria stopped, folded another piece of bread and butter and ate another oyster.

Veronica also ate an oyster, but without tasting it, she was trying, quite unsuccessfully, to visualise the Judy Griffiths she knew now as a girl of seventeen who couldn't live without night life.

"She doesn't look a bit that sort," she said.

Gloria swallowed her oyster.

"No, that's what Avis said. But still waters run deep, and I was going to tell you it didn't stop at eating and drinking in the best places, for she had to be dressed for the part. Avis said that what Dennis Edwards said he'd spent on her clothes was something fantastic. Avis says that the girl seemed hardly able to agree to wear the same frock twice."

"Really!" Veronica unconsciously ate an oyster.

Gloria swallowed two of hers and then leant across the table and lowered her voice.

"The wretched Dennis Edwards, who seems to have been quite a nice kind of lad, his only fault was that he was in love, couldn't carry on in that way on his bit as a bank clerk, and so he took to helping himself to any odd bits that were lying about."

Back to Veronica came the day when the half crowns had been missed off Martin's mantelpiece, and Judy's obvious distress and her own surprise at that distress.

"She helped him?" she queried.

Gloria shook her head.

"Not that they could prove, but she suggested it. Avis says that Dennis Edwards didn't want to give Judy Griffiths away, and the stories had to be simply dragged out of him. It seems that he had some fairly well to do relations that he used to go and stay with, and that she suggested to him that he might see a bit more of them, and that if he looked round he could probably pick up a few odd pounds. Then when that wasn't enough she sent him round seeing all sorts of friends. Of course he didn't always get money, sometimes he nipped the bit of jade off the mantelpiece, and sometimes he laid his hand on the odd bit of jewellery." Gloria ate another oyster. "Naturally, in the end people began turning suspicious; I mean you can't keep losing the odd bit of Dresden every time the same person calls without noticing it, and his circle grew smaller and smaller, and the rich relations stopped inviting him to stay. Nobody seems to have turned actually nasty and called in the police, he just wasn't welcome, that was all, and then—"

Gloria returned to her plate. "She has," thought Veronica, "a most infuriating way of eating her lunch, she always seems to need to take a mouthful at the more important points of her story." She watched all the oysters go but two, then, unable to contain herself, said:

"And then?"

Gloria's eyes shone.

"This is where we come to the real dirt. It was all very confused in the case, Avis says, and it was very difficult to pin anything on to her, but definitely she got the idea—"

Gloria ate another oyster, but Veronica couldn't wait for her to swallow it.

"What idea?"

Gloria spoke with her mouth full.

"Forgery."

"Forgery!" said Veronica. "Good God. Forged what?"

Gloria ate her last oyster and lit a cigarette.

"I'm frightfully vague about this bit, because I never have known what those young men do behind the iron bars in a bank, but he copied somebody's signature, somebody who used to cash a lot of cheques. Only really whoever it was only cashed half their cheques, and Dennis Edwards cashed the others. He said that he had to do it, that he was being dunned left, right and centre for money, and there was a suggestion that it was Judy Griffiths who taught him how to forge. I mean she thought of the idea, and got him to bring home a copy of the signature, or whatever it was. He was caught in the end, but by then it wasn't one kind of forging, it was all sorts, and the money he'd got away with was nobody's business. He couldn't account for it all but it was believed she'd parked most of it. In any case one day he found himself with handcuffs on, waiting for his trial. That was the really sad part. Avis says that in spite of it all he was still nice, and did his best to shield Judy Griffiths, and he did it so well that she only appeared in the case as a witness for the defence, and she wouldn't have been there then only his solicitors insisted. Avis says it was marvellous the way she got away with it. She stood up there in the box and told some cock and bull story about how she'd never loved him but stood by him because she knew how weak he was, and though they tried everything to prove that she'd had all the money spent on her they couldn't pin anything on her, she'd been too clever, and always got him to pay cash for everything. The judge seemed to believe her, anyway she got out of the case all right, but not out of it from the point of view of the public. He'd lost his head when he was arrested and tried to brain a policeman, and he got seven years and went to Dartmoor or somewhere. The police had to smuggle her out of court by a back way, because there was a crowd of women waiting outside to boo her."

Veronica beckoned to her waiter and ordered coffee. She felt stunned and bruised. The story threw such a totally different light on the Judy she knew. Whatever she'd expected to hear it was not this. Judy leading a boy on to pilfer for her, and then persuading him into real crime. Judy being hustled by a back entrance out of the law Courts.

"What a dreary sordid story," she said.

Gloria looked pleased with herself.

"I told you it stank. Did you tell me that she was something or other to do with your local vicar?"

Veronica nodded.

"She's a kind of guardian governess to his wards, full of good words, the life and soul of the parish."

"She's running true to type. That was how she fooled Mrs. Bramble. All the time that she was leading poor Dennis Edwards up the garden path she was going down once or twice a week and helping Mrs. Bramble with her clubs for the unfortunate." Gloria giggled. "She was a good one to do that."

"Was she engaged to this man?"

"No. Avis says there was a lot of chat about that. Although she'd led him round by the nose from the time she was seventeen till she was about twenty-two or three, she'd never been engaged to him."

"Or anything?" asked Veronica.

Gloria paused while the coffee was served.

"Avis said 'no.' There's a very pretty name for her sort; Avis wonders it wasn't used in court. As a matter of fact, I suppose she'd been seeing things were looking pretty hot, because for more than a year before the case came on she hadn't seen much of him, but there were some telegrams and letters he'd sent her begging her to see him, if only for a minute. Avis said if they'd been sent to her she'd have been so ashamed she'd have dropped down dead in the witness box."

Veronica sipped her coffee, then she put down the cup.

"She oughtn't really to be another day in the vicarage. I wonder what'll be my best way to handle her story. People like clergy are so generous, so apt to believe the best about people."

"There isn't any best about her." Gloria tapped out her cigarette on the ash tray. "If there's a train to-night I should think he'd put her on it."

Veronica didn't see it being as easy as all that. She knew the easy, happy relations between Martin and Judy. She knew how difficult it would be to him to make the break for Polly's sake.

"I shall want evidence. It's my word against hers." Then a thought struck her. "Do you know what date all this was? I suppose it will have been reported in the papers."

Gloria looked thoughtfully at the wine waiter.

"I think a Kümmel would sit nicely on those oysters." She watched the liquid poured into a glass. "Avis would know. I'll ring up and ask her."

Veronica leant forward.

"Look, Gloria! I really do think this is rather important; I mean it's my duty to get her sent away. You see, since my husband died I stand in the place of squire to my village. I don't want to be rude, but you are apt to forget things. Do you think you could remember to ring her, and then ring me?" Then she had another idea. "You've taken an awful lot of trouble already. I should call it quits if after you've got me the date of that case you went to Mellis and picked yourself a hat."

Gloria gave her a shrewd amused glance.

"I never say no to a good offer."

## CHAPTER SEVEN

THERE are days which from the first opening of an eye, to its closing, everything goes wrong. Such a day was the Monday after Veronica's talk with Gloria. She awoke to see, as her maid drew back her curtains, sheets of rain battling against the window. Veronica had schemes for the day; it was her custom at intervals to go down to the vicarage, and there, button-holing Martin, take him round his garden and make him express wishes for the coming season. She would then return home and order all his choices extravagantly from a nurseryman. Martin had very simple tastes in the matter of flowers; he had a fondness for cheap old-fashioned roses, and clumps of bulbs, which he loved for their colour and not for the size of their blooms. He was very apt to say about his flower beds, 'They looked nice as they were last year,' and it was very difficult to get him to enthuse about anything new and expensive. All the same, Veronica had got a hold on the vicarage garden, and she had established the right to plan it out with Martin, and to-day was the day she intended to talk to him about bulbs for the Spring. Veronica was not a woman who liked even the elements to thwart her, so she eyed the rain sourly, and snapped at the maid for putting down her tea tray carelessly.

On the tea tray was a pile of letters, and Veronica turned them over idly, and saw with a sudden quickening of her heart beats, Gloria's sprawling hand-writing.

*My dear* (Gloria wrote), *There was no need for anyone to go searching the files of "The Times," because Avis had the cuttings. You can borrow them, she says, if you like, but they won't be a damn bit of good to you. I told you that Judy Griffiths looked as smug as anything while she was in the witness box, and that she got the judge on her side. Well, Avis said it was too sick-making for words the way she got away with it, and in the accounts of the trial she's hardly mentioned at all, and then, from her answers to the questions she was asked, you would think, if you only read the paper and hadn't been in the court, that she had been Dennis Edwards's guardian angel, instead of his evil spirit. If you take my advice you will go to your parson with the real story, for if you show him these cuttings he'll get the wrong idea altogether.*

*Sony I could not be more good to you. Come and lunch with me one day soon. Love, Gloria.*

*P.S.—I got the divinest little hat at Mellis's. I hope seven guineas was the sort of price you meant.*

It was not until she had read Gloria's letter that Veronica knew how much she had counted on those cuttings. It was going to be maddeningly difficult to make Martin even listen to a story about Judy unless she had got evidence to substantiate it; it was maddeningly difficult at any time to make Martin listen to a story about anybody. If there were anything charitable he could say to refute it, he would; and this story was so long, and so sordid, that she could imagine herself being stopped before she was half-way through it. She knew—and dreaded—the stern look that would come over Martin's face, and she could imagine him saying, "He that is without sin among you, let him first cast a stone at her."

Coming down to breakfast, abstracted and angry, her eye fell on her head gardener, who was arranging a mass of white chrysanthemums in the corner of the hall. She stopped beside him, looking at the plants with a frown.

"Aren't those the white chrysanthemums that you showed me in the greenhouse last week, and that I told you to take up to the church on Saturday for the altar vases?"

The gardener straightened his back, and nervously rubbed his hands dean on his green baize apron.

"Yes, milady, but I didn't take them down, milady, on account of them not being wanted."

"Not wanted?" Veronica was flabbergasted; it was an understood thing that, on six Sundays out of seven, she provided flowers for the church altar and on the odd Sunday when she did not send them the altar looked very shabby.

"Then who sent those white chrysanthemums on the altar?"

The gardener rubbed his hand once more nervously on his apron.

"I understood that they, was in the nature of a thank offering, milady. You see, I was down at the churchyard on Friday, seeing to the flowers on the family graves, and Miss Griffiths comes by: 'How lovely those brown chrysanthemums are,' she says to me, and I said, 'You should see the lovely white blooms we have in the greenhouse for Sunday,' and she said, 'Oh, didn't Mr. Richards tell you they won't be wanting flowers this Sunday? Fred Peters and Rosie are buying them. It's because of the baby.'"

Veronica's eyes narrowed.

"Miss Griffiths is merely engaged as governess to the vicarage, and she had no right to tell you the flowers were not wanted, and you had no right to accept such a statement from her."

The gardener twisted the end of his apron anxiously.

"Oh, but I didn't, milady. As I was getting on my bicycle to come home, I see Fred Peters on his bicycle coming up the road from Upper Saltings, so I said to him, 'Fred,' I said, 'is that right that you and Rosie are doing the flowers for the church on Sunday?' And he looked shy-like, and then he said, 'Well, Rosie thought it would be kind of nice to do something, on account of her going to have a little one being an answer to prayer,' and that Miss Griffiths had said, 'How about flowers for the altar?'" The gardener looked down at the chrysanthemum pot. "These are only the ones that were full out, milady, and would be no use by next Sunday. I've some more in bud I'm bringing on for that."

Veronica's voice was like a chip of ice.

"I will have a talk to Mr. Richards about the flowers. I don't intend that we should waste our time and greenhouse space growing things that are not wanted."

The gardener, left to himself, put his final pot into place, and then was creeping back to his gardening when he was stopped by the butler. To those who knew the butler merely from his front-door aspect, or his appearance at the lunch and dinner table, he seemed more of a machine than a man, but at this moment he was human. He dug the gardener in the ribs with his elbow, accompanying the dig with a fine expressive wink.

Towards the middle of the morning the weather cleared, and Veronica ordered her car and set off for the vicarage. She was still feeling in an irritable mood. She hated to be in a state of indecision; she had so counted on those press cuttings, and at the moment she could not make up her mind how best to use Judy's life story without them. Downstairs at the vicarage she could find nobody, so in the way that Bertha found peculiarly irritating, she opened the kitchen door and walked in.

"Good morning, Bertha! Where are they all?"

Bertha gave her a look that expressed those things that her tongue could not say. Her voice had a modicum of politeness in it.

"Miss Matthews is out having a word with the mothers of her Sunday School class, on account of those that didn't show up yesterday. Miss Polly's at school. Reverend's out visiting in Jimson. Miss Griffiths is down the garden with Ben. They're gardening."

Judy was conscious that Veronica had a fondness for overseeing the vicarage garden. She did not actually want to annoy her, but against that it riled her independent spirit that Martin, who had a little garden, should be henpecked by a woman with vast estates into planting out his little piece of land, not as he wanted it, but as she chose. It was not, though, to circumvent Veronica that she had done what she had, but it had been an accident. At luncheon one day Polly had said, "Can I have some bulbs to plant in my garden?" and Martin had said that of course she could, and had asked Judy to see to the buying of them. Judy, without thinking, had replied that the best plan would be to get one of those cheap odd lots of bulbs such as were advertised, and then Polly could have a little of everything, and the rest could go into the garden. "I should like," Judy had said, "to put a ring of crocuses round the trees on the lawn." Martin's face had lit up. "I should like that; in fact, I meant to do it, but Lady Blacke said that bulbs were meant to go in the beds, and it was a pity to put them into well-kept turf." Judy had laughed. "If you had any well-kept turf it might be true. But without meaning to be rude, nobody could call the vicarage lawn well-kept turf, and we haven't improved it by playing cricket on it all the summer."

The result of this talk was that an inexpensive bag of bulbs was ordered, and it had arrived that morning. Judy always wanted a garden, and the sight of those bulbs was too much for her; she was not going to worry about a little rain, but was going to start planting right away. Such gardening as was done at the vicarage beyond the work put in by Polly and Judy, came from old Ben who, when he was not busy being sexton and had time off from his milking, did an hour or two. He alone knew how he was paid, or what hours he worked. Now and again he would waylay Martin in the church-yard and, touching his forehead and giving his head a sideways jerk, would murmur, "I reckon it's sixteen and thruppence," or "Fifteen and eight-pence, sir." Judy had been present at one of these reckoning days, and had asked Martin if he knew for what Ben was paid. Martin had been quite shocked. "Oh no, and Ben wouldn't work for me if I questioned his bill. He was gardener to old Dickson before me, and he used to help Dickson with his bees, and he feels he's far more right to the garden than I have. Why, even Lady Blacke's man only brings the stuff down; he never puts it in—he knows Ben wouldn't stand for it."

Judy determined to garden herself, and knowing gardening to be good for the children, had been very tactful with Ben. She had asked his permission before she had as much as pulled out a weed, and though by now both she and Polly gardened whenever they felt like it, she made periodical visits to Ben to ask him where the work was most needed, and tactful questions of that sort.

This morning she went across to the churchyard to look for Ben. She found him with a piece of sacking round his shoulders to keep off the rain, stacking some dead flowers on the rubbish heap that, in spite of arguments with Martin, he kept where he had always kept it, at the back of the vestry.

"What they sees in putting a lot of dead bits on top of them as has gone, I don't know," he said bitterly to Judy. "They think as if they put a couple of roses or that in a jam jar on top of their grand-mother they're doing the old lady proud for a month or two. If I've told them once I've told them a hundred times—if you want to do right by the dead, give 'em something fresh or nothing. I won't lie comfortable in my grave when I'm gone if I know there's a jar full of nasty brown water and dead flowers sitting on my stomach."

Judy made sympathetic murmuring sounds, and then broke into the subject of the bulbs.

"They were ordered for Miss Polly, really, but there are a lot over; do you think I might plant them about in clumps in the grass?"

Ben liked his opinion asked, and he liked to take time over his answers; now he pursed up his lips, and shook his head, and nodded at Sloe, who was trying to find a rat at the back of a grave stone.

"There is the chance. Sloe's a very digging sort of dog, but if you didn't mind I should like the fun of putting them in." She smiled at him. "I wanted rings of crocuses round the trees on the lawn."

Ben had a soft corner for Judy; he now shifted his sack on his shoulders.

"There's nowt here that can't wait; I'll come and give you a hand."

Stooping together under the trees, while they made their holes and put in their bulbs, Ben and Judy talked.

"Making rings like this, there'll be visiting come Midsummer," Ben told her.

"Who's going to visit who?"

"The little folk. Seems they can't keep their feet out of a ring, not round Midsummer."

Judy looked up surprised.

"You talk as though you'd seen them, Ben."

Ben went on planting his bulbs.

"I have, too. Way down there, there's a ring they made their-selves. Many's the time I've heard a little piping, and stooping down like, I've seen them at their gallivantings. This year there'll be more, maybe."

"Because I've made rings for them?"

Ben burrowed inside the sack for another packet of bulbs.

"Partly, but more on account of a little gorse plant that've spring up by the front door. That be a mark, surely."

"Mark of what?"

Ben straightened his back.

"There's loving where the gorse blooms."

Judy and Ben were still deep in fairies and their habits when Veronica came out on to the lawn. The grass was still wringing wet, and she stepped across it distastefully, wishing that Ben would keep it shorter, and annoyed at the whisks of water that brushed across her ankle bones.

"Good morning, Miss Griffiths. Good morning, Ben. What are you two up to?"

Ben's whole attitude changed at sight of Veronica. He looked stubborn and disobliging.

"Planting bulbs, same as you can see."

Judy was conscious that the occasion called for tact; she did not want to make any coldness in the vicarage. She burst into hurried apologetic speech.

"We had to get some bulbs for Polly's garden, so we bought some extra for ourselves, just a cheap little lot, you know. I wanted—" She broke off, remembering that what she wanted in the vicarage would certainly not appeal to Veronica. "I mean, Mr. Richards likes crocuses under the trees."

Ben fixed Veronica with a spiteful gaze.

"They like the same things, seemingly."

Veronica felt herself growing cold with temper, but she had too much *savoir faire* to show it. This matter of the bulbs was outwardly only a small thing, but she knew—and she had not the faintest doubt that Judy calculated—that it was one of the small things which was welding Judy into the vicarage, and forcing her outside. She was spared answering directly, for Martin came round on to the lawn.

"Jimson's outside, Miss Griffiths," he called. "Would you like me to fetch Polly if you're busy with your gardening?"

Judy had noticed the way Veronica's nostrils flared out at the sides, and a certain tautness about her, and read the signs aright as temper, and was thankful to get away.

"No, thanks awfully. I couldn't have done much more; my back's aching." She turned smiling to Ben. "We've had a lovely morning, Ben. I expect Miss Polly will want to put some in this afternoon. Is that all right?"

Ben nodded.

"Surely." Then he stooped and picked up the sack of bulbs and the gardening tools. He turned to Veronica before he trudged away.

"You seen little gorse bush which have sprung up by the front door? That didn't come from no nursery man, and didn't cost no money; more'n you can say for all they new-fashioned Salvias and such."

Veronica joined Martin.

"You know that old man's past his work. I think you'd better look round for a decent gardener, who could keep the church-yard tidy. I'll be responsible for the extra wages."

Martin was surprised—not for the first time—that Veronica, who had known the Saltings longer than he had, could so hope-lessly misunderstand the mentality of the people.

"Dismiss Ben! First of all, Ben wouldn't go. He would simply say, 'I belongs to be here,' and then there would be a Parish strike. The Rural Dean would be driven demented with complaints about me, and for peace and quiet I would have to leave."

Veronica smiled with her lips, but she did not feel amused.

"Aren't you ridiculous?" She walked beside him round to the front of the house. "By the way, I think we ought to get this matter of the altar vases cut and dried. We've gone to great trouble in my greenhouses to bring on some large white chrysanthemums ready for the church. This last week my gardener was casually told by Miss Griffiths that our flowers wouldn't be wanted, as the policeman and his wife were giving them. Now, I think the best plan is that I always provide the church flowers, and if the people want to make a thank-offering they can put it in the poor-box."

Martin stood still and shook some raindrops off some late and battered Michaelmas daisies.

"'And He saw also a certain poor widow casting in thither two mites. And He said, Of a truth I say unto you, that this poor widow hath cast in more than they all: For all these have of their abundance cast in unto the offerings of God: but she of her penury hath cast in all the living that she had.'" Veronica always felt at a disadvantage when Martin quoted the Bible.

"But, my dear man, Mrs. Peters is not a widow; the cost of the chrysanthemums is not their all, and if they want to cast their two mites, I have suggested the poor-box."

Martin's voice was concerned; he considered Veronica generous, and felt it a pity that she should spoil that generosity, as she so often did, by a wish to be the only giver.

"To you giving is a little thing—you give every day—but many of my people are sparing of their giving, and as Christ said, it's an easy thing for the rich to cast their gifts into the treasury, but when the poor do it it means much more. Grateful as I am for all your good gifts, I would rather see less from you, and the difference made up of small sums from every home. To give what's hard to spare—that's what we all need to learn."

A thought came to Veronica—this was her moment to introduce casually a thing she had often wanted to say.

"But, my dear Martin—I really must call you Martin; it's ridiculous for us to go on calling each other Mr. Richards and Lady Blacke—what is the rich person to do? You've never made a call on me that I've refused. I admit I'm a rich woman, but is it my fault that I can never give what's hard to spare?"

Martin had been thrown off his stroke by Veronica's suggestion that he and she should take to Christian names. He was Martin to Aunt Connie, and to Mrs. Bramble, and Uncle Martin to Chloe, but otherwise no woman called him by his Christian name. The rights and wrongs of being called by his Christian name by a woman had never come into his mind, for Mrs. Bramble had treated him like a son, and no other woman had suggested doing it. He supposed that if Lady Blacke—he flinched from the thought of calling her Veronica—thought it was all right to call him Martin it was all right, but he wished she hadn't suggested it; it made him feel awkward with her, and in some way undermined their position to each other of priest and parishioner. Having got to this point in his thoughts he collected himself. Lady Blacke—whether she called him Martin or not—was his parishioner, and as such had asked him a direct question that concerned her soul. Still fingering the Michaelmas daisy plant, he thought deeply before he answered.

"Giving isn't always a matter of money. To some people the most difficult thing to give is simple kindliness, and understanding."

Veronica flushed.

"You mean I haven't those things?"

He nodded.

"Yes. There are many people in the Three Saltings who trade on your generosity, but how many are there that come to you for sympathy when they are in trouble? How many are there who feel the better because they've had the chance to talk things over with you? How many are there who feel the happier because you're in the room?" Veronica did not like her failings laid out in front of her any more than most people, and that Martin should be the one to see these failings so clearly hurt her bitterly. A fountain of self-pity welled up inside her. "Martin was wrong; somebody, probably that miserable Judy, had put these ideas into his head. Of course people in the Saltings didn't exactly drop in and out of the Manor House; they were put off by the difference between their station and hers. But that was the fault of the people of the Saltings; she was willing enough to he friendly and kind." Self-pity is the easiest of all sources of emotion. Veronica's eyes flooded with tears.

"It hurts me, Martin, when you talk like that, and I think perhaps you're being a little unjust. Money and position make an automatic barrier; I would like to be friendly with everybody if they would let me."

Martin, his eyes on the Michaelmas daisy, failed to see Veronica's tears. In any ease, his mind was on her soul, and had he seen the tears he would have put them down to contrition, and thought them very suitable.

"Is that the truth? I know a woman as rich and as well placed as you are. She used to come down to my poor dock-side parish, and the people's faces lit up at the sight of her. There was hardly a house in which at some time or another she had not discussed problems, in which money had no part, over a cup of tea across the kitchen table. She is a Mrs. Bramble, and I have to thank her," his voice warmed, "for her splendid Miss Griffiths."

For one second it was on the tip of Veronica's tongue to blaze forth all she knew about Judy, but a look at Martin's face dissuaded her. He was in his most detached and spiritual mood, and would, she knew, stop her before her words were half out with a reprimand, and probably a quotation from the Bible. She was also too much a woman of the world not to see, even in the temper she was now in, how stupidly she would be playing her cards if she were to choose this moment to lay them out. But, his 'splendid Miss Griffiths.' And the tone of his voice when he said it was as much as she could bear. She pulled her mink coat round her.

"Oh, well, it's chilly standing here. I'll drop the question of the altar flowers; it's your parish, and you know what you want, and you do know the one thing I really care about is to be of help to you."

Martin looked up.

"That's splendid; and do think over what I've said. It's a thing that I've had in mind to talk to you about for some time. Simple kindness is worth such a lot."

Veronica laid a hand on his arm.

"With you to help me, Martin, I could learn."

Martin looked in surprise at her hand, but he took it to be a hand asking for help and not a hand intending to caress.

"It's not my help you want. You will get that from God."

Veronica couldn't go on standing on the path with a hand lying on Martin's sleeve that got no pat or friendly pressure. In any case, the conversation this morning seemed, for all her efforts, to refuse to turn in the direction in which she wanted it. Of course she knew Martin was right, and that if she did need help praying was the way to get it—but it was maddening the way a parson could turn aside every personal remark by handing it, as were, to God.

It was when Veronica was in the car, preparatory to starting home, that she had the one good moment of her morning. Just as Perkins was starting the car Jimson came rattling up the drive. Veronica tapped on the glass.

"One moment, Perkins."

She waited until Jimson was at a standstill, and what she had to say would clearly reach Judy. She leant out of the window.

"Good morning, Polly. Good-bye, Miss Griffiths." She turned with a smile and a wave to the front door, "Good-bye, Martin."


Chloe came down to breakfast singing. Sterndale grinned at her.

"Cheerful? It's a beast of a day."

Chloe looked happily at the rain on the window. "Well, it's November."

Sterndale finished a mouthful of sausage.

"What are you doing to-day?"

Chloe poured herself out a cup of coffee.

"I'm going to lunch at the Vicarage and staying on to tea, to look after Polly, as Judy's going to help Mrs. Brown give the house a turn-out."

"Good. Glad you're being useful."

"I don't mind being useful if only Aunt Connie wasn't there. I can't think how Judy stands her. I get the dumps after half an hour alone with her."

Sterndale gave her a teasing look.

"There's Martin. Perhaps he'll keep you company. And I know you'd rather be with him than anybody."

Chloe fetched herself a sausage.

"I admire Uncle Martin most awfully, but he's more like a god than a man; when it comes to ordinary things I don't find an awful lot to talk to him about. I like somebody who likes the same things as I do—films and things like that."

Sterndale kept his face still, but his eyes were twinkling.

"More a person like Michael Evans?"

Chloe flushed.

"Well, I must say Mike's very easy to talk to."

"Oh, so he's Mike now, is he?"

Chloe grew even pinker.

"Yes, and he said at the rehearsal yesterday that he liked being called Mike, so I don't see why I shouldn't."

"Nor do I," agreed Sterndale. "Would you like me to see if he can come over to tea this afternoon?"

"He is coming over for a rehearsal. I thought you could both come to tea at the Vicarage." Sterndale got up with a resigned sigh.

"And I suppose I shall be put on to play beggar-my-neighbour with Polly and Aunt Connie while you and Mike hear each other's parts." He came over to Chloe, pulled her out of her chair and turned her face up to his, "You like him, don't you?" Her eyes pulled away from his; she was looking at the floor, scratching the carpet with her toe.

"Well, I rather do."

He held her more firmly.

"Look up at me, duckie." Unwillingly she turned her eyes to him. "Do you really like him. Because you know it wasn't so very long ago that Martin was the only man in the world, and you don't want to make any mistake about Mike, because at least he knows his mind, and if you're going to skid off on to another man you're going to hurt him rather badly."

Chloe looked anxious.

"Do you think that when you can't see anything without wishing a special person was there to see it with you, and when you don't get much fun out of doing anything unless you do it with a special person, and when that special person comes you feel kind of hot and fat inside because you're so glad to see them, that you're in love with them?"

The description, however curiously phrased, fitted in so exactly with how Sterndale felt about Judy that his face saddened. How well he knew the greyness of any enterprise in which Judy was not included, and how well he knew that swelling of the heart that Chloe described as 'hot and fat,' which overcame him as Judy came into the room.

"I should think almost certainly you were in love, but you're much too young to marry, you know."

Chloe wriggled.

"Nobody said anything about getting married."

"No, but somebody's soon going to. Poor Mike is getting as thin as a piece of wire, he'll have to say something soon or burst."

"Well, if he did," said Chloe, a singing happiness at the back of her voice, "I could be engaged, couldn't I? But I daresay he never will. There are lots and lots of days when I don't think he likes me as much as he did the day before."

Sterndale let her go, and gave her behind an affectionate smack.

"I must say it does sound as if you really were in love this time, but you won't get married before you're eighteen."

Chloe looked thoughtfully put at the wintry landscape.

"That would suit very nicely; I'll be eighteen in April. I think I should like my bridesmaids dressed in sort of daffodil colour."

Sterndale laughed and went to the door, but it was a half-hearted sort of laugh. Lucky Chloe to speak in that gay way of bridesmaids, but if only Judy would love him he wouldn't say that a date in five months' time would do very nicely, he would want a special licence and make the marriage tomorrow.

"You are a baby," he said. "Socks and a romper are what you want, and not bridesmaids."

Chloe skipped after him.

"You'll bring Mike to tea?"

He nodded.

"I will."

The winter came early that year. In December the first scurries of snow blew over the Downs, and many nights there was a frost. All the weather prophets in the Saltings had been prophesying an extreme winter, and they wagged their heads, pleased to find themselves right.

"What did I tell'ee," said Ben. "They swallows didn't set off a full three weeks afore their time for nothing."

"Nature don't waste," Fred Peters stated. "Reckon she didn't put that mort of red berries around for nothing. She knew the birds would be starving hungry before the winter was through."

"Seems like I had a guidance," Mrs. Beam wheezed, "buying all that extra chest liniment. When the weather cock on the church blew so far round to the east I said to myself, 'That's the first time that I remember seeing that bird so far round.' And it must have guided me, for when the traveller came a few days later I'd chest colds on my mind and ordered three times more than my ordinary of the liniment."

To Judy the winter held no terrors. She was entranced at the sight of the Downs patched with snow. She was physically well and was feeling mentally well for the first time in years. The recuperation of her nervous system had been gradual, and it was only now that she was clear of the bog of despair that she could appreciate the glory of being free of it. Because she was well in mind she was able to take a strong grip on herself and crush her instincts, which called to her to make some show of her growing love for Martin. She longed to make excuses to be with him, to think out little kindnesses and comforts for him, and she longed above all for some physical contact. It would have been such heaven to put her arms round him. But never once did she let any of these wishes get the better of her. She remained cool and detached and entirely inside her position of companion to Polly. If anything she erred on the side of coolness, for in fear of giving herself away she avoided those occasions when she could legitimately have had Martin to herself.

There were troubles which Judy had to contend with, things which worried and fretted her, but even these, glowing with her new-found happiness, she was able to ride. There was, first and foremost, Veronica. There could be no doubt, ever since that day when she had heard Veronica call Martin by his Christian name, that she was watching Veronica deliberately forcing a climax between herself and Martin. She was becoming more possessive, her methods were so subtle that Martin neither noticed them nor grasped their significance. She had arranged that he should dine at the Manor House more often, and for every occasion she produced a legitimate reason for his being there—there was this case she wanted to discuss and that, or it was the heating plant in the church, or it was supplies of coal for the poor of Lower Saltings. There was, too, something in her manner which had changed. Judy was very unwilling to believe in changes in people's manner. Her natural instinct was to say to herself, "You're probably imagining it." But over Veronica she couldn't brush the change aside in that way. Veronica had a manner as if to say, "You and I share a secret," and she looked, Judy sometimes thought, as if she was going to give her a meaning nudge in the ribs.

There was also the trouble of money. Money was definitely disappearing—tiresome, silly little sums, but nevertheless it kept going. It was practically always money which, for some purpose or other, Martin was going to entrust to Judy. Martin had a habit, of which Judy could not cure him, of depositing silver to be used for a specified purpose on his mantelpiece, and then announcing at meal times that it was there and for what it was to be spent. It did not matter very much that the money was going, because the sums were small, and Judy, rather than bring the subject to light, replaced them herself. She knew this to be a moral weakness, but the mere mention of missing money brought her out in a cold sweat, and she would rather have parted with her last farthing than brought the matter to light and caused discomfort in the house. But that somebody was pilfering was certain, and that somebody must be either Bertha, Polly or Aunt Connie. Of the three Judy was inclined to suspect Aunt Connie, but she would not allow herself to give shape to this suspicion. Suspicion was a vile thing, unless you had evidence it was better not to let your mind play on who might be the culprit.

It was nearly Christmas. Judy was taking Polly in to Eastbourne to meet Andrew and to do Christmas shopping. Veronica, a very rare thing for her, was lunching at the Vicarage. There was to be a dress rehearsal of "The Ghost Train" that night, and she had spared Perkins, with rather a poor grace, to assist in the stage lighting. Polly was in a great state of excitement, and in spite of all Judy's restraining efforts, kept forgetting that she was at the luncheon table and bounced up and down on her chair and occasionally indulged in a little singing.

"Christmas is coming, the geese are getting fat," she chanted, "Please to put a penny in the old man's hat."

"Even with Christmas coming and Andrew coming home one doesn't sing at the table," said Judy.

Martin smiled at Polly.

"Though you are not old men I have remembered to put out some pennies for your's and Andrew's hats. There's half a crown on the study mantelpiece."

Judy looked at him reproachfully.

"You did promise you'd give any money direct to me. How'm I to teach Polly never to leave money about when you set her such a bad example."

Aunt Connie was eating in a quick, nervous manner, as if she thought somebody might snatch her food away from her. Between mouthfuls her eyes darted from face to face. She gave one of her neighing giggles.

"We all know you like to have the money in your hand, Miss Griffiths, but it's my nephew's money and he can put it where he likes."

Martin looked anxiously at his aunt, she was not improving, in fact she was definitely deteriorating. This hurried eating was a sign, and sometimes the control of her hands was not very good—food halfway to her mouth fell off her fork or splashed on to her chin. There was no question but that Doctor Green was right. He had sent for papers about homes run by nurses where, though there was no restraint, attention was given. He had talked the homes over with Judy and on her advice had written to Mrs. Bramble and sent her on the pamphlets asking in which, if any, she thought an old lady could be happy. Because he knew that he was planning to send her away and because she was not responsible for what she said Martin checked back the reproof that he would have given, and instead said gently:

"I know you didn't mean that, Aunt Connie." Aunt Connie laughed again.

"You think you know a lot, nephew, don't you? But I know some things that would surprise you."

Judy, equally conscious of those brochures in the post and sensitive to what Martin must be feeling, broke in:

"Miss Matthews is quite right, it's not for me to tell you what to do with your money, but Polly and I'll know how to spend it, won't we Polly?" Veronica looked up with a sweet smile.

"I'm sure of that. I should think you're a very good spender, aren't you, Miss Griffiths?"

The remark seemed harmless enough, but once more Judy had the feeling that Veronica was suggesting that she knew something, something which she, Judy, did not want brought to light. However, she refused to give any sign that she was resentful. "I don't know, I've never had much to spend."

"Really?" Veronica opened her blue eyes widely. She turned to Martin. "Miss Griffiths doesn't give that impression, does she?"

Martin took the remark at its face value. His eye ran over Judy, and he said, with a note of warmth:

"She always looks very nice to me."

Judy, knowing that Veronica would take this up, spoke hurriedly.

"That's because you're a man, and don't know one garment from another, but if you were a woman you'd know that I look very 'off the peg.'" She turned back to Veronica, "It's nice of you to say I look as though I knew how to spend money, and up to a point it's true; when you can't afford to have things made for you you automatically become a rather clever buyer. I expect if you suddenly had to get ready made things you'd find it terribly difficult at first."

The meal was nearly over, Martin was folding his napkin preparatory to saying grace, Veronica had not much time for a retort. "No wonder she got away with it in the witness box," her mind registered. "Anything more smug than she is I never heard. I should believe her myself, if I didn't know." Out loud she said:

"Yes, coming down from expensive clothes to cheap ones must be very hard."

Martin got up to say grace. Judy tried to keep her mind on the grace, but she found it difficult.

Veronica's inflexion bothered her. "She thinks that she and I have got a secret. I do wonder what it is. If I wasn't certain she didn't know about me—" She gave her shoulders a mental shrug.

"Don't be an imaginative fool, of course she doesn't know. How could she?"

Grace was no sooner over than Polly was out of the room and off to the study. She came out again in a second, and looked reproachfully at Martin.

"You've forgotten again. There's no half-crown there."

Martin took her hand.

"You're wrong, Pollikins. I know exactly where I put it. Come and see!"

Polly and Martin and Aunt Connie went into the study. Veronica followed them, but only as far as the door, for her eyes were glued to Judy, who unconscious that she was being watched, was standing in the passage flushing and paling by turns. "Extraordinary," Veronica puzzled. "I suppose, having started Dennis Edwards on a career of stealing she picked up the habit herself. But really, half-crowns! She doesn't look the sort for petty sins."

"There!" said Polly. "It isn't there, is it?" Martin, with a worried frown, called to Judy.

"I say, come here a minute, Miss Griffiths." Judy, under Veronica's eye, pulled herself together, and with a look of resolution came into the study. Her tone was easy and laughing.

"You see, Polly, what comes of leaving half-crowns about. They get taken away."

Polly, with a cry, flung herself at Judy and hugged her.

"You're teasing. You took it." She looked at Martin. "She took it."

Martin gave Judy a questioning glance.

"You didn't, did you?"

Judy detached Polly.

"Yes. I thought a fright might cure you, and be a lesson for Polly."

Martin laughed.

"It will be a lesson to us, won't it, Pollikins?"

Aunt Connie was over by the window; now, with the muscles of her face twitching, she came to Judy and gripped her arm.

"Did you say you took it?"

With an effort she could only just hide, Judy kept her tone easy and natural.

"Yes. Mr. Richards and Polly are so careless with money."

Aunt Connie lowered her voice.

"So you took it, did you? That's stealing."

Judy saw Polly was scared, so she rumpled her hair.

"Run upstairs, darling, and dress; we ought to be starting." She turned to Aunt Connie. "It's not really stealing. It's just a way of teaching Polly to be careful." Without giving time for an answer, she followed Polly out of the room.

Aunt Connie was confused. "Why had that hussy said she had taken the half-crown. She herself had taken it. She was sure she had. Or hadn't she? It was so difficult to remember things; she kept getting muddled. But that hussy had admitted that she took money." Aunt Connie licked her lips. "That was something. But Martin was so stupid; he wouldn't see his danger." Throwing her nephew a malevolent look, and muttering to herself, she too went out of the room.

Martin watched his aunt go with such an expression of pain that Veronica could barely hold herself back from putting her arms round him and saying, "Don't look like that, darling. I'm here, and nothing will hurt as much, if only we share it." But she was held back, apart from her normal self-control, by a complete mis-reading of the look of hurt. To her Aunt Corinne was of supreme unimportance; what she supposed to have distressed Martin was Judy's trumped-up story about the half-crown.

"Don't look so worried, Martin." She patted his arm. "It was only a ridiculous little sum."

Martin's mind had been miles away. How long did letters take to Italy? How soon could he hope for an answer from Mrs. Bramble? He pulled his mind back to the study.

"What did you say?"

"I said you shouldn't look so worried; it was only a small sum."

He couldn't get on to what she meant.

"Polly's half-crown, d'you mean? Miss Griffiths had it."

His tone was so matter-of-fact; it was so obvious that the thought of petty pilfering from Judy had never as much as flicked across his mind, that Veronica was almost winded. It seemed to her so clear that Judy had taken the money, however ludicrous it might seem, that it was incredible Martin hadn't realised it. She spoke before she had time to think.

"My dear Martin, I'm afraid she did take it. The half-crown doesn't matter; but I think perhaps it's a straw showing the way the wind blows. Don't you think, perhaps, as she has sole charge of Polly, that you engaged her without quite enough inquiry? What d'you know about her past?"

Martin was disgusted. He felt as if he had seen Veronica treading on, and soiling, something beautiful.

"How dare you suggest such a thing? How could you think that Miss Griffiths would steal? And how can you say I didn't know enough about her when I engaged her? I engaged her on the recommendation of Mrs. Bramble, and that's enough recommendation for me. Besides, Miss Griffiths carries her own recommendation about with her; it's written in the strength and goodness in her face."

Veronica's heart stood still. Her hands turned very cold. It was not so much Martin's words that scared her, but the look on his face. He had spoken with no consciousness of himself, and so it was as if a veil had lifted and she could see into his heart. She was convinced that he had no idea what lay there—that, perhaps, he would never know; but that did not mean that the danger wasn't there. In all her jealousies and imaginings Veronica had not, until that moment, faced the possibility that Judy had a place in Martin's heart; she had only been afraid that one day she might have. Her acceptance of what she read put Veronica's back straight against a wall. She had to fight now if she was to win happiness, and there was no time to reason how. If Martin were fond of Judy, and Judy the schemer that her history proved her to be, then at any minute she might make a move.

A woman who could get a wretched boy into such a state that he would steal and forge for her would find a simple person like Martin child's play. If Judy planned to marry Martin Veronica had no doubt she would do it, unless—and here she was swept away by an idea—unless she got there first. She pulled herself together. Her face softened; her voice was gentle.

"I forgot that Mrs. Bramble found her for you. She must be a wonderful woman. I wish I could meet her."

Martin's face cleared.

"So you shall. She's in Italy at present, but she'll be back in the spring."

"In the spring." Veronica's voice was musing. "I wish it was the spring now. That we hadn't got the long cold winter ahead of us. It comes so hard on the poor."

Martin gave her a glance of approval. She was improving. She was learning to think from the angle of other people.

"We must trust in God; He won't make the burden harder than they can bear. And He's put people like yourself to help them through."

Veronica dropped her voice to a whisper.

"People like ourselves. I don't need all that money, Martin. I would like to do much more good with it than I do. Why don't we spend it together? I'm terribly lonely, and I'm fond of you. Why don't we marry?" She saw his eyes widen with amazement, and he made a move to speak, but she stopped him. "No, don't answer now. Think over what I've said. And don't think of it only from the point of view of you and me. Think of your people, and perhaps later on of your dock-side people. Think if perhaps what I'm suggesting isn't God's will." She moved to the door. "And think, too, that perhaps it means happiness for two lonely people. Think it over, Martin. I'll come for your answer to-morrow."

# Chapter Eight

MARTIN spent much of the night on his knees. He had been so startled by Veronica's suggestion that he had at first been unable to think clearly. He had no thought of marrying anybody, and had never considered Veronica other than as his parishioner and the patroness of the parish. His first reaction was to refuse her proposal out of hand. Then as the evening wore on his conscience troubled him. Was there a truth in what she said? Was it God's will that he should marry? Veronica lived in an extravagant way; there was a great deal of unnecessary luxury at the Manor House. Was it possible that all that wealth should be in his care, to use for God's poor? He brushed aside her last words about happiness; he was happy as he was in his simply-run home; if happiness came into the question at all it was as to whether he ought to sacrifice his happiness. There were so many needy; so much good could be done with money—not by occasional generous cheques as now, but by an outpouring of almost all that Veronica had. As things were she would never give away all she had, but perhaps as his wife—with him to guide her— she would grow to see how little was needed for contentment.

It was at this point that he began to pray. He prayed for guidance, that he might see clearly and not be blinded by his own unwillingness to marry. He was still on his knees when a cock, somewhere in the village, crowed, and he knew that morning could not be far off. He had been kneeling in silent supplication, trying as far as he was able to leave his mind free, so that he might be receptive. The crowing pierced through the silence and disturbed him. He raised his head, and as he did so the light on his desk fell on his prayer book, and it seemed to him that he was called to pick it up. It opened at the marriage service, and twelve words sprang before his eyes. "With this ring I thee wed, with my body I thee worship."

Martin closed the prayer book; tired though he was, his face was lit with a radiance as though the sun were shining on it.

He knew with every fibre of his being that God was there to be communed with; but so direct an answer strengthened his faith and would uphold him when his courage was dim. He didn't kneel again, but raised his head and said quietly:

"Thank you, Lord."

The day was bitterly cold. It was snowing, and as well there were thunder clouds over the downs. At breakfast, Judy noticed with anxiety how deadly tired Martin looked. Andrew and Polly were in first-day-of-the-holidays spirits, and noisy in consequence. Judy tried to quieten them.

"Be quiet, you two toughs!"

Andrew and Polly were pleased with the soubriquet, and roared with laughter. Martin, who was reading a letter, looked up. Judy was glad to see that, though tired, he did not seem worried by the children: he was distrait, but when he focused on them his look was only amused. He laid down his letter.

"What are you doing to-day?"

"We're going to see everybody this morning," Andrew explained, "so they know I'm back."

Judy looked at the window.

"We'll start early, then, for it looks a beast of a day."

Polly leant towards Martin.

"And in the afternoon we're going to make Christmas decorations."

Martin glanced at Aunt Connie, who was slowly chewing at a piece of toast. Seeing she had not finished, he got up and said a grace silently to himself.

"Could you come to my study, Miss Griffiths? I want a word with you."

Aunt Connie's eyes darted to Martin.

"Is there need for secrecy? Anything you want to say can be said here. The children can go upstairs."

Martin's eyes rested on her sadly. He came round the table and gently patted her shoulder.

"This is a rather private matter."

Polly bounced about on her chair.

"I know, it's Christmas presents."

Martin was unwilling to take cover behind somebody else's mis-statements, but with a sick woman such as Aunt Connie to deal with he was grateful for Polly's suggestion.

"We all have secrets at Christmas."

Aunt Connie sucked in her lips and let them out with a smacking sound.

"You can say what you like, nephew, but you can't deceive me. I know what's happening."

Martin sighed and opened the door, and held it for Judy. Andrew and Polly, seeing they were to be left alone with Aunt Connie, gave each other a look, then Andrew hastily swallowed his last drop of tea and got up.

"Come on, Poll; come on, Sloe! Let's go and see Bertha."

In the study Martin closed the door on himself and Judy, and motioned to an arm-chair.

"Will you sit down? I want to talk to you." He was silent a moment or two, and then said, "How difficult it is to see what's right."

Judy's heart was beating faster. What was on Martin's mind? Was his wanting to talk to her something to do with his looking so wretched? She eyed the arm of his chair wistfully; what she would have liked to have done was to have sat on it, and pulled his head to rest against her, and leant down until her cheek touched his forehead, and then with her arms rounds him have said, "Come on! What's the trouble?" Because such thoughts were weakness and led nowhere, Judy took a pull on herself and made her voice sound brisk.

"Right and wrong about what?"

Her tone made Martin jump. He looked apologetic.

"I'm sorry; I'm slow at coming to the point." Judy only just held herself back from saying, "No, darling, you're not. Take all the time you like." Martin felt in his pocket and brought out the letter he had been reading at breakfast that morning.

"This is from Mrs. Bramble. It's about my Aunt. I'll read you what she says:

> "*Don't send your Aunt to any of those places, for although I dare say she would be perfectly happy, you won't believe that she is, and will worry yourself into your grave. I have a much better suggestion. My old Nannie is still alive, and she should be pensioned off. and I have a cottage ready to put her into. The difficulty has been that—as is the way of Nannies—she must have someone to look after. Your Aunt Connie seems to me exactly what Nannie needs, and the cottage—which she can call her own—is probably what your Aunt needs. Let me know by return if this arrangement suits, and I will put things in motion.*"

Judy beamed.

"Isn't she marvellous! She can always arrange anything."

Martin searched her face.

"You think it will be all right? That my Aunt won't feel she's pushed out?"

"Not if Mrs. Bramble arranges it. I expect she'll invent some way of letting Miss Matthews think she's inherited the cottage." She spoke fearlessly. "After all, Miss Matthews isn't able to think clearly."

Martin was relieved.

"I'll be thankful to have things settled. The letter came as a bit of a shock. It seemed to make things so final for the poor old lady. However, you are right. In Mrs. Bramble's hands the matter is sure to be arranged so as not to hurt her." He turned the letter over. "There's a message for you. She says:

> "'*Thank Judy for her last letter, and tell her I'm glad she is so happy, and say by that I know she took to heart what I said to her when I sent her to you.*'"

Judy saw again the Otis Club, and the sofa in the lounge on which she and Mrs. Bramble had sat, and she could feel Mrs.

Bramble's kiss on her cheek, and hear her voice say, "Don't forget, Judy, that mere peace of surroundings does not make for peace of heart. You have your own part to play in your own healing; make your heart receptive—don't feel it's wrong to be comforted; deliberately try to put the past behind you. Will you promise?" And she could recall her voice answering, "I can't promise, but I will try." She gave a rather wry smile. She had made her heart receptive all right. For the rest, she had not consciously had to try. Martin and the children and the Saltings had filled her life and crushed the sadness and bitterness out of it. She got up.

"She's a wonderful friend."

Martin put the letter back in his pocket.

"Splendid!" He looked at her inquiringly. "Did her advice lead you to happiness?"

Judy stopped and thought.

"Not exactly. Her advice was right, but I didn't need it. What she wanted for me happened, anyway."

"She's a great believer in happiness." Martin once more took the letter out of his pocket. "She's preaching it to me." He turned over the sheets and read:

"'Don't fix your mind so much on Heaven that you miss happiness here below.'"

"It's strange what a lot is said about happiness. But happiness comes from the work you love, and I have that."

Judy was at the door; she gave a little despairing shrug that he did not notice.

"If happiness in work is all we need, then you and I ought to be very happy people."

In the kitchen Bertha was being what the children thought was entrancingly Christmassy, for they found her filling pies with mince-meat and singing "God rest you Merry Gentlemen." One of Bertha's greatest charms, from the children's point of view, was that she was free of the usual grown-up fusses about food. Now at sight of them she stopped singing in the middle of the line "let nothing you dismay," and handed each of them half a mince-pie.

"And eat it up quick before Miss Griffiths or Miss Matthews catches you."

"Judy wouldn't mind," said Andrew, sitting on the table. "When she came down to see me at school she let me eat simply heaps of cakes, and it was just going to be lunch."

Bertha watched him with approval.

"You're looking fine. Less of a hank of bone than when you came home last holidays."

Polly, with her mouth full of mince-pie, swung between the table and the dresser.

"He's awfully posh now. He's got a room to himself."

"You never?" Bertha's tone was properly full of admiration. "What's that for?"

Andrew turned his head away; his voice was off-hand.

"I got nightmares and woke the others up." Bertha took another spoon of mince-meat out of the jar.

"You don't look much like nightmares now. I was quite surprised when I saw you, for Miss Griffiths said you were seeing a doctor."

"So I did." Andrew kicked the kitchen table. "He gave me some stuff. It was bright yellow and smelt awful, so before I drank it I gave some to Matron's cat. It seemed all right, so the next day I had some; but as a matter of fact the cat wasn't all right really, for one of our boys said he had trod in where it had been sick."

Polly was shocked.

"How mean to make the cat sick." She sat on the floor beside Sloe. "I hope you don't give any to Sloe."

"I didn't mean to be mean. It oughtn't to hurt a cat to have a tonic."

Bertha had been putting two and two together.

"I reckon Miss Griffiths ought to pop down and see you every term."

"Wish she would." Andrew held up a finger. "Hark! there's the telephone. Shall I answer it?"

"No good you doing it; it'll be for the Reverend. Where is he?"

"In the study with Judy."

Bertha wiped her hands on her apron.

"Oh, I'll do it, then."

She came back in a minute humming "Good King Wenceslas" in a truculent way.

"It was Lady Blacke. She wanted to speak the Reverend, but I told her he was engaged with Miss Griffiths. She says to tell the Reverend that she'll be here tea-time. I nearly said 'No need to tell him; the day to telephone is the day when you're not coming.'"

"Bother!" said Andrew. "I'd forgotten all about her. Does she still come as much as ever?"

Polly hugged Sloe.

"Worse. Every single day she comes, and not one of us wants her, and you'd think she would see it."

Andrew jumped off the table and hugged Bertha round the waist.

"Darling Bertha, before you tell Judy she's coming, will you ask us to tea with you? If Judy knows she's coming she must think it would look rude if we weren't there."

Bertha beamed down at him.

"Wheedler, aren't you? All right, then, I invite you. What d'you want?"

Andrew ticked off his fingers.

"Scones. Cherry cake. Cake with sugar on it, and—"

"Now, then, now then!" Bertha remonstrated. "What d'you think we are? The mint? Haven't come into a fortune, you know, while you were away at school. Think we've found the crock under the rainbow?"

Polly looked up.

"What crock?"

Bertha went to the cupboard and got out some butter.

"If ever you see the end of a rainbow, where it touches the ground there'll be a crock of gold."

"Goodness!" Polly pulled one of Sloe's cars through her fingers. "But doesn't everybody run and get it?"

Bertha greased some tins.

"No, 'tisn't once in a lifetime you see the end of a rainbow. But when you do you'll find your crock."

Andrew punched Bertha in the ribs.

"Who's a liar? 'Tisn't true, Poll; she's made it up."

Judy opened the door.

"Oh, here you are! The weather's getting worse; if we're going out we'd better go."

Andrew sidled round the table, his voice was transparently innocent.

"Bertha's asked me and Polly to tea. Can we have it with her?"

Judy laughed.

"I expect so, but tell me first what the catch is."

Polly scrambled up off the floor.

"It's not a catch, Judy; Bertha honestly invited us."

Judy laughed again.

"If you don't tell me what the catch is, I'll say 'No'."

Bertha chuckled.

"She's got you two rumbled. Better speak out."

Andrew slipped his arm into Judy's.

"Lady Blacke's coming to tea."

Judy turned in surprise to Bertha.

"Is that what the telephone was?" Bertha nodded. "How very odd; she doesn't usually ring up—she drops in. Was it about something special?"

Bertha shrugged her shoulders.

"She didn't say. She just said to tell the Reverend that she'd be here tea-time." Bertha paused. "But now I come to think of it, she did say it rather meaning-like."

Judy felt she was being too curious about Veronica's business.

"I dare say it's something to do with 'The Ghost Train.' They had a dress rehearsal last night."

Bertha picked up another tin.

"And very good it was. I slipped in for a bit. It wasn't so much a dress rehearsal for those taking part, as for the men that make the train noises. Wonderful it was, for all the world like a train rushing through."

"How did Miss Chloe get on?" Judy asked.

Bertha winked.

"Lovely. But she and Mr. Evans didn't need to do no play-acting. They play a young couple, and it came natural like."

Judy smiled happily.

"Dear little Chloe."

The door shut on Judy and the children. Bertha shook her head. "Dear little Chloe," she thought. "That's right, and I wish her happiness. But it's 'Dear little Judy' that I'd like to say."

In the hall, as Judy and the children were going out, they met Martin. Judy remembered Veronica's message.

"Lady Blacke's rung up; she said to let you know she would be here to tea."

The passage window was facing Martin, through it came a dull wintry light. Could it, Judy wondered, be her fancy that Martin had turned paler. He stood quite still after she had spoken, as though she had startled him, then a quiet "Thank you," and he went into his study and closed the door.

Andrew raised an enquiring face to Judy.

"Is something the matter with him. He looks awfully green."

Judy called Sloe before she answered, and then she only said that Christmas was a tiring time for clergymen; but inside she felt an uneasiness. Martin did look green, he had, now she came to think of it, been rather silent and unlike himself since yesterday, when they all came back from Eastbourne. Was it to do with Lady Blacke in some way? She had been alone with him probably after she and Polly had left. Had she said something then to disturb him? And if so, what?

Andrew, quite unmoved by the cold, paid a round of visits.

"We must," he said to Judy, "go to the Browns, and I must see Mr. and Mrs. Peters, and Mrs. Beam, and Ben, and Chloe, and Mrs. Reynolds, and I expect we'll meet lots more as we go along."

Polly skipped up the road.

"It's obvious you've been away, my boy, or you'd know you couldn't see all these. This is Mr. Peters' day in Upper Saltings, and Chloe has gone in to Lewes to have her hair done and have lunch with Mike, and anyhow you'll see them this afternoon because she's bringing Mike in to meet you. They'll be here for tea, but we'll get them to come out to the kitchen after tea; you'll like Mike, he's awfully nice, isn't he, Judy?"

Judy was only listening with half an ear, her mind was still on Martin, turning and twisting, struggling to find what lay behind his tired strained look; and, because there was that part of her life which had to be a secret, feeling scared. Could Veronica know anything about her? Had she said anything? She pulled herself together at Polly's question, it was an easy one to answer, she knew better than anyone in the Saltings, better even than Chloe, how really nice Mike was.

"Yes, darling, he's a grand person." Then, trying to throw off her vague uneasiness, she started to run, "Come on, both of you, let's have a warm up."

The morning was a success. Most of the Brown children were at school, but Mrs. Brown and her two youngest were in, and Mrs. Brown was as delighted to see Andrew as if he were one of her own.

"Good gracious, Master Andrew, you ain't half grown," she said admiringly. "I must tell Brown how you was looking."

Even the enchanting thought that he was figuring in correspondence sent to a prison could not distract Andrew from his amazement at the change in Mrs. Brown.

"You look quite different."

Mrs. Brown smiled.

"It's my teeth. Miss Griffiths got the money for me to have new ones and took me in to have my old ones out."

Andrew regarded her with his head on one side.

"It isn't only your teeth, it's you that's different. You look as if—" He felt round for what he did mean, "as if you laughed a lot. You didn't look like that last holidays."

Mrs. Brown gave a look at Judy, which expressed more than her inexpressive tongue could ever say.

"That's Miss Griffiths. No-one ever had a friend like her."

Judy was embarrassed.

"Nonsense," she said briskly. "And we must be going, as Andrew has a lot of visits to pay. The children will be up on Christmas Eve to help your children with the decorations and to bring the Christmas tree."

Peters, as Polly had prophesied, was out, but Rosie Peters made a most satisfactory hostess. They had hardly opened her gate before she had some hot milk on her stove to make them cups of chocolate. While it was boiling Andrew and Polly ran outside to have a word with Bess. Rosie at once opened a cupboard and took out a parcel; her cheeks were pink.

"This is a little something I made for you for Christmas, Miss Griffiths, dear."

Judy looked at the parcel.

"May I open it now or do I keep it until Christmas Day?"

"You open it," said Rosie, "and then we'll do it up again. I don't want everybody knowing I made it."

Judy took the red Christmassy ribbons off her parcel. Inside was a nightdress of flowered chiffon, most beautifully made. Judy was quite overcome; for she knew that such a nightdress was outside Rosie's dreams of night-wear, and that not only loving labour had been put into it but quite a startling amount of imagination.

"It's beautiful." She kissed Rosie. "How angelic of you. But it's much too good for me."

Rosie took the night-dress from her and folded it and did it up again in its parcel. She gave Judy a glance out of the corner of her eye.

"Nothing could be too good for you, Miss Griffiths, dear. But if you don't want to wear it just now put it away in a bottom drawer."

Judy was just going to make a laughing retort to that when the children came back.

"It's most extraordinary," said Andrew.

"Wouldn't you think even if he did go and live in another house a mother would know her own son? But Bess is no more interested in Sloe than if he was just an ordinary visitor."

Polly had spied the parcel. "What's in that?"

Rosie stirred the cups of chocolate.

"Just some sewing I've done for Miss Griffiths." She put the cups in front of the children. "You remind her, Miss Polly, where I've told her to put it."

As the shop bell jangled Mrs. Beam, wheezing more than ever, came out from her back room to her counter. She was pleased to see Andrew, but took it as her right that he should have called.

"Good morning, Master Andrew. I was expecting you to pop over last night."

Andrew was nosing round the shop.

"I couldn't, we didn't get home in time, and supper was early because Bertha wanted to see the dress rehearsal of 'The Ghost Train.'"

Mrs. Beam looked at Judy.

"Reverend forgot to book his seats, so I took your lot, the five in the middle of the front row, as is proper." Then she added, with wheezy satisfaction, "Them at the Cedars is on your left and Doctor Green's lot on your right. When her ladyship came in to book she was quite upset and said she had meant to sit with all of you, but I said things were fixed and gave her a seat the other side of Doctor Green's lot. It's a good seat, I said. There's nothing you won't be able to see from there."

Judy read all she was intended to read into this statement. She refused even obliquely to be led into a discussion of Veronica.

"I can change with her," she said casually. "It's dull for her sitting alone."

Polly and Andrew flew at her.

"Don't you dare," said Andrew. "We want you, we don't want her."

Mrs. Beam nodded and looked approving.

"That's the way to talk, Master Andrew."

Judy saw that expression in Mrs. Beam's eye that meant that she was planning to set her news system in motion. She moved to the door.

"Come on, children. If you want to see Mrs. Reynolds and Ben before lunch you've got to hurry."

Mrs. Beam waited until the bell on the door had ceased jangling and then she called out as quietly as her wheezes would allow:

"Miss Griffiths, if you're going to Mrs. Reynolds ask her to pop down here. I want a word with her." Mrs. Reynolds was doing her housework to a mutter of her lines from the play. She was delighted to see the children, and in spite of Judy's expostulations cut them a large slice of cake.

"If you liked," she suggested, "you two could pop into the spare bedroom and see all my and Miss Chloe's things for the play. They're hanging in the wardrobe." When the children had gone she lowered her voice. "I had to get you alone. I think to-day's the day. Miss Chloe went off in such a state this morning and couldn't eat any breakfast."

"I hope it is," said Judy. "It would be lovely. They are both such darlings."

Mrs. Reynolds looked at Judy and sighed.

"You must forgive me saying it, Miss Griffiths, for it's not my place, but I wish it was double news we were expecting. Mr. Adam doesn't say anything, but he's thin, and not the man he was."

Judy knew the kindness that prompted Mrs. Reynolds to speak. She answered gently.

"There's no happiness for anyone in marriage without love."

"No." Mrs. Reynolds shook her head. "That's truth that is. But sometimes love comes, and 'tis better to be two than one, my dear."

Judy felt a lump rise in her throat. How true that was, how much better to be two than one; but what Hell to be the wrong two. How much better to be one all your life than make that mistake. The children were coming down the stairs so she could not answer, and she was thankful, for what she could have said was her secret.

Ben was in the churchyard. He was pleased to see Andrew.

"You've grown and you look less sickly than you did."

Polly skipped up to Ben and held his hand.

"We're going to make paper decorations this afternoon."

He smiled down at her.

"That's right, 'tis a festival meant for little ones like you." He turned suddenly to Judy: "There's just one blossom to flower on that there little gorse. You want to watch that flower, you can't loose she."

The children were interested.

"What little gorse, Ben?"

Ben gave a nod towards the Vicarage.

"It's growed by itself along of your front door."

"And why must Judy see the flower doesn't come off?"

Ben looked brave.

"We can't loose she. 'When gorse be out of bloom, then love be out of tune.'"

The thunder-storm which had been hanging round all the morning rolled over the Saltings in the afternoon. There were crashes of thunder and lightning forked the sky, and in between the roarings and crashings there were sheets of hail.

Judy had tea ready in the drawing-room. There was a large cheerful fire of logs burning.

"They'll need warming up," she said to Bertha. "It's a depressing sort of day."

Bertha looked grimly at the armchair on the right of the fire.

"Pity that old screeching cat's got to sit there; spoils the view, as one might say."

Judy gave Bertha a reproving look.

"Bertha! You know I won't listen to that sort of talk."

Bertha was quite unrepentant.

"I know that's what you say, but if you weren't calling her an old so and so in your mind you wouldn't be human." She opened the door and listened. "There's a car. 'Tisn't Jimson coming so quiet, and 'tisn't Mr. Evans' little red car, it'll be her ladyship."

Judy's vague disquiet of the morning about Veronica's visit had crystallized during the afternoon into nervous dread. All those old symptoms of her pre-Saltings days had recurred to worry her. Her solar plexus felt taut, almost painful, and her mouth was dry. She was shocked at herself for she had thought she had her nerves in hand, besides, what was she scared of? Veronica came to tea often enough; why, because for once she rang up to say she was coming, should she get in such a state about it.

Veronica had slept almost as little as Martin. In the night hours she had gone through agony. All those fears natural to a woman in love had swept over her. Had she been wise to speak? Had Martin hated her for it? Had she said enough, or should she have let herself go, and instead of stressing her money, have frankly admitted that she loved him?

There had been a time in her life when a sleepless night enhanced Veronica's beauty, taking away her English rose prettiness, and in its place—by drawing the colour from her cheeks and putting blue shadows under her eyes—giving her an ethereal, rather moving loveliness. But now that her twenties were behind her, she had to be in radiant health to look her best. Because to-day she was pale, and there were what she frankly admitted to herself were "bags" under her eyes, she had taken extra care with her make-up. But her make-up hid nothing. In fact, because there was extra rouge to hide that she was pale, and extra tinting on her eyelids to distract from the bags beneath her eyes, that she was either ill or worried stood out. Judy's natural impulse was to hold out a hand to the sick or sorry, and she forgot herself in being nice to Veronica. She pulled forward a chair and helped her out of her sable coat. Veronica liked her things admired, so she said, stroking the fur:

"How lovely this is."

Veronica did not want a *tête-à-tête* with Judy. She had succeeded in the daylight hours in dulling her fears and convincing herself that Martin's answer would be "Yes," but even so Judy was a problem; she would have to go, and that would make trouble; the children would be upset. Devoutly Veronica wished that Judy was settled with, paid off and gone.

"Yes, I love furs." She sat down and held out her hands out to the fire. Her voice was imperious. "Where's Mr. Richards? I said I was coming. Did Bertha give him my message?"

"Yes, he knows. He's coming in to tea." Judy laid the coat on a chest in the hall. She felt wretched. Why could Veronica call Martin by his Christian name when she couldn't? And since she did call him Martin, why couldn't she speak of him as Martin to her? Calling him Mr. Richards like that made her so very much the paid governess.

Aunt Connie came in. Thunder upset her, and her face and hands twitched. She settled herself in her arm-chair, and examined the tea-tray to see that everything was in front of her, and that Judy was not taking upon herself to act as hostess.

"Where are the children?"

Judy was always gentle with the old lady.

"Chloe's bringing Michael Evans and Mr. Adam to tea, so we shall be rather a crowd; so the children are having theirs with Bertha."

Aunt Connie chewed over this statement, and then burst out:

"You want the men to yourself. You don't want their attention distracted."

Judy's voice remained gentle.

"They'll be in here as soon as tea is over." She listened.
"There's Jimson."

"You always know when my nephew is about, don't you?"

Judy was conscious this was only too true. Her ear caught
the rattle of Jimson long before others heard it. She would have
been able to pick Martin's footsteps out among hundreds. Her
checks burned, and she turned to the window to hide them, but
Veronica had seen them, and she thanked heaven she had said
what she had yesterday. Judy was certainly up to something.

Martin had been sitting with an old farm labourer who was
dying. Ever since he had come to the Saltings he had been moved
by the quiet way in which these old country men slipped from life
into death, as though it were no more than climbing over a new
downside. He felt lifted up, and away from the ordinary world.

Judy saw at once from Martin's face that he was in one of his
exalted moods. She knew that when he was like that he could
scarcely hear the conversation around him; that he would sit
with his cup of tea beside him forgetting to drink it, and if he
took anything to eat he might swallow it without being conscious
that he was eating. He gave everybody a vague detached smile,
and sat down at the far end of the room. After his sleepless night
he still looked white and drawn; Judy felt he must be chilled.

"Why don't you come nearer the fire," she suggested. "It's
biting out."

Veronica had been saying to herself, "When he comes into
the room, the moment he looks at me I shall know his answer."
Counting the moments as she had until she saw him, knowing
the question that she had put to him to be vital, she supposed
that he, too, was thinking of nothing else, and his smile, which
included her without apparently seeing her, was the last thing
she expected. Her inclination was to go across to him and say
"Well?" Judy's harmless suggestion about the fire seemed to

her an impertinence; it was she who should be looking after Martin's welfare. To make this clear to Judy, and to make Martin conscious that she was in the room, and why she was there, she got up and slipped her arm through his.

"Yes, come along! I'm quite warm now; you take my chair."

Martin did not seem to notice Veronica, for he answered Judy.

"I've been with old Pettigrew."

"So I guessed," said Judy. "Has he gone?"

"No, but he won't live through the night. I'm going back after tea. He's quite conscious. I think he'll be glad to go; he said that he hoped the Lord would put him on to work in the fields, 'Which be work that I know,' he said, 'and at which I'd not be likely to look a fool.'"

"How grand!" Judy spoke softly. "I hope when I come to die that I feel it's as simple as all that—just changing over from one job to another." This complete understanding between Martin and Judy was more than Veronica could bear. She had no idea who old Pettigrew was, and felt she was being deliberately kept out of the conversation. After her nervous sleepless night her self-control was not as good as usual, and she was just going to break in with a biting remark, when a car stopped outside, and Sterndale, Chloe and Michael came in. Chloe dashed across the room and threw her arms round Judy's neck.

"Darling, I'm going to marry Mike, and I want you to be the very first person to know beside Sterndale."

Judy hugged her.

"I am so glad." She nodded at Michael. "Many congratulations!"

Martin took Chloe's hands.

"God bless you, my dear; I hope you'll be very happy."

Sterndale came over to Judy.

"It was only as a great favour that I was allowed to be told. Both Chloe and Michael had made up their minds that you must be told first."

Chloe gave Judy another hug.

"Of course she had to, because she's the nicest person Michael and I know; we're both agreed about that." She turned to Martin. "Isn't she the nicest person you know, Uncle Martin?"

Martin gave Judy a smile.

"I certainly don't know what we should do without her."

The situation was more than Veronica could bear; no one had spoken to her, all this praising and kissing of Judy! She lost all sense of caution, and was determined only to show Judy to these people as she really was. Two spots of colour burned in her cheeks; her voice was staccato.

"You seem to have a wonderful knack for making friends, Miss Griffiths, which reminds me that I was going to tell you that I had heard about a friend of yours—Dennis Edwards."

No one in the room—not even Aunt Connie—could fail to notice the effect that name had on Judy. Almost unconsciously she pushed Chloe from her as if she needed air. The thunder was rumbling outside, and it seemed to express the electric atmosphere in the room. She spoke in a kind of desperate whisper; she saw that all her dreads of the day had been real; that Veronica knew her story, and that nothing could stop her repeating it.

"Yes?"

Veronica looked round the room, taking in Sterndale, Michael, Chloe and Martin.

"You'll wonder why I'm telling you this, but I've been waiting for her to tell you herself, and as she hasn't, it seems to be my duty."

There was silence, broken by Judy's nervous breathing, the hissing of the tea-kettle and the thunder outside. Through these sounds Veronica told her story, just as she had learnt it from Gloria.

"And so," she finished, "he got penal servitude, and she got off scot free."

"You're a liar!" said Sterndale.

Chloe's voice was full of tears.

"I don't believe a word of it."

"Ask her if it's true," said Veronica. "Ask her if she knows Dennis Edwards."

Judy looked round. Her eyes took in Chloe and Michael and Sterndale, and came to rest on Martin. He looked stunned, and he said nothing. She knew too well that twisted, garbled version of her story, and how like the true one it could seem; but somehow she had thought that Martin would not believe evil of her so easily. She was too hurt at the thought of how she was appearing in his eyes to think of defending herself; if he was going to believe her guilty, then she had nothing to say. She spoke quietly.

"I am leaving," she said; "I'll go up and pack. I've just time to catch the six o'clock train. I had thought that I had buried my past—that even I could be happy—but you can't escape things in this world."

She turned to the door, but before she had got to it, Michael was there, and had his back to it. He spoke directly to Martin.

"You're not going to be such an idiot as to accept a story like that." He waited for a clap of thunder overhead to die away. "I've known Judy since we were kids."

"Mike," said Chloe, "you've never told me."

He stopped her.

"You listen to this, because it's serious. Dennis Edwards and Judy's father were partners, as Lady Blacke says: my father was a parson in the same town. When Dennis's father died, Dennis was brought up by the Griffiths's, and all that part of the story up to going to London is perfectly true, only the most important thing is left out. Dennis was a thief from the day he was born; I was at school with him, so I knew even more about it than Judy did. He was more or less expelled from school for stealing, and I'd have never bothered with him again, only Judy was so sorry for him. Even when she was quite small she worked like a slave to keep him straight. When I said I couldn't be bothered with him any more, I remember Judy cried and said, 'But he hasn't got anybody but us.' I was jolly glad—and so was everybody else who was fond of Judy—when Dennis got sent off to a bank in the north. He never ought to have been in a bank at all, only his expelling from school had been unofficial, and he managed to rake up a good character. I went off school-mastering after that, and didn't see Judy for quite a time, and then one day when I was in London I ran into her. She wasn't much older than you are, Chloe, but that day she looked a hundred. I took her out to lunch and, almost by accident, got on to what had happened. Dennis had turned up again. He'd deliberately got transferred to a London bank, to be near her. In his odd way he'd always loved her, and now he was pitching the tale that she'd got to marry him; that he couldn't go straight without her." Michael looked round the room with such bitterness that you felt that if he'd had Dennis Edwards there he would have banged his brains out on the floor. "Getting money out of him!" He gave Veronica a disparaging look. "I don't know where you got that cock-and-bull story from. She begged and she borrowed, she used all her own money, and sold such little bits of jewellery as she had to get him out of scrapes. I was only one of her friends, and we all said the same thing. 'Let him go; he's not worth bothering about.' And she always made the same answer: 'I must bother about him, because if only I could love him it would be different; he would go straight; but I can't and I never will. You've heard the end of the story, but not the truth even of that. When he was really caught he squealed, like the rat he is, and looked round for some way of getting out of his mess, and so he dragged in Judy. But what Lady Blacke hasn't told you is what the Judge said about her. He was a wise old bird, and saw the story quite straight from the beginning. He took a lot of trouble, because fools that had been taken in by Dennis were screaming for Judy's blood. He said, 'This young woman has sacrificed her life and her happiness in pity for a weak, useless man, and she leaves this court without a stain on her character.'"

The storm had passed by the time Michael had finished speaking. It was raining, but a thin wintry sun was piercing the clouds. Nobody in the room seemed able to speak or move, until they were suddenly galvanised by screams from the children, who could be seen running across the lawn. Judy at once became herself. She opened the door.

"Bertha! Why have you let those children go out without their coats, and in their house shoes?"

Bertha's voice was exasperated.

"They nipped out without my looking. There's a rainbow; they think it finishes in our garden, and they're after the crock of gold."

Martin threw open the drawing-room window and called to the children to come back, but they were out of sight.

"We'll have to fetch them," said Judy.

Judy and Martin met Polly and Andrew on the slope of the lawn. Polly was so excited that she spoke in a kind of howl. She held out in her hands an earthenware honey-pot, full of silver.

"We found it, we found it. It's the crock of gold."

The rest of the party were standing in the drawing-room window. At the sight of Polly, Aunt Connie pushed through Chloe and Sterndale, and came across the lawn in a fumbling run.

"It's mine, you naughty child. I buried it where she wouldn't get it."

Chloe and Michael ran after the old lady.

"Come on in!" said Michael. "You'll catch your death of cold out there. Send those kids in," he called to Judy. "Miss Matthews wants that honey-pot."

"It's not a honey-pot," said Polly. "It's the crock of gold from under the rainbow."

Veronica stood just outside the window, on the garden path. Her eyes were on Martin and Judy. Because he knew that she saw what he saw, Sterndale's voice was full of pity.

"Suppose I put you into your car. You and I aren't wanted here."

Judy was trying to get a grip on herself, but she was almost crying.

"You believed what Veronica Blacke said; the others didn't, but you did; I saw your face. That's why though you know the truth now, I've still got to go."

Martin took her hands.

"I didn't believe her." The words seemed pulled from him. "But when she was slandering you I saw something that I had missed before, and when you said you were leaving me, everything was clear. Last night God led me to read the marriage service; I thought it was to guide me in another matter, but it was for more than that. We aren't meant to go on as we are; we've met each other for a purpose. Will you marry me, Judy?"

Bertha had her head stuck so far out of the kitchen window that she was straining her neck, but the pain that she was enduring she considered worth while.

"Such a beautiful way they looked at each other," she said to herself contentedly. Then she drew her head back into her kitchen. "I wonder if I could spare a minute to pop over to Mrs. Beam?"


THE END

# FURROWED MIDDLEBROW

FM68. *Touch not the Nettle* (1939) . . . . . . . . . . . MOLLY CLAVERING

FM69. *Mrs. Lorimer's Quiet Summer* (1953) . . . MOLLY CLAVERING

FM70. *Because of Sam* (1953) . . . . . . . . . . . . . . MOLLY CLAVERING

FM71. *Dear Hugo* (1955) . . . . . . . . . . . . . . . . . MOLLY CLAVERING

FM72. *Near Neighbours* (1956) . . . . . . . . . . . . . MOLLY CLAVERING

FM73. *The Fair Miss Fortune* (1938) . . . . . . . . . . D.E. STEVENSON

FM74. *Green Money* (1939) . . . . . . . . . . . . . . . . D.E. STEVENSON

FM75. *The English Air* (1940)* . . . . . . . . . . . . . . D.E. STEVENSON

FM76. *Kate Hardy* (1947) . . . . . . . . . . . . . . . . . D.E. STEVENSON

FM77. *Young Mrs. Savage* (1948) . . . . . . . . . . . . D.E. STEVENSON

FM78. *Five Windows* (1953)* . . . . . . . . . . . . . . . D.E. STEVENSON

FM79. *Charlotte Fairlie* (1954) . . . . . . . . . . . . . . D.E. STEVENSON

FM80. *The Tall Stranger* (1957)* . . . . . . . . . . . . . D.E. STEVENSON

FM81. *Anna and Her Daughters* (1958)* . . . . . . . . D.E. STEVENSON

FM82. *The Musgraves* (1960) . . . . . . . . . . . . . . . D.E. STEVENSON

FM83. *The Blue Sapphire* (1963)* . . . . . . . . . . . . D.E. STEVENSON

FM84. *The Marble Staircase* (C.1960) . . . . . . . . . . ELIZABETH FAIR

FM85. *Clothes-Pegs* (1939) . . . . . . . . . . . . . . . . SUSAN SCARLETT**

FM86. *Sally-Ann* (1939) . . . . . . . . . . . . . . . . . . SUSAN SCARLETT**

FM87. *Peter and Paul* (1940) . . . . . . . . . . . . . . . SUSAN SCARLETT**

FM88. *Ten Way Street* (1940) . . . . . . . . . . . . . . . SUSAN SCARLETT**

FM89. *The Man in the Dark* (1939) . . . . . . . . . . . SUSAN SCARLETT**

FM90. *Babbacombe's* (1941) . . . . . . . . . . . . . . . . SUSAN SCARLETT**

FM91. *Under the Rainbow* (1942) . . . . . . . . . . . . SUSAN SCARLETT**

FM92. *Summer Pudding* (1943) . . . . . . . . . . . . . . SUSAN SCARLETT**

FM93. *Murder While You Work* (1944) . . . . . . . . SUSAN SCARLETT**

FM94. *Poppies for England* (1948) . . . . . . . . . . . SUSAN SCARLETT**

FM95. *Pirouette* (1948) . . . . . . . . . . . . . . . . . . . SUSAN SCARLETT**

FM96. *Love in a Mist* (1951) . . . . . . . . . . . . . . . . SUSAN SCARLETT**


*titles available in paperback only

**pseudonym of Noel Streatfeild